THE KILLER INSIDE

Cass Green's debut adult novel *The Woman Next Door* was a No.1 e-book bestseller and her second, *In a Cottage in a Wood* was a *Sunday Times* top ten and *USA Today* bestseller. *Don't You Cry* was her third standalone thriller. She is also an award-winning author of fiction for young people. Her first novel, *Dark Ride* won the RONA Young Adult Book of the Year and the Waverton Good Read Award. *Cracks* was recommended on Radio 4's Open Book programme and *Hold Your Breath* won the Oldham Book Award. She is the Writer in Residence at East Barnet School and teaches crime fiction at City University and children's fiction for Writers and Artist's Yearbook.

 @CassGreenWriter

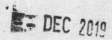

Also by Cass Green

The Woman Next Door
In a Cottage in a Wood
Don't You Cry

THE KILLER INSIDE

CASS GREEN

HarperCollinsPublishers

HarperCollins*Publishers*
1 London Bridge Street
London SE1 9GF

www.harpercollins.co.uk

This paperback edition 2019
1

First published in Great Britain by
HarperCollins*Publishers* 2019

A catalogue record for this book is
available from the British Library

ISBN: 978-0-00-828724-5 (PB)
ISBN: 978-0-00-833637-0 (TPB)

Typeset in Sabon by Palimpsest Book Production Ltd,
Falkirk, Stirlingshire

Printed and bound in the UK by CPI Group (UK) Ltd,
Croydon, CR0 4YY

MIX
Paper from
responsible sources
FSC™ C007454

This book is produced from independently certified FSC™ paper
to ensure responsible forest management.

For more information visit: www.harpercollins.co.uk/green

Dedicated to The Sibs: Helenanne Hansen and Charlie Green

SUMMER 2019

There are three people alive inside the whitewashed family home at one pm on this sunny afternoon in late July. And because not much happens on this quiet road in this quiet seaside town, the first gunshot could perhaps be mistaken for a misfiring exhaust.

But at this time of the afternoon, there is only a young man walking an elderly West Highland terrier on the road and he is lost in the music pumping through high-end, noise-cancelling headphones. Oblivious to the shriek of the seagulls and the rhythmic smash of surf against rock, he doesn't hear the sharp retort of the gun or the screaming in its aftermath either.

By the time the second shot comes – at 1.34 pm – he is long gone. The only witness to the violence is a seagull perched on the back wall, which tumbles into the air in outrage at the sound.

It is less than a minute later when the gun fires for the third time.

SUMMER/AUTUMN 2018

ELLIOTT

That festival was a big deal in our part of the world.

Just up the road from the seaside town we called home, the End of the Summer event was usually a low-key, family-run affair with a number of acts you've probably never heard of.

But this year was very different. For some complicated reason involving a favour by Dave Grohl, The Foo Fighters – one of the biggest bands in the world – were headlining. The band is the mutual favourite of me and my wife Anya and as soon as I heard about it, I knew we had to be there.

Tickets went on sale at nine am on a day in June, when my Year Five class was doing guided reading, followed by maths. I told them they were going to watch *Planet Earth* as a treat for being good (not true – they had been little bastards the day before) while I endlessly pressed redial on my phone with one hand, the other attempting to access ever-crashing ticket websites on the school computer. When it got to ten am I had to stop briefly to let the class out to play, before racing to the staffroom to continue.

When I got the automated message telling me, with totally unwarranted cheerfulness, that, 'Due to exceptional demand, tickets to the End of the Summer festival are now sold out,' I said, 'Bollocks,' loud enough and with sufficient heat that some of the older guard in the staffroom gave me pinched looks.

But then, the weekend before the event, a miracle occurred.

My friend at work, Zoe, knew someone roadying, and she was able to get her hands on two extra tickets; one for me, and one for Anya.

We were ecstatic. It was the very last weekend before the schools were back and it felt like a perfect way to end the summer.

And anyway, Anya needed cheering up.

We'd only been 'trying' as they say (such a weird expression because actually, we were quite good at it) for six months or so. But each time her period arrived, she became more dejected and withdrawn. The last time she'd claimed she 'had a real feeling' even though she was only overdue by a day or two. She made me laugh by saying things like, 'Will you still fancy me when I am big with child?'

Maybe the humour was a disguise for how high her hopes had been raised.

On the day of the festival, we woke up to mizzling, nasty rain in the air and a low-slung sky. Anya was quiet that morning. I tried to chivvy her with some lame jokes, but she just smiled weakly and it was somehow worse than rolled eyes. When I asked what was wrong, she said she had a bit of a headache and I decided not to press.

Clad in wellies and waterproof coats, we arrived at the festival in a downpour. Our feet were sucked into claggy, viscous mud straight away and we were sweating inside our jackets.

I took the decision that the best way to fight off the vagaries of the weather was to drink as much as possible.

By late afternoon, I didn't mind the mud.

And finally, at six, the sun came out.

We'd seen a weird kind of emo rock band and a folk-punk duo I like, plus some comedy in one of the tents. The main event was still to come.

I made my way back to Anya with two more wobbly pints of cider in my hands that I'd had to queue painfully long for. Her head was turned away from me and, as I reached her and said, 'Hey,' she seemed to startle.

'You're shaking,' I said, noticing her hand as she took the plastic glass from me. 'Are you cold?'

She gulped a long mouthful. Her eyes when they met mine were oddly bright. She seemed to be crackling with energy in a way that happened sometimes. It was very sexy.

'It's nothing,' she said and turned to look at the stage. This was clearly a lie.

'Hey,' I said again, placing my hand on her slim arm, which was covered in goose bumps. 'Did something happen?'

She shook her head vigorously. 'People are dickheads, that's all. Some bloke knocked into me and wasn't very sorry.'

'Where is he?' I said, turning to look at the thickening crowd.

'Gone,' she said and gave me a wonderful smile that seemed to come from nowhere. 'Let's forget it, okay?'

'Okay, if you're sure.' I took a swig of my pint.

I allowed myself to relax and soak up the buzz of the crowd. Soft evening light bathed us. The nearest group of people included a small girl whose face was painted like Spiderman, and a man in shorts with an Oasis T-shirt that seemed to have come from younger, slimmer times straining over his belly. He was bellowing about seeing Oasis at 'Glasto' to a small, middle-aged woman with a long-suffering expression.

Anya took a sip of her pint and did a little turn to survey the crowd. She was wearing what she called her 'festival

4

dress', a long, hippyish affair with thin straps and a brown hem of mud, her waterproof coat tied around her waist. I didn't resist the urge to kiss her freckled shoulder and she gave me a quick, warm smile.

There was a palpable thrum of excited energy in the crowd. The thing we'd all been waiting for was happening any moment now.

I heard someone call my name and turned to see Zoe squeezing her way towards us through the knots of people, grinning.

Zoe was almost six feet tall with her afro and, even though I had repeatedly told Anya that I hadn't really noticed, you'd have to be insane not to recognize that she was kind of gorgeous. She wore thick-framed glasses that would have made anyone else look like Morrissey on a bad day, but highlighted her big, brown eyes, and she always had on brightly coloured lipstick. She could be stern when needed but the kids adored her; she had even won over some of the racist old parents round here.

The fact that she stood out at all was one of the downsides of living in this small, seaside town. I was born and raised in the crowded, multi-cultural heart of London and, well . . . it was an adjustment. I'd been asked more than once here – with a note of suspicion – if I was an Arab, because of my dark colouring and beard.

This place had its downsides, which sometimes made me want to run screaming back to the city, but it was also beautiful, cheap enough, and, therefore, home.

Zoe was my best friend at work – and, by default, probably in the town – but I sensed a tightening in Anya's expression whenever her name came up. So, I tried not to talk about her too much. That Anya could ever be a bit territorial and jealous was, frankly, something I still found flattering.

Anyway, Zoe was looking great at the festival, in some

sort of orange catsuit thing with a thick yellow scarf around the front of her hair. She pulled me into a hug and I could sense Anya tensing next to me.

'Everything okay?' Zoe said, turning to Anya.

She gave her an odd sort of look, but I didn't think anything of it then.

Anya's smile was tight. 'Yeah, brilliant,' she said. 'And we're so grateful for the tickets, aren't we, Ell?' But she reached for my fingers at the same time and it felt like she was making a point.

Zoe didn't seem to notice anyway. She began to tell me a story about one of the mothers saying her son didn't have any time to do an after-school club any more because 'one of his tutors' was changing days.

'*One* of them?' she said now. 'He's ten years old!'

Our school didn't have too many pushy parents, but a slow gentrification process was happening in the town, which meant a new demographic of parent. We didn't have any Octavias or Gullivers. Yet. Kept things interesting, anyway. I listened to the story and laughed at the right bits but was acutely conscious of Anya standing silently next to me the whole time.

After a few moments a tall woman with a shaved head and Cleopatra-like eyes came over, clutching two bottles of beer, one of which she thrust at Zoe.

'Oh cheers,' said Zoe. 'This is Tabitha. Tab . . . Elliott, my partner in crime at school. And his wife Anya.' We all nodded our hellos.

'By the way,' said Zoe, turning to me again. 'You still okay to get started on the Charney Point visit? It has to be done quickly because they're closing for a major refurb in October.'

This was a trip for Year Five to go to a Viking museum that was about ten miles down the coast. I'd logged it onto the school calendar and needed to remember to fill out all the risk assessment stuff. I made a mental note.

'Safe in my hands, Miss,' I said with a little salute. Zoe grinned and then our attention was diverted by a change in energy in the crowd. The background music abruptly stopped.

I always love that moment when the band is just about to come on. The anticipation reaches a kind of critical mass. You can feel the wave of energy that's gathering force before it crashes down over you, drenching you in euphoria.

There was a loud roar as the lights at the side of the stage began to strobe the crowd, even though it wasn't yet dark.

Anya squeezed my hand and whispered, 'I didn't know.' She was grinning wildly now, happier than I had seen her all day.

When she saw my look of bafflement, she nodded at Zoe and Tabitha, whose fingers were entwined.

I stared.

'I didn't either.'

Zoe saw us looking over at her.

'There's only so much diversity Beverley Park Primary School can take, isn't there?' she shouted with a grin.

I laughed, but it was forced. Surely, *I* wasn't someone Zoe felt she had to hide anything from? I was her mate. But had she actively kept it from me, though? Had I ever bothered to ask about a boyfriend or a girlfriend, even though Anya repeatedly tried to pump me for this sort of information? Well . . .

My thoughts were interrupted by a thunder of cries from the crowd, so loud I felt them thrumming through my feet, and the band bounced onto the stage.

Dave Grohl shouted, '*Are we fuckin' ready?*' and everyone went wild.

A few songs in and my throat was aching from shouting and singing along. Forests of arms in exultant Vs waved before us and I couldn't control the daft grin on my face. I glanced at Anya and saw she was trying to crane her neck to get a better view. The group in front of us were all unusually tall.

I nudged her and pointed to my shoulders, waggling an eyebrow suggestively.

She shook her head and laughed, mouthing, 'No way.'

I got down onto my haunches and patted my shoulders again.

'Come on!' I yelled. 'I can take it!'

Anya was giggling now, eyes gleaming.

'I'll break your neck!' she shouted. I turned and gave her a hurt look.

'Are you casting aspersions on my manliness?'

Chortling almost helplessly, she hitched up her long skirt and carefully wound one leg over my shoulder, then the other, holding onto my head as she wobbled into position.

In truth, she was an awful lot heavier than I'd expected her to be at this unfamiliar angle. Plus, I realized that I was actually quite drunk. But I was a determined man. As I struggled to my feet, Anya sliding around on top of me, I felt a warning twinge of pain in my lower back and a burst of masculine pride all at the same time.

The band began to play the opening chords of 'Everlong'.

Despite the pain increasing by the second in my back, warm, sweet contentment spread through all my synapses. Anya's hands were in the air, my fingers clasped around her slim ankles. My mind was fuzzy from cider, but I knew somehow this would be one of those moments I wouldn't forget. I even pictured myself doing this with a child one day; carrying a little boy or girl on my shoulders and pointing out planes, dogs, cars . . .

We'd be the sort of parents who still went to gigs, too.

I don't really know what happened next. It felt as though she shifted and I slightly lost my balance. For a heart-lurching few moments I thought we were both going to smash face down into the people in front.

She shouted above the music, '*Down!* Let me *down!*'

I crumpled awkwardly to my knees and Anya climbed off my shoulders so abruptly she almost wrenched my head off.

'What happened?' I said, rubbing my neck. It came out more angrily than I'd intended, but I was in pain.

'You almost dropped me, that's what happened,' she said. Her eyes looked huge, stricken, in her ashen face. Then she said, 'I want to go home.'

For a moment all I could do was stare at her. Anya was usually the last person dancing when they turned the lights off. I'd literally never heard her say anything like that before. I didn't know what to do with it.

'I mean it, Ell,' she said and that was when I saw her eyes were brimming over with tears.

'What's wrong? What is it?'

'I don't feel well.' She swiped at her eyes with the heel of her hand. 'There's something going around at work. Maybe it's that. Or maybe it was that kimchi earlier. I should have had the burger, like you did.'

The thought of leaving before the end of this much-anticipated gig made resentment burn like acid in my guts. I wanted to say, 'I'm not going anywhere. You do what you want,' like a disappointed little kid. The words were right there, about to spill out. Then I saw how sickly and green she looked. What kind of person would that make me? Especially as I had almost caused her to break her neck.

I pulled her into my arms and could feel her trembling.

'Okay,' I said, and began to lead her through the crowd.

It took us for ever to get through the press of sweaty, beaming faces that turned to frowns as we pushed past. The air smelled of sun cream, beer, and sweat, with the odd sweet waft of weed.

9

When we got to the gates I turned to her, to make one last bid.

'Are you absolutely sure about this?' I said.

'I need to go home,' she said, and with that she threw up all over my shoes.

Twenty minutes later, we were in an Uber. Anya had barely said a word since being sick. I'd hurriedly offered her water and called the cab, then she'd sat on the side of the road with her head in her hands until it arrived.

Inside the car, she leaned her head back against the seat and closed her eyes. My happy drunkenness was quickly morphing into a flat, depressed feeling.

I gazed out of the window as the car got onto the brief stretch of dual carriageway, but, before we were able to reach any kind of speed, we hit a traffic jam. I sighed and sat back in my seat. The air was filled with the desperate wail of an ambulance then the blue lights of a police car flashed past us in the burgeoning dusk.

The sight tapped into a deep, unhappy place inside me, a place where memories too painful to share were kept. I looked across at my sleepy wife, as if she were a talisman against these feelings. To my surprise, her eyes were open, and she was staring right at me. It was unnerving; like she knew what I had been thinking about.

Picture a little girl waking up in her bedroom with primrose walls on the morning of her tenth birthday.

She still has her toy Simba in her arms, even though she pretends she doesn't cuddle him at night. It had been a babyish present, but she secretly loves him. In fact, she loves everything about The Lion King, *which is why, when her mother suggested it as a theme for the party, she couldn't hide the excitement. Some of her friends might think it's a bit silly when you are in Year Five but she doesn't really care.*

She bounds downstairs and sucks in her breath when she sees the transformation happening in the den. Balloons in every shade of green are hanging in cascades along one wall and a huge, painted sticker says 'HAKUNA MATATA', over a table that already groans with food.

A woman with a white apron on bustles past her and places a tray of sausage rolls on the table, next to a bowl of animal-shaped chocolate biscuits. The table is covered in some sort of matting stuff so it looks like it is wearing a grass skirt.

There are cupcakes with swirly green icing shaped like leaves, and some have orange snakes curled up on the top, complete with tiny forked tongues. She reaches out a finger and touches one of the tongues to find it is made from thin liquorice strips. Resisting the temptation to eat one, she turns away, not wanting to spoil its perfection. Sometimes, she thinks, the Before is better than the actual event. Sometimes she thinks about this so much that she cries because holidays and Christmas and parties are hardly ever as good as she hopes they'll be.

The food has been talked about a lot before the party because Lottie from school is bringing her brother with her and he has something wrong with him. They have to be really careful with the food, which doesn't seem fair when it is her party.

Still, she won't let that spoil it. It's going to be the best party ever.

It's not her fault that everything goes so badly wrong.

ELLIOTT

We had a restless night. Anya tossed and turned, and the room felt stiflingly hot. I finally dropped into a deep sleep sometime in the early morning and woke at ten to the sound of gentle rain against the window and a grey sky.

Anya was already up, her side of the bed cold.

My head was throbbing, but I forced myself to pull on running gear. Much as my body and mind resisted it, it seemed as though exercise might help and, anyway, I deserved the punishment. Yawning, I walked through to the kitchen. I was expecting to see her reading the papers on her iPad, her favourite mug steaming next to her. But now I noticed there were none of the usual weekend smells; toast cooked until almost black the way she liked it, and strong coffee that she made as though it was an art form. I wouldn't have been that bothered if we had instant, was the God's honest truth. But I guessed I was finally getting used to the good stuff.

The kitchen felt gloomy and I snapped on the main lights. There was a note on the table.

Ell,

I've gone over to Mum and Dad's for the day. I'm still feeling a bit shit and I think I need some of my mum's TLC. We both know what a terrible patient I am.

Not sure what time I'm back.

X

I didn't see why she had to go over to Julia and Patrick's because she was feeling ill. It seemed a bit selfish too, especially as Patrick hadn't been in the best of health since his heart attack the year before. It was true that she wasn't a good patient; whoever invented the term 'man flu' clearly hadn't met my wife. But I would have been perfectly happy to make her tea and deliver dry toast, or whatever you're meant to do, when needed. And if I was being really honest, Julia was more of the 'pull yourself together' school of middle-class woman than your cuddly supplier of chicken soup.

The truth was that Anya had form for doing this. Every now and then she would have a couple of days of being a little withdrawn when she would gravitate towards her mum and dad, instead of me. Yes, I know that sounds hurtful, and it was, a little.

But you have to understand what they were like as a family. Tight-knit, fiercely loyal to each other. Once you were 'in' you felt special too. It was a golden circle. I'd thought families like this only existed on television until I'd met the Rylands.

I looked at the note again.

The kiss – single – didn't lessen the uncomfortable sensation that the note was a little cold, by her usual standards. There would usually be a little joke, or a 'Love YOU', which was a thing we did.

I thought about the events of the evening before. Her odd mood. The atmosphere when Zoe arrived. Me almost dropping her from my shoulders. Her wanting to go, then being sick. That weird vibe in the Uber . . .

The fact that some of these memories had hazy edges gave me a prickling feeling of shame. How many pints of cider had I drunk? Five? Six?

Had *I* ruined our day out? An unpleasant feeling began to creep over my skin. Sometimes, when I drank too much, it made me conscious that 'Nice Respectable Teacher Elliott' was a thin veneer over the treacly darkness I feared lay inside me.

I bashed out a text.

No worries. Hope you feel better. Love YOU xxxx

Outside, I turned left and began to run along the coast road. It was raining, that fine rain that deceived you into thinking it didn't mean business, but which soon drenched you through to the bones. My hair clung to my head and I was breathing like an old man, filled with my usual conviction that everything about this activity was wrong and unnatural.

Drum and bass thumped through my earbuds, which usually spurred me on to run harder, but just felt annoying today. I switched the music off and all I could hear was the roaring of waves hitting the shore, my own rasping breath and the hiss of the odd car going through puddles as it passed me.

The sea was to my left; silvery grey in the rain, lace-edged waves licking at the slick, shining sand. There was a low wall and scrubby grass between the road and the beach down below, yellow signs dotted here and there that warned of unfenced cliff, with a dramatic stick man falling to his death.

This road seemed to go on for ever, past bungalows on the other side that already had a closed-up-for-winter, sad look about them, and the café that still gamely had bright beach towels and deckchairs with 'witty' slogans for sale on its covered porch.

After a while I turned right, heading up the hill that led

to Petrel Point, where there was a World War Two lookout and a great view.

This was a savage bit of the run, and there was an easier route via a path leading from a car park on the other side, but the view at the top made it worthwhile.

As I made my way up the hill, the usual metamorphosis began to occur. I slowly began to transcend the feeling of hating running and everything connected with running, as my body warmed up and my stride became more fluid.

I'd never run in my life until we moved here. At first, I did it because it seemed like the sort of thing people in their thirties did when they left London and, frankly, I was a bit lost. The endless space around me felt as though it might suffocate me, in a weird way, and I couldn't get used to everyone looking the same. Why are people so obsessed with having space? Buildings make me feel secure. I've never had much of a desire to be the tallest thing on the horizon.

Don't get me wrong, I'm not one of those people who thinks London is the be-all and end-all of civilization. I wouldn't want to have stayed where I grew up, in a shitty council flat in one of the more depressing bits of north London. It was just a bit more of an adjustment than I'd expected it to be.

Anya grew up in the next town along.

Lathebridge is a genteel place, with its famous Grand Hotel on the front that hosts a small arts festival every year, and its white regency houses along the seafront.

Casterbourne is more crummy arcades and charity shops than cream teas and literary folk, but it was cheap enough for us to buy a small house, with help, and well, there was always the sea. Right now, a silvery band was spreading across the horizon and promising brightness to come. It was one of the things I'd come to love about living here, that the weather could change so quickly. I could see for miles as I reached the top.

I was starting to feel simultaneously better and absolutely knackered, so I looped round past the fort and made my way back down towards home.

I pictured what Anya was probably doing right now. She'd be on the long sofa in their living room – *sitting room* – probably curled up watching telly and maybe drinking her beloved green tea.

I had an idea; maybe I'd have a shower and just turn up. No one was going to object, were they?

Many, perhaps most, people felt quite differently about their parents-in-law.

When friends made disparaging jokes about their own, bemoaning Christmases and birthdays in their company, I smiled along as though I got it, but really, mine were two of my favourite people in the world.

When I first met Julia and Patrick, I was a little nervous of what they would make of me. I worried that a primary school teacher who came from my sort of background would be a terrible shock to their middle-class sensibilities. All manner of Tobys and Julians and whatever, with Oxbridge degrees and jobs in the City, must have been queuing up.

I had enough of a chip on my shoulder without them even knowing my full story. They still don't know about my so-called father. Only Anya does.

But the minute I met them, I felt welcome. Sometimes I marvelled at how quickly they'd accepted me. Almost like they had been waiting . . . and there I was.

Anya told me about her sister, Isabella, who had died of an infection when she was a few days old and whose solo picture – a small, red face in a white blanket – sat among all the ones of the sister who lived. Anya confessed that she felt guilty for having no feelings about this stranger at all and I could understand it, a little. But I think it was one of the reasons they were all so close, as a family. They were grateful for what they had, and maybe conscious that it could be taken away in a few failed breaths.

I was a bit taken aback that Anya was really called Anastasia. Julia only brought that out to wind her up though, as she hated that name. As a tiny girl they had called her 'Stasi', but it was a little too East German Torture Squad when written down, so it morphed into Anya, which she used as her official name now.

Patrick was a barrel of man with a hearty laugh and a propensity to see the positive in everything. He came from working-class roots, growing up in Liverpool and going on to work in shipping. Sometimes he made a comment about me and him having things in common, but we didn't, not really. Very occasionally, you would witness him on the phone dealing with someone difficult and there would be the smallest flash of something else – something sharp-edged that was swaddled by his comfortable home life. He liked to go hunting now and then in Scotland, and I was grateful he never felt the need to ask me along for a father-son-in-law bonding session over dead, furry animals. Not my thing, in any lifetime.

Julia worked in publishing as a literary agent and was lively, fun company. She tended to clasp me in perfumed hugs and say things like, 'Darling, how is my most favourite son-in-law?' as though there were competition for the title.

That's not to say that I hadn't found her intimidating when I'd first met her. She'd peered at me over her glasses with a slight frown and, for the first half hour in her company, I'd felt a little like I was under a microscope. Then she'd seemed to change, just like that, and was warm and welcoming. I never really knew what it was that turned her around. Maybe she just saw how I felt about her daughter and approved of the sea of love that was on offer.

18

Anya was their everything. That was clear to anyone who knew them. She was the golden child – the one who survived – and they would do anything to protect her.

Neither of them ever mentioned my own mum. I think they found it hard to know what to say.

I sometimes imagined how it would have gone if my mum had lived long enough to meet them. I pictured Julia, dressed with her usual style, smelling of some sort of subtle perfume, then Mum in those shapeless dresses that were the only things that fit her and leggings, feet overflowing from her shoes like uncooked dough. She would have smelled of smoke because she would have been so nervous about meeting them and she'd have said, 'Come on, Elliott, don't give me that look. It's one of my few pleasures in life and I only have one or two a day.'

I hated myself for thinking like that and I'd put up with any number of worlds-colliding awkward meetings if she was still here. But she had been dead for ten years now, following a massive heart attack, and it was becoming harder and harder to picture her in the world at all, let alone in mine.

My so-called father, well . . .

I think about the issue of 'bad blood' a lot. You would too, in my shoes.

A few nights before we got married, I'd had a huge attack of nerves, entirely based on the idea that Anya wouldn't want me if she knew everything about me. I'd got royally pissed and, because I am unable to stop myself from making sarcastic quips to big, angry men, ended up with a black eye and a wobbly tooth.

Anya was furious, and I blurted it out. I decided she needed to know that part at least. I told her about the man who was my father by pure biology alone: Mark Little. He got life for beating a man to death who'd been working in a post office Little was trying to rob at the time. I don't remember any of this. Part of my mum's disabilities came from him having thrown her down some stone stairs when I was a newborn baby.

He had hepatitis and died in Brixton Prison. And that was the end of him. At least, in the corporeal sense. I try not to think about it, but I find it very hard to forget that fifty per cent of my DNA comes from him.

Anya had held me tightly that night and told me she loved me and that it was going to take a lot more than a 'gangster dad' to change that.

She didn't know everything about me.

I could only test her love so far.

IRENE

Irene placed her chunky Nokia next to the sink and stared out at the small rectangle of back garden.

Why wasn't Michael picking up? It was the third time she had called him this week and it kept going to voicemail. Her son could be very elusive sometimes.

The grass was emerald bright after all the rain and badly in need of a cut. Michael had promised he would be round this week to do it.

When her husband Colin was alive, the garden was kept in an immaculate state. He spent hours out there, in all weathers, digging flowerbeds and tending their small vegetable patch.

Now and then she pulled up a weed or two, but she wasn't able to do much these days and relied on Michael, for this and other little jobs about the place.

Sighing, she put the kettle on and then, from nowhere, she was sideswiped by a scene.

The two boys, aged maybe ten and five, playing football on that lawn. It wasn't so tidy then; strewn with plastic toys, footballs, and cricket bats. This wasn't one specific memory, just an ordinary afternoon that would have played itself out many times. It was so vivid on the canvas of her

21

mind now, she felt as though she could step right back into it.

Liam, her little firecracker, was probably cheating again, running around his red-cheeked brother with a cheeky grin that meant he got away with an awful lot more than he should. Michael, always so concerned with fairness, would have been huffing and puffing with the injustice of it all. Liam wouldn't have been able to resist stoking the flames, goading his big brother and maybe calling him a mean name. They would be fighting before she had the chance to rush out and prise them apart.

Michael was so much bigger and stronger than his brother, but would never really hurt him, even when he was pushed. But still they fought like cat and dog and at the time it drove her doolally.

She smiled now, remembering it. It felt as though those long days of the boys' childhood would go on for ever. But no one told you that they would be gone one day.

She was always so tired then. Her supermarket job left her exhausted every day, with an aching back and sore feet. Little time for much beyond making tea and hanging out washing before sitting in front of the television.

Irene wished she could step back into that afternoon, just for one hour. She'd wrap herself in it, bathe in every single second. There would be no, 'I'm too tired to play' or, 'Go and watch telly, boys, I'm busy.' There would be cake and sweets and as much Coca-Cola as they wanted to drink. She wouldn't even bother with the diet stuff. She'd play all day if that's what they wanted.

She swiped at her eyes.

Silly old baggage.

Glancing now, despite herself, at the space next to the cupboard where the cat bowls had lived until recently. Stupid still to be upset about this, when there were so many awful things going on in the world. Michael had brushed it off a bit when she'd told him.

But she couldn't help the sadness that surged now as she thought about the comfort that old moggy had been.

The kettle seemed to have boiled already. She wasn't sure she even felt like a cup of tea now, or the sandwich she was planning to make.

Michael was always nagging her to look after herself properly, but it was difficult, when she was on her own.

She hoped he was alright, whatever he was doing.

What was he doing?

He pretended that he was happy, but she knew he wasn't, not really. How could they be happy, after what had happened, any of them?

Abandoning all thoughts of tea now, Irene went into the sitting room and picked up the photograph that sat on the mantelpiece. Liam, aged eight, all gappy teeth and sparkling eyes. He was always such a beautiful child. When he was a toddler, people used to stop her to comment on his auburn hair and those big, light brown eyes. Once, when she was up in London for the day visiting her mother, a man in the street gave her a card and said he was from a modelling agency that represented children. Modelling!

Irene had been dying to tell Colin about it when she got home, but he hadn't been excited at all. He said that Liam already ruled the roost and it wouldn't do him any favours to make him a bighead. She never called the modelling man.

It was a shameful thing she kept locked away inside; the fact that Liam had always been that tiny bit easier to love than his older brother.

Michael was always sick; always complaining about something or another.

And as an adult, he had all his weird theories about things;

that there was a secret group of powerful people who controlled everything we did, that the state was constantly monitoring us. Irene couldn't really keep up and just humoured him when he went into one of his rants.

Liam, though, seemed to have sprung from her womb raring to go at life. He sparkled with some sort of vitality that pulled you in.

He could have been anything, really. She gazed at the picture in her hands. He was still so open then, at primary school. Later, his smile became uncertain and wary. That was when things started to go wrong for him, at secondary school. He was always drawn to the bad lads, the cheeky ones at first, then worse. Something about extreme behaviour in others seemed to draw him like an insect to a lit window, and just like that insect, he would destroy himself, bashing against the glass.

For a minute she allowed herself a fantasy.

Liam was working in some sort of well-paid job in an office. He had a nice car and liked to go on holidays to hot places, where he bought her daft souvenirs. He hadn't settled down yet, but was getting serious about the latest girlfriend, a nice girl he'd met at work. Michael's marriage was still going strong and he hadn't lost his job. Maybe he'd had a promotion and they would celebrate with Prosecco. Everyone was always going on about Prosecco and Irene hadn't ever tried it. For a moment the fantasy was so real and delicious she could almost hear the sounds of them all around her.

Irene leaned forwards and covered her face with her hands.

It killed Colin. That was for sure. Even though they had their differences – God knows they did – Colin still loved his son. For a time after they got that postcard, their last contact with him, Colin had raged about the 'lack of consideration' and the 'utter thoughtlessness for anyone else'. But

24

when it was evident that Liam really wasn't coming back, even when Colin was sick . . . well, it did for him.

All the postcard said was, 'I have to go away. I'm sorry. Don't look for me. Lx'.

His passport was missing. He'd been talking for ages about how he wanted to 'get away'. Ever since he was a little boy, really.

And now it was just her and Michael left.

She went back into the kitchen to check her mobile again.

Where are you, Michael?

ELLIOTT

Gloomy at the prospect of going back to work after the weekend, I'd stayed up too late the night before watching a trashy horror film and drinking a few beers.

In the morning, I was feeling scratchy and tired and not at all like a man who'd just had six weeks off.

I found myself thinking about Mum again, which immediately led me down an unwelcome rabbit hole.

Nowadays I would probably be called a child carer or something, but it didn't really seem like that at the time. I just had to do a bit more on occasion than most kids my age.

Mum had rheumatoid arthritis that used to flare up quite often, leaving her skin grey and her eyes deadened as she crab-walked gingerly around our small flat. She had strong drugs that were supposed to help but she said they made her sick, so she had periods of not taking them. Her weight had always been a problem and I can't exactly say we had the best diet, so she was what you'd call clinically obese.

We lived in a ground-floor flat that was a stone's throw from Holloway Road.

'Like the prison?' Anya said once, eyes wide.

Like the prison. Our estate was one of those blocks of flats built in the 1930s.

Morningside House was a big rectangle of brown and white buildings with a scummy grass area in the middle. The 'No ball games' signs were ignored but so much of the grass was covered in dog shit that it wasn't exactly a draw anyway. I mostly played football in the playground after school.

There were benefits to living on the ground floor here, in that you never had to use the pissy-smelling stairs. The lifts never worked. But there was much more chance of being broken into, not that we had anything worth stealing. Mum had her bag taken right off our kitchen table when we were in the other room, eating our favourite meal (Findus Crispy Pancakes and oven chips) and watching *EastEnders*. We never even heard the door being jemmied open.

But that was lucky, for where we lived. There weren't quite as many stabbings as you hear about now, but there were still a number, plus the odd shooting. More than anything, though, people opted for the good old-fashioned methods; knuckle, boot, and skull. Maybe the odd car jack or iron bar.

On one side of us was a family with three sons who seemed to spend the better part of the day beating seven shades of shit out of each other. Every now and then you'd hear the mum, Marie, shouting that she would 'burn down the fucking house one day, with youse-all in it'. It sometimes seemed quite a reasonable idea.

Brendan was the father, a hairy-faced bull of a man whose glower alone could send me scuttling into the house if I happened to come across him outside the flats. The three sons – Frank, Kieran, and Bobby – were all a little older than me but the youngest, Bobby, had enough of a sphere of influence at school for me to avoid ever passing on stuff I saw or heard from their household. Like the time I saw Marie kick him up the backside at the front door because he couldn't open it fast enough. All it took was one look from him, anger and humiliation glittering hard in his eyes, for me to know to keep my mouth shut.

When Mum's pain got too bad, she would sometimes go to bed and not get up for a day or two. She took Valium – had been on it for years – from the days when GPs thought nothing of prescribing it for every period of stress or mild sleeplessness. She wasn't a huge drinker but she knew that if she combined it with alcohol then it would knock her out. That was all she wanted. I don't think she even liked the taste of alcohol very much.

My neighbour on the other side was an elderly Scottish woman called Mrs McAllister, known as Mrs Mack. She had neat, grey curls and bright eyes behind thick glasses. Her mouth seemed to transmit disapproval without the need for words.

There had always been a polite distance between her and Mum. Mum said she thought Mrs Mack disapproved of us, once speculating it was because of Mum's brown skin. Or maybe it was because she knew about my father. When she said that it gave me a weird feeling in my stomach. Like there was a thread that tied me to him, still. That I was somehow the same as him.

The whole thing with Mrs Mack started on one of those days when Mum had taken to bed. I came in from school and could tell straight away that she was home, but that something was wrong. There was a stillness, a kind of hesitation in the atmosphere, like the house was waiting for me.

Her bedroom door was closed. I popped my head in and could see the mound of her in the bed, smell the sweetish smell of her bedroom, a mix of smoke, the air freshener on the side, and a uric tang from the damp patch on the ceiling.

Afternoon light was bleeding through the thin orange curtains, highlighting crumpled tissues on the floor next to the bed and an empty can of beer.

This was the sort of detail Anya would never have been able to understand. A gulf of distance so large would open up between her and what she thought my mum was, that I wouldn't be able to face trying to explain. So, there was only so much I told her about it.

As for the other stuff . . .

If I could just keep her away from the darkness, you see, and in the light where she belonged, maybe we really had a chance long term. Maybe I would stop feeling that she was an incredible gift I only had on loan.

That day I had been desperate to speak to Mum after school. We'd been given a letter in History about a trip to the Imperial War Museum and it was going to cost parents ten pounds. Museums weren't free then, so I'd never been, and being a bit obsessed with old war movies, had always wanted to go and see all the tanks and guns. Mum was on benefits and I knew that ten pounds was a lot, but it seemed reasonable to me that we could spare this when it was for school. Especially if Mum could afford a can of Stella when it suited her.

I wandered into the living room and booted a cushion covered in a greasy sort of green taffeta across the room with as much savagery as I could muster. It knocked down a dusty cactus that sat in a knitted pot-cover on the table by Mum's chair. I glared at it for a moment, then prowled into the kitchen.

Rooting in the fridge, I saw Mum hadn't got to the shops like she'd said she would. I knew that I'd be trying to find enough change in her purse for some chips again. I was always starving then, right in the middle of a pre-pubescent growth spurt. My knees were like knots in pieces of string, my elongated thigh muscles giving me almost constant pain. I found the crust of a loaf, and slathered on the last of the peanut butter, before folding the whole thing into my mouth at once. It was never enough. Hunger felt like something living inside me, a growling beast that nagged and heckled.

I wandered out to the front of the flats, not knowing what I wanted to do, but feeling like the whole place was wrapping itself round me and squeezing air from my lungs.

Mrs Mack had a series of little pots outside her house, along with a ceramic toadstool and a Smurf holding a fishing rod. I looked down at it, with its annoying blue face, and before I knew what I was doing, I'd slammed my toe into it so hard it went clattering down the length of the path running in front of the houses. My toe hurt through my trainer and, before I could run off, her front door was open, and she was peering out at me.

'What was that?' she said. I stared back at her, too numb to speak.

She regarded me through her horn-rimmed glasses like I was a specimen in a jar and said, 'What are you doing, lurking out there anyway?'

'Not lurking,' I managed to grunt. Then, 'Going to get chips.' I didn't know why I added that. It was the first thing that came into my head. I didn't even have the money for any chips.

She looked at me for a few moments more. 'I've made a cottage pie,' she said. 'Do you like cottage pie?'

I shrugged. It wasn't so much confusion about my feelings on cottage pie (I was hazy on exactly what it was). Guilt at what I'd done, coupled with the horror that she would notice it any second, was stoppering my throat like a wad of cotton wool. My cheeks throbbed with heat and I stared down at my shuffling feet, willing time to move on so I was anywhere but here.

'Come on,' she said, opening the door up wider. 'You're like a string bean. You need something better than chips inside you.'

I hesitated for a moment, calculating how I might be able to hide the evidence of my Smurf-destruction, and reasoned it would be easier to keep her distracted for a while.

I went into her hallway and the smell of cooking meat immediately flooded my mouth with longing. I had to swallow to stop myself drooling like a dog.

It turned out that I liked cottage pie very much indeed, along with pudding thrillingly steamed in a tin and served with thick custard for afters. I liked the biscuit tin with the picture of the Scottish Highlands on the cover (I only knew that because she told me) and I liked the proper Ribena, gloopy and sweet, that she had instead of Value blackcurrant squash we sometimes had.

I don't know why that day was different to the others. But she should never have invited me in.

IRENE

Irene's hands trembled as she checked inside her handbag for her purse. It would involve a bus ride to get to Michael's flat and she got anxious about travelling anywhere on her own lately. But she needed to know what was going on.

She thought about ringing Linda. She still had her number.

The shameful truth was that she was a little frightened of Linda, with her screechy laugh and her sharp tongue. No wonder she and Michael hadn't lasted, although Irene wasn't naïve enough to think that her eldest son had been blameless in the marriage.

It was drizzly outside, and Irene felt a strong desire to turn straight back as she began to walk down the street. Everything felt so loud after being on her own for the last couple of weeks – roaring traffic and the jarring sound of human voices.

When the boys were little, and scared about something, she used to say to them, 'Just put one foot in front of the other,' and that's what she did now, making her way to the bus stop and joining a small queue of people there. A young woman with a pram was jiggling it backwards and forwards in an attempt to distract a baby that was emitting hiccupy sounds of misery. The woman's eyes had lilac smudges beneath them and her long red hair was greasy at the roots. Irene gave her a sympathetic smile and the woman looked surprised for a moment, almost as though she felt caught out in her thoughts, then she rewarded Irene with a returned smile.

'How old?' Irene said, peering into the pram and seeing a baby so tiny it still bore the wrinkled, shocked look of the newly hatched.

'Three weeks,' said the woman quietly. Irene looked up to see her eyes were now brimming with tears.

She patted the hand that was holding the handle of the pram and said, 'It will get so much easier. I promise you that, sweetheart,' and the woman nodded her thanks and lowered her eyes.

Climbing onto the bus, Irene felt a stab of guilt at what she had said. If only sleepless nights were the hardest bit of parenting. She hadn't expected to be worrying herself sick in the wee small hours about her children when it had been thirty-four years since she had given birth.

When, twenty minutes later, she arrived at the street where Michael was renting the attic room, she looked up and down for his car. But there was no sign of it.

That didn't mean anything in itself, she told herself, as she got to the terraced house where he lived. He might just be out.

Her stomach turned over as she pictured him lying on an unmade bed with an empty bottle of pills next to him. It would be so unlike him to do something like that though, wouldn't it? He had never been the one to take drugs. Not after his brother.

But life hadn't been especially kind to him lately. Breaking up with Linda had really cut him up, however much he'd claimed he was 'better off without her'.

Irene was glad they didn't have any children of their own, even though she would have loved grandchildren. It would have made the break-up even harder on everyone.

Gathering herself, Irene went to the front door and located the buzzer for the top flat. There was no name, just 'Top flat'. It wasn't the sort of place anyone would put down roots. When Michael got made redundant from the print company he'd worked with for many years, he'd been given a small pay-out, which was keeping him afloat. When she'd asked him about getting a new job, he told his mother he was 'assessing his options'. He was forty, but that wasn't very old these days, was it? Forty felt like nothing much now, not to Irene, anyway.

There was no reply from the top flat. Irene pressed the buzzer again and then got a shock as the front door was suddenly flung open. A young black man with a woolly hat and a beard, a cigarette halfway to his mouth, seemed as surprised to see her and for a moment they both stared at each other.

'You going in?' he said after a moment and Irene blurted out, 'Do you know Michael? He lives in the top flat?'

The man scrunched his brow for a minute then recognition dawned. 'That fat ginger bloke?'

Irene bristled, but forced herself to remain polite.

'He's my son,' she said. It was answer enough for the other man who avoided her direct gaze then and said, 'Not for a while. Ask Rowan on the second floor. She usually knows what's going on.'

Irene thanked him stiffly and, as he bounded down the steps behind her with an air of gratitude to be getting away, she came into the cramped hallway. There were two bicycles to one side, and on the other an ornate and old-fashioned wooden sideboard with a speckled mirror. It was covered in a sea of post and fast-food flyers and, looking around awkwardly, Irene began to rifle through, separating the letters from the flyers.

She quickly found one, then two letters addressed to Michael, but on closer inspection, they looked like junk mail. She put them back.

The steps were steep, and covered with a treacherously rucked carpet, so she climbed slowly but was still a little out of breath when she got to the top floor. She took a moment to collect herself, then rapped on the door to Michael's flat. She waited, then did it again, but there was no response.

'Michael? Love?' she called out, hating how quivery she sounded. Nothing happened.

Reluctantly, she walked back down the stairs and found herself hesitating on the second floor.

She felt silly knocking on doors and speaking to strangers about her business, but, in for a penny, in for a pound, she guessed.

Some very strange sounds were emanating from inside the flat there. It sounded like someone was giving birth, having an argument and playing the drums at the same time.

Irene steeled herself once again and knocked gently on the door. Nothing happened for a moment and so she did it again with more confidence this time. The music, if that's what you could call it, abruptly stopped.

The door opened, and a very overweight woman peered blearily out at Irene. She was somewhere in middle age, with hair in pale-coloured dreadlocks held back by a red scarf. Her skin bore the look of a lifelong smoker and there was a sweetish smell that even Irene recognized wafting out of the flat. It no doubt explained the slightly unfocused look in her eyes.

'Can I help you, darling?' she said in a surprisingly high-pitched, girlish voice.

'I'm looking for my son, Michael,' said Irene. Suddenly

she found she was close to tears. Her knees were hurting, and she was gasping for a hot drink. All she wanted was for someone to say, 'There's nothing to worry about. Michael's fine.'

The woman looked at her and something Irene couldn't place passed across her face. Maybe something had happened between her and Michael. Irene couldn't help herself immediately hoping he had used protection and then being disgusted with herself for even thinking like this.

'I haven't seen him in two weeks,' said the woman, frowning now. 'He hasn't been answering any of my messages.'

'Oh.' Irene felt herself sagging and leaned a hand against the doorframe.

She hadn't wanted it to be anything other than a silly old bat with too much time on her hands worrying about nothing. But this strange person now looked as worried as Irene felt.

'Look, you'd better come in,' said the other woman.

ELLIOTT

It was probably thinking about all that childhood stuff earlier, but when I got to the school playground, my eyes seemed to fix on Tyler Bennett straight away.

Tyler was one of those kids it was very hard to like, even though I wasn't meant to say that. He was a three-foot-high block of truculence, with a sulky face and the ability to be ever the wronged party in a dispute.

He was standing now just inside the school gates with a mutinous expression, clearly waiting for someone. The bell was just about to go so I wandered over to him. He greeted me with the sort of look dogs give when they suspect someone is about to take their bone away.

'Alright, Tyler?' I said. 'What are you doing? Bell's about to go.'

He ignored me and peered out of the gate, little brow so scrunched his eyes almost disappeared.

'Are you waiting for something?' The bell rang out clearly.

'C'mon, mate, time to go in.' I touched his shoulder and he reacted as though he had been hit, pulling his arm away violently.

'Woah!' I said, taking a step back. At that exact moment, as if conjured up from nowhere, a huge, bullet-headed man appeared at the gate, brandishing Tyler's school bag and breathing heavily.

'What are you doing?' said the man, presumably young Tyler's progenitor.

'I'm not doing anything,' I said reasonably, because I'd met plenty of parents like this one. 'I was just telling Tyler the bell's gone.'

'Did you touch him just then?'

I stared at the man for a second. 'I tapped him lightly on the shoulder in a friendly way,' I said, my face entirely straight. 'Because the bell had gone.'

'That true, Ty?'

Tyler shrugged. After an agonizing moment's pause he added, 'S'pose,' and I was ridiculously grateful to the little sod for not making this worse just for sport.

'Right,' said the man. 'Well, he was waiting for me, wasn't he?' He moved closer to his son, as though making a point, before handing the bag to Tyler, whose gaze was flitting between us in wide-eyed fascination. The man's eyes narrowed further and he said, 'Wait, do I know you?'

'I'm a teacher at your son's school, so I imagine you may recognize me,' I said, giving the man a broad smile. His type hated that. You can really wrong-foot aggressive people with a bit of sunshine. I should have stopped there, but my annoying weekend, a residual irritation with Anya for abandoning me, and the toxic swill of my thoughts earlier all conspired against me. Before I turned away, I found myself muttering, 'You have an *excellent* day, now.'

The man's cheeks darkened. It was unnerving to see aggression painted even more boldly on his face.

'You've got a real attitude, do you know that?' he said, his voice a low rumble that got me in the gut, just as it was intended to.

'I can assure you I haven't, Mr, uh . . .' My brain flailed

for Tyler's surname before it came to me. 'Mr Bennett. I'm just trying to do my job and get your son in for the start of the new term.'

The man was frowning now, staring hard at my face, and then a malicious grin broke out over his.

'I know who you are,' he said.

I formed my mouth into a pleasant smile. 'Well, as I said, I work here.'

'Nah,' he said, shaking his head. 'Not from here.'

Did he? I couldn't think how. His accent was a little more London than the local one, but I still didn't know him.

'I don't think so, Mr Bennett,' I said. He made a snorting sound, then muttered something under his breath. All I caught was, 'for you . . .'

'I beg your pardon?' I said.

Bennett did a sort of 'nya nya' thing, then shook his head and walked off without saying anything else to his son. Tyler's thumb had snuck into his mouth during this exchange, something I hadn't noticed him do before. I attempted a friendly smile.

'Come on, buddy,' I said. 'I'm no happier than you are that the holidays are over. Let's go in.'

As I got to the building I turned, and my heart seemed to jolt out of its place. Bennett was standing across the road, staring right at me.

ELLIOTT

I felt on edge all morning after that encounter. I'd dealt with aggressive parents before, as I said, but there was something about him that had really chilled me. There had been the hint of a smile there, like he'd been contemplating actions further down the line that he would enjoy very much, and I wouldn't. And why did he think he knew me?

At breaktime I looked out for Clare, Tyler's class teacher. I wanted to know whether she had ever been on the other end of the Tyler paterfamilias's displeasure.

She wasn't about – maybe on playground duty. I went to make myself a coffee. There was a sink full of dirty mugs. With a sigh I cleaned one as best I could with hot water and something that had once been a dish scourer, then decided to be the bigger person and do the lot. I was up to my elbows in suds when Zoe appeared next to me.

'You're *really* good at that,' she said in an earnest-sounding voice. 'Would you like to be our Sink Monitor this week?'

I mouthed, 'Piss off,' at her and threw a bit of foam. She laughed and flicked it away.

'So . . .' I said after a moment. I grinned and waggled my eyebrows.

Her cheeks flushed.

'What?' she said.

'Tell me all about Tabitha then,' I said, nudging her in the side. She looked down, failing to hide the way her eyes instantly lit up.

'What do you want to know exactly?' she said, getting out one of the clean cups and reaching into her handbag for one of her horrible green teabags that tasted of garden mulch.

'Well, I don't know,' I said. 'You've kept so quiet about it, I don't know anything. I feel like . . .' I bit off the end of my sentence.

'What?' she said, serious now. It was my turn to blush.

'I dunno,' I said. 'It just seems weird not to tell me.' I stopped, then said quietly, 'That . . .'

'That I'm a lesbian?' she said at the top of her voice. Several heads shot up from the various battered chairs around the room. Mary Martinson, who had been a teaching assistant here for about a thousand years as far as I could tell, was staring with her mouth actually open from the sofa in the middle of the room, a plastic bowl of salad in her lap.

I didn't really know what to do. I hadn't intended to force Zoe to out herself like that in the middle of the staffroom. I made myself a cup of coffee I no longer wanted. I could hear her breathing heavily next to me as she reached for the packet of Value ginger nuts that some kindly soul had left for all to eat.

I must have looked as awkward as I felt. Zoe touched my arm. I looked at her and she said, 'Why would I?' in a quiet voice.

'I don't know,' I said. 'It's none of my business. But I thought it might just have come up in conversation, like, I dunno, I talk about Anya.'

Zoe nodded and gestured for me to come over to a quieter bit of the room with her. There were only a couple of minutes left of break and I had things to do, but this felt important, so I followed, with my unwanted coffee.

'I don't know why I did that just now,' she said, taking a sip of her tea. She flashed me a quick, vulnerable smile. 'I'm still kind of finding my way, in all honesty.' I waited, and she continued. 'I was with a bloke for years. Bit of an arsehole. One day I'll get shitfaced and tell you all about it.' She puffed out her cheeks and sighed, then continued, in an even quieter voice. 'I didn't expect to fall in love with a woman, but it seems I have.'

When she put down her mug I gave her a little mock punch on the arm.

'Sensible decision,' I said. 'Women are lovely. Blokes are hairy, horrible things.' Her loud laugh turned heads again.

'I knew I could rely on you for a deep, philosophical conversation,' she said. 'Thanks for helping me work through this complex issue.'

'Anytime, doll,' I said in my best old-time American accent.

She laughed and then her expression turned serious again.

'And you?' she said. 'Everything okay with you guys?'

I looked back at her, puzzled and not a little discomfited.

'Me and Anya, you mean?' I said. 'Why?'

She looked flustered and gave a slightly forced laugh. 'Oh, nothing, nothing,' she said. 'Just with leaving early and all.'

'No,' I said. 'She was just under the weather, no biggie.'

'Right,' she said. 'Right,' then, with a bright smile, 'Anyway, things to do, kids to corral!'

I didn't manage to see Clare until afternoon break because I was on lunchtime playground duty.

I watched Tyler for a bit at lunchtime. He was part of a football game that mainly involved screaming at the top of his lungs and denigrating the prowess of his team mates. I found myself wondering again about his home life so, when I saw Clare in the staffroom, I asked if I could have a quick word.

Clare was a small, serious woman in her forties. She had a couple of kids and a husband who, as far as I could gather, did as little as he could in their upbringing. She often seemed to be sighing at her mobile phone and generally had a care-worn sort of air about her.

We sat down on the sofa. She peeled the lid of a tub of yoghurt and began to spoon the contents into her mouth in small, neat movements.

'So,' I said, 'tell me about Tyler Bennett's dad.'

She made a face and then said, 'What do you want to know?'

I told her what happened that morning at the school gates. She sighed and put down her yoghurt and spoon.

'Well, he's an ex-soldier,' she said. 'His name's Lee. Emily, Tyler's mum, died of breast cancer.'

'Shit,' I said. 'I didn't know.'

'Hmm.' She fixed me with a serious look, and her next sentence came out in a rush. 'I probably shouldn't pass this on,' she said, 'but he's an ex-offender. I think there were some issues with the mother after he came back from Iraq. Possibly PTSD or something like that. But whatever went on, they had got over their differences when she got sick.'

'Right,' I said thoughtfully.

'I do find him a bit prickly,' she went on. 'But I think he's just trying to cope on his own, so I generally cut him, and the boy, a bit of extra slack. Can't be easy for them.'

'No,' I said. 'Can't be easy at all.'

As I made my way back to the classroom I thought about poor little Tyler and the big tough man who was trying to be both mum and dad in that sad household.

I felt sorry for him. But I didn't like the sound of 'ex-of-fender' and the implication of domestic violence.

It was a little too close to home.

IRENE

There was a ginger cat lying across the middle of the carpet. It wore a grumpy expression and gave a silent, shivery mewl as she stepped over it and looked for somewhere to sit down.

A quite astonishingly ugly dog – a pug, perhaps; Irene didn't really 'do' dogs – wandered over and made snuffling noises while pawing at her foot. It was almost spherical, neck wrinkles spilling onto its fat little body.

'Come on, Elvis,' said the woman, and scooped the animal up, 'you need to be on good behaviour for our visitor.'

The room was dimly lit, some kind of Turkish rug slung over the window. It didn't fit, and daylight streamed from the sides. Otherwise the room was lit by a series of lamps. There was a sofa so low to the ground, Irene worried about getting back out of it again, covered in a pale orange sheet and piled with cushions. Most of them had colourful prints that Irene thought of as Moroccan.

On various surfaces were remnants of half-melted puddles of candles. Along with the sweet drug scent, Irene could smell garlic and some sort of musky perfume from the woman.

'Can I get you anything to drink? You look a bit peaky,' said the woman, in that girlish voice. The dog panted in her arms, ham-like tongue lolling, giving it an even more unappealing look.

Irene carefully lowered herself onto the sofa, which gave even more than she'd expected. She tried to cover up her discomfort by smoothing her skirt over her knees and fixing the woman with a dignified stare. She wanted to decline the offer, but she really could do with a cup of tea. For a moment she worried that the woman might only have strange druggie tea, then said, 'Yes please. Do you have tea?'

'Only PG Tips, I'm afraid,' said the woman and Irene felt relief flooding her veins.

'Then yes please,' she said.

The kitchen was behind a beaded curtain and Irene could see the woman (Rowan, was it?) collecting cups from a tree mug as the kettle boiled.

When she came back into the room, she was also carrying a few misshapen biscuits on a plate, along with Irene's drink. Irene took the slightly chipped mug, which seemed clean enough, and eyed the strange biscuits now on the coffee table, which was otherwise covered in copies of a magazine called *Spirit and Destiny* and an almost full ashtray.

'Have a biscuit,' said Rowan, taking one herself and biting into it with a loud crunch. 'They're made from hemp and flax seeds. Really good for you.'

Hemp definitely sounded druggie. And this person looked very much like the sort who wouldn't wash her hands after touching an animal. Irene declined, even though her stomach was rumbling, and took a sip of her tea. It was strong and milky, just how she liked it, and she could feel it restoring her almost straight away.

'I'm Rowan,' said the woman. She was looking at Irene in that way people do when you get to a certain age; as if you're daft. The dog settled onto her lap and regarded Irene with the occasional nasal wheeze, like it had a head cold.

'Yes, I know,' said Irene and was taken aback to see the bright eagerness on Rowan's face now.

'Oh, did he talk about me then?' she said. 'Michael?'

'Sorry, no,' Irene said quickly. She hadn't intended this to be cruel but the other woman's mouth turned down at the sides.

Oh Michael, she thought. *This isn't your sort of person.* She wondered if that was why he went away. Had he got in too deep with this woman?

'He's talked about you a lot,' said Rowan, blowing on her tea. Hers was in one of those impractical teacups with a huge circumference and a tiny handle. Steam curled up from it and she seemed to cradle it more for comfort than from a desire to drink. 'Very warmly.'

Irene couldn't help the rush of pleasure at hearing these words. It wasn't something she would have assumed at all. Sometimes she thought she was an annoyance to her eldest son. She didn't trust herself to speak and instead nodded and took another sip of the tea.

Rowan watched her carefully. Irene got the strange feeling that the other woman knew exactly what she was thinking. Michael wouldn't have liked that. He was always private.

'Yes,' she continued, 'he said that you're the strongest woman he has ever known.'

Irene put the mug onto the table too briskly, so that the tea almost slopped out of the top. She mashed her trembling hands together in her lap. Impossible to hold onto any reserve now.

'Did he really?' she managed, emotion coagulating in her voice.

Rowan leaned forward and clasped her own hands together, as though praying. The dog slid off her lap and went into the kitchen, where Irene could hear it lustily slurping from a water bowl.

'He really did.' She paused. 'Look,' she said and gave a deep, wheezy breath inwards, 'I know all about . . . well, Liam going missing.'

'Oh,' said Irene. 'That's not quite what . . .' She picked up the cup again for something to do, even though she no longer wanted the tea. It felt strange to say he was 'missing' but wasn't that word painfully on the money in so many ways? There was a long, strained silence. Then she said, 'Where is Michael, Rowan? Where has he gone?'

'Well, that's the thing,' said Rowan. 'I think he's gone looking for him.'

'What makes you say that?' This came out too sharply, but Irene couldn't help it. It touched on the same painful well of hope that allowed her to get out of bed each morning. 'Has he heard from him?'

Rowan blushed now, unexpectedly, and stared down at her cup. It was very bizarre. She didn't seem like a woman easily given to embarrassment. Then she looked up and there was something in her eyes that Irene felt herself drawing away from.

'What is it?' she said tightly.

'It came out wrong just now . . . about looking for him.'

Irene was beginning to feel exhausted from this visit. It was an emotional rollercoaster. Now she was getting irritated with this woman and her riddles.

'What do you mean?'

'I mean,' said Rowan with excruciating patience, 'that I think he's trying to find out exactly what happened to him all those years ago.'

All those years ago . . . As if it were a hundred. As if it were a thousand. As if it didn't matter any more.

'Mrs Copeland,' said Rowan. 'You know Michael believes Liam is dead, don't you?'

ELLIOTT

I was cycling home when it happened.

I'd naïvely thought, moving from London, that it would be easy to cycle here. I'm not exactly sure what planet I was on, thinking city drivers were the aggressive ones, but the way they hammered round the narrow lanes here at all hours had come as a bit of a shock. Still, we only had one car and Anya needed to drive to the next station along for the better train connection to London, where she worked, so I cycled in every day.

I was on the road that led from the top end of town when I heard the sound of a car behind me. It didn't overtake as I'd expected it to where the road got wider. I turned to look behind me, but the driver had on a baseball cap and sunglasses; plus, they were sort of hunkered down in their seat. The car was a dark SUV – black or dark blue, I couldn't really tell.

An uneasy feeling rippled up my neck and I pedalled harder, knowing that the turning to lead me off this road was coming up soon. The car just seemed to purr malevolently along behind me for ages. I thought about that movie *Duel*, where the guy is terrorized by a never-revealed maniac in a huge truck. The road was coming closer and I pedalled even harder. I was almost there when I heard the roar of the engine behind me – right there. Awash with shock, I wobbled and then toppled sideways, crashing onto the narrow pavement. The car zoomed away with an angry roar around the corner before I got a chance to see the number plate.

'Shit!' I said. Pain sliced through my knee, which was caught under the bent frame of the bike. My hands blazed with a burning, stinging pain. Looking down, I saw a constellation of tiny stones and beads of blood on both my palms. The front wheel of my bike was all bent from hitting the pavement, and I'd jarred my back.

'Bastard, bastard,' I said with feeling and hobbled towards home, having to hold the front half of the bike off the ground all the way.

I was surprised and grateful to find that Anya was there when I got back. She didn't normally get in until about seven.

I'd taken the bike down the alley to the backyard and I opened the kitchen door to find her standing at the stove, stirring something in a pan. When she saw me, her face went from pleasure to concern in half a beat.

'Did something happen?' she said, wiping her hands and coming over to me.

'Fell off my bike,' I said. She made a sympathetic noise and took my backpack from me. 'Well, I say that, but I was essentially forced off it by some tosser who thought I was Dennis Weaver.'

'Oh no!' she said, and it made me smile, despite the fact that most parts of my body were hurting right now. One of the things about being married that had never stopped thrilling me was the near-telepathy over cultural references.

She came over and turned my palms round, then gently kissed the grazes. It hurt but I managed not to wince.

Anya helped me wash the grit out, as I told her all about

what happened, and then she gently applied antiseptic. Her brow was sweetly scrunched, as if she was doing highly skilled surgery.

My right knee ended up with a large plaster across it, which was bound to come off straight away, but I let her apply it anyway.

'So,' she said, as she put away the first aid kit and washed her hands. 'Did you get a look at the guy's face? The one in the car?'

'No, not really,' I said wearily. 'He had on a baseball cap and sunglasses. Anyway, it all happened . . .'

I paused.

'What?' said Anya, turning back to me.

'It's probably nothing,' I said. 'Just that I had an encounter with a parent today and he was a bit aggressive.' I filled her in on what had happened.

'Do you think it was him who knocked you off your bike?' she said. Her back was to me and she turned on the gas under the pan again, before starting to stir. 'You really didn't see him? Can you describe him at *all*?'

I thought about it for a moment, touched by how seriously she was taking this.

'No,' I said after a few moments. 'I can't believe he'd do that. I mean, it really was nothing.' I paused again. 'It's just that . . .'

'What?'

I blew air out through my mouth. 'I don't know, Anya, he just said this really strange thing about *knowing me*. I swear I've never spoken to the man before.'

'Knowing you?'

'Yeah . . . sort of like we'd had a beef before.'

We were both silent for a moment, thinking about this.

'Do you think he might be confusing you with someone else?' said Anya, turning to me now.

I shrugged. 'Who knows?'

As I said it, I thought about the way the man had looked at me when he was standing outside the school. Stock still, staring, his eyes cold. Aggression seeming to radiate off him. I experienced a small chill.

I went over to her and wrapped my arms around her narrow middle, leaning down to rest my chin on her shoulder. She smelled better than any person I'd ever known, and I breathed her in for a moment.

'You're feeling better?'

She nodded, looking down at the stove top.

'I'm . . .' I began '. . . I hope I wasn't a dick the other day.'

She twisted her head and gave me one swift kiss on the lips before turning back to her stirring.

'Don't worry about it,' she said, which didn't exactly reassure me.

'What are you cooking?' I said.

'Making a cheese sauce,' she said. 'For a mac cheese.'

I smiled into her neck. I was obviously forgiven. Despite all the things that my palate had been introduced to in the last few years – from crocodile steaks to guinea fowl, quinoa to (unforgettably) coffee that came out of a civet's bum – I still hankered for the comfort foods of my childhood, sometimes. This was one of the few things my mum used to cook from scratch and eating it made me think of being cosy on the sofa and watching telly together on winter evenings.

'To what do I owe the honour?'

She turned and pecked me on the cheek.

'I just thought the first day back marshalling the little monsters of Beverley Park might warrant comfort food,' she said. 'Especially now I know you've had to deal with thuggy dads and stave off maniacs in trucks.'

'Well,' I said sheepishly, 'it wasn't exactly a truck . . . but thanks.'

She started to stir more vigorously. I took the hint and moved away, going to the fridge to find some juice.

'I meant to tell you,' she said. 'Managed to lose my phone yesterday.'

I hadn't clocked that we hadn't had a text exchange today, what with everything that was going on.

I paused with the juice carton in my hand. 'That's a bummer,' I said. 'Have you used the finder app?' We had a program that showed you where your phone or laptop had last been used. It had been very handy when I'd lost my laptop last year, enabling me to track it down to a café on the seafront.

She carried on stirring, her back to me.

'Yeah but it's clearly been unlocked and disabled by someone.' She flashed me a quick, bright smile. 'Don't worry,' she said. 'It was a bit knackered anyway. I treated myself to an iPhone 8. I'll give you the new number, wait . . .'

She fished the phone from her back pocket and tapped at the screen. My own phone buzzed with her message, but I ignored it, a little distracted by what she'd said.

'Why did you change the number?' I said after a moment.

She shrugged. 'Oh, it was just a security thing . . . they prefer you to do that when it's been stolen . . . or whatever.'

I didn't reply. I'd never heard that before. Plus, it was unlike her to blithely spend money like that; and then I remembered that she had been with Patrick and Julia yesterday. They would have given her the cash for the new phone.

Those were the kind of things that rankled a bit, much as I loved my parents-in-law. It was the assumption that they could just spare, what, seven hundred pounds like that. As though it meant nothing.

When dinner was ready, we settled in front of the Sky planner with our food on trays.

I got through my portion quickly and was rising for more when I looked over and saw that Anya had basically rearranged hers, barely touching her food.

'Not hungry?' I said and she shrugged.

'Just a bit tired, is all.'

It was a strange evening, overall. I was aching all over from my earlier tumble and took myself off for a hot bath after we'd watched two episodes of a crime drama we'd been following. It was a good one, but watching the murder victim being covered in dead roses by the masked killer who had been hiding in their attic wasn't exactly a mood-lifter.

Before I went for my bath I looked over and saw Anya staring at the television with the oddest expression on her face.

It was a hard, angry look; quite unlike her, really. She'd turned the telly over to some sort of dating reality thing and it was almost like she was glaring at the contestants currently making idiots of themselves.

'Hey, you don't have to watch that, you know,' I said and for a second she snapped her gaze towards me in a way that made me stop in the doorway. Her face relaxed into a smile then and she gave a big yawn, arms above her head so the baggy sleeves of her favourite cardigan slipped down over her slim, freckled arms.

'I like enjoying the discomfort of others,' she said with a grin. 'Plus, I get to be really judgemental.'

'Well, I'll leave you to your schadenfreude,' I said as I went through to the bathroom.

'You and your fancy book learnin',' she said, in a daft American accent, before throwing a cushion at me.

She went to bed before me and I thought she was asleep when I came in later. I was a natural night owl and Anya was the opposite. I slipped gingerly under the duvet in the dark, wincing as my knee stung and my lower back throbbed.

But she turned to me straight away, bringing her face close. I saw the gleam of her wide eyes and felt her warm breath on my face.

'I love you,' she whispered.

'I love—' I started to say but then her mouth was on mine, hard, mashing against my lips so that after a moment I tasted blood. Then she was pushing the duvet away and climbing onto me. She was ready and, despite all my aches, I was too. I slid inside her with a groan. She started to rock quickly, fists pressing onto my chest, so I could feel each of her knuckles grinding into my skin. Even though it hurt, it was so exhilarating and unexpected I found myself unable to hold back after a few moments.

'Ah, sorry,' I said sheepishly. She stopped moving and leaned down, kissing me tenderly on the bruised place on my lip.

'No need to be,' she said. 'I was almost there before you came into the room. I was having a very hot dream.' She paused. 'And then there you were.'

'I'm glad I was,' I murmured and, as she turned round, I pulled her in towards me and let my sore, happy body melt into the bed.

The sound of smashing glass woke us at three am.

ELLIOTT

The first thing I did, half asleep, was flail an arm under the bed, still programmed to reach for that baseball bat of my youth. But as I properly woke up, I leaped out of bed so fast I cracked my knee – the other, non-injured one – against the bedpost. Swearing, I stumbled out of the room in the T-shirt and boxers I slept in, then crashed down the stairs, almost falling on the way.

Bursting into the living room, I couldn't see anything unusual, so I walked into the kitchen, wincing at the cold tiles beneath my bare feet. The cold air, laced with rain, was the first thing I noticed, right before I almost stood on the broken glass.

The brick lay in the middle of the kitchen floor. Standard red house brick. My first, strange, thought, was that would have come from the house a few doors down that was currently having a loft conversion. But who would do this?

'Oh my God.' Anya was behind me now, her face ashen.

'Right?' I said, my jaw tight. I was suddenly picturing Lee Bennett and his smirking face. As if on cue, my grazed hand throbbed and I discovered I was clenching my fist.

Could it really be him? Surely not?

'Okay,' I said, 'I'm calling the police.'

'Wait!' said Anya, grabbing hold of my arm. Her hand felt hot against my goose-pimpled skin. 'And tell them what?' she added, her face creased with disapproval. 'That a bunch of kids threw something through the window? What do you expect them to do? Send in Special Branch?'

'What if—' then I bit off the end of the sentence.

'What?'

I felt stupid even saying it out loud.

'What if it's that Bennett bloke from school?' I said, with heat. 'What if he tried to knock me off my bike too?'

She gave me a strange look. Obviously thought I was being ridiculous. I *was* probably being ridiculous.

'Ell,' she said, 'if it's him, then I think you'd need more evidence before you start accusing him.' I was surprised, having expected her to dismiss my paranoia.

She went on, gently placing her hand on my arm. 'But look, you know how stretched the police are round here. You've seen the same reports I have. Let's just assume it was kids and get the window fixed, yeah?'

I hesitated, knowing she was right. The local paper had been covered in screaming headlines a few weeks back about the low rates of arrest for robberies around here. Apparently, the police had almost stopped investigating minor crimes like that. This wasn't even that serious. I had no real reason to think Bennett was behind this anyway. I was probably putting two and two together and coming up with a paranoid five.

Anya left the room, coming back in with my trainers in her hand. She had her sandals on now.

'Well, we can sit here and wait with the wind blowing through the window, or we can clear it up and sort out a glazier.'

We got to work.

The glazier took hours to come. I insisted Anya go back

to bed, which she reluctantly agreed to, then set up camp in the living room, with my iPad on my lap and the sound turned low.

It took no time to find Lee Bennett's Facebook page. It was pretty much exactly what I'd expected. Selfies with his shirt off; posts with such gems of wisdom as 'Mourinho really has fucking lost it now. Time to go' and a couple of pictures with Tyler in them, mainly at football matches. He hadn't made much effort over his settings, so I delved back a bit until I found some with a woman in them.

She was blonde, and delicate-looking with a pointy chin and large eyes. She and Bennett together, clearly on holiday, with tall cocktails, tans, and lots of flesh on show. Only one with her and Tyler, where he was sitting on her lap on a train and clearly reaching for something out of shot.

The thought of anything happening to Anya caused a tight feeling in my throat, not unlike the sensation just before you throw up. What if, for whatever reason, he was going after me and putting *my* wife in danger? He thought he knew me. Maybe he was incubating some perceived slight based on mistaken identity.

I must have dozed a little because when my phone started to ring from the floor next to me, I leapt from the chair in shock. It was the glazier, telling me he was outside.

It was almost four thirty am when he was finally done. He was a taciturn Eastern European man, who had barely said a word the whole time he was here. I presumed he was usually called out to deal with robberies and the aftermath of fights in bars. I was a bit surprised to discover that all he was prepared to do was board up the thing. Seems you had to pay all over again to have the actual window replaced, at a sensible hour.

He was probably wondering why we didn't patch the

window up ourselves, just for the night. But there was no way we could have gone back to sleep; it wasn't a huge window, but it was quite big enough to allow someone in who had any kind of malign intent. I had, after all, hoped my days of sleeping with a baseball bat next to the bed were long gone.

Anyway, I didn't imagine the man was complaining, judging by the eye-watering amount of money he charged before I was wearily able to send him on his way.

In the bedroom, Anya was sleeping deeply and making small, endearing sounds through her nose. I climbed into the bed, desperate to warm my frozen limbs against her body, but I knew it would wake her up. One of us might as well get some sleep on this miserable night. So, I forced myself to keep away from her sleeping form, huddling into the duvet, trying not to think about how soon it would be before I had to get up again.

I reached for sleep, telling myself to clear my mind. I counted down in eights from four hundred, a trick I'd read on some website for insomnia, and got all the way beyond zero, but my mind still buzzed and sparked like a faulty strip light. I kept thinking about Lee Bennett, and Anya's weird mood lately.

Almost inevitably, however much I tried to yank them back to the present, I found my thoughts drifting back in time.

Mum, sitting in her favourite chair, fags on one arm and a glass of lager on the table next to her, gusts of husky smoker's laugh at *The Vicar of Dibley*.

Our windows had got broken a couple of times, on the estate. But we didn't summon twenty-four-hour glaziers who charged two hundred quid an hour. We boarded it up until a man who knew a man came and sorted it as a special favour to Mum.

When the alarm went off, it felt as though I'd only been

asleep for minutes. Parts that hadn't ached previously now hurt – elbows, the other knee, and, weirdly, my neck. Anya had to leave early to get into London and when I came out of the shower she was almost ready to leave. She was drinking a cup of coffee and staring out of the window.

She was dressed in a silky blouse and black trousers, her glossy red hair in a ponytail and a slash of bright red lipstick standing out against her pale, freckled skin. For about the millionth time I wondered what on earth I did right to end up with someone like her.

It was only after she had gone that I remembered my broken bike. I'd intended to leave with her and get her to drop me at school. I didn't know anything about buses here. It took a good half an hour to walk and I was meant to be in early today for the weekly staff meeting.

I was sweating profusely by the time I got to school.

The meeting was almost over as I came into the staffroom and I caught Zoe's eye. She pulled a doomy face and sliced a finger across her neck.

'Elliott,' said Jackie Dawson, our head teacher. 'So glad you could join us.'

I smiled sheepishly. 'Sorry. I had an accident on my bike.'

I knew it was a mistake the second the words left my lips because I saw Jackie's eyes sweep over my sweaty, but clean, light blue shirt and grey trousers. I didn't look remotely like a man who had just taken a tumble onto a road.

'I mean,' I added quickly, 'I came off it last night and, er, it took me longer to get to school this morning.' I found myself holding up my scratched palms as proof.

Jackie liked me, but for some reason this morning her expression was cooler than I would have expected. She nodded after a moment and said, 'Okay, well I'm sorry to hear that. But can we have a quick word before you go off to your class?'

'Sure,' I said and something uneasy twitched inside me.

Meeting over now, staff scattered to collect belongings and down the dregs of drinks.

I followed Jackie to her office, which was down a corridor in a part of the school. She gestured for me to close the door and my worry increased.

Jackie had been the head here for ever, as far as I could tell. Late fifties with curly brown hair, she had a mumsy softness about her appearance that belied how tough she really was.

'I won't keep you, Elliott,' she said. 'But I have to tell you that a parent has made a complaint against you.'

I let out a heavy sigh.

'Okay,' I said. 'I bet I can guess who. Tyler Bennett's dad, by any chance?'

'Yes, that's right.'

'Look,' I went on, leaning forward in my seat. 'It really was nothing. This guy just took against me, I think.' I paused. 'Didn't like the cut of my jib.'

Jackie was blank-faced. 'He said you pushed Tyler and then you were rude to him.'

A hot blast of outrage. 'That's ridiculous!' I said. 'I didn't even touch Tyler.'

As I said it, I remembered this wasn't strictly true. But it was such a gentle push to his shoulder, so it hardly counted.

'Are you sure?' said Jackie, her expression now softer. She wasn't enjoying this any more than I was.

'Yes,' I said. 'Absolutely. It's something and nothing.' Part of me wanted to tell her about the bike incident and the brick. But that just made Bennett's allegation sound as though it had more merit, so I kept quiet.

She looked relieved. 'I knew it would be, Elliott, but unfortunately we have to follow procedures, as you know, when this happens. I'll get you to write up exactly what occurred and I'm going to have to inform LADO too.' She was referring the Local Authority Designated Officer, appointed to look into any issues to do with safeguarding.

This was such bullshit. What a waste of time for everyone concerned.

Trying to quash the weariness I was feeling from my voice, I said, 'Of course. I'll get onto it.'

I had a strong desire to slink out of the office and go straight home but I forced myself to head down to my classroom. My hands were throbbing and my back hurt. Today was not shaping up well so far.

Halfway down the corridor I saw Zoe, who made that face again.

'You okay?' she said.

'Yeah. Tell you about it later.'

I got my class started on their English project, which this term was all tied up with a Viking theme, hence the visit to the museum. They were writing letters to their families at home as Viking settlers.

Ryan Reece, the class wag, shouted out, 'Sir? Do Vikings rape and pillinge?' to which I gently put him right on the word 'pillage' and got round any tricky issues by telling them that some historians felt their bad boy reputation had been exaggerated a little.

It was hard to focus though, that morning. I kept thinking about the complaint that Lee Bennett had made. Writing it all out was just going to be a drain on my time. And what for? It was such a pointless sort of disagreement, over nothing. I was angry with myself too. I knew that if I hadn't been sarcastic with him, he wouldn't have taken such grave offence.

It was something that used to occasionally get me in trouble at school, this need to make the smart comeback, both with teachers and other pupils. I knew that I did it, yet somehow I still never managed to rein it in. This was the first time I'd had a complaint like this though.

While the class had a rare five minutes of quietly getting on with their work, I opened a document and started to make a note of what had happened yesterday morning. I felt uneasy when I remembered what I said to Jackie, that I hadn't physically touched Tyler at all. Was it too late to say so now? I made a decision. I'd include it in the report and deal with the fact that I remembered differently when I gave it to her.

The other thing I intended to do was find out what sort of car Lee Bennett drove. Because if he was in such a strop that he was prepared to knock me off my bike for it, I might have an even greater problem than I first realized.

At the end of the day I lurked in the playground on the guise of checking an outdoor display of bamboo fencing that last year's upper school had made. Tyler was late coming out and I wondered if he had been given a telling-off as he crossed the playground, all slouch and sad-sack trousers. His thick, pale ankles with pooled off-white socks ended in a pair of non-regulation trainers. He held his trendy but impractical messenger bag so low that it scuffed along the surface of the playground.

I pretended I was looking around but kept one eye on the gate for any signs of Lee. And there he was. Standing just outside and smoking a fag, which he extinguished and chucked onto the pavement. His expression didn't change when he saw his son, but he rubbed his knuckles on the boy's head in a way that looked mildly uncomfortable.

They began to walk off towards a side road and I was willing to bet that was where, like many of the local parents, he parked his car. I hurried across the playground to follow them, ignoring another parent's attempt to catch my attention. I caught sight of Milly, a reception teacher, who was watching me for some reason, but I ignored her too and hurried out of the gate before I lost sight of them.

I was about to dash across the road when a white Range Rover, driving far too quickly, screeched to a halt by the yellow zigzags outside the school gates, about two feet from me.

A woman with oversized sunglasses and even bigger hair was glowering at me over the steering wheel, as if I was the unreasonable person in this scenario.

'Hey,' I called. 'This is a school! You don't drive like that on this road. You could kill a child!'

She made a 'wanker' gesture at me. I crossed the road and I find myself calling, 'Yeah? Well you too,' as she drove away.

A couple of parents clucked sympathetically at me, but I was too distracted to respond. I hurried into Caversham Road and cursed when I saw that I had missed them. Two cars were currently having a standoff, not wanting to give way, and there was a lot of angry honking and beeping. I swear half these families lived within a five-minute walking radius. We used to give out badges to reward children for walking to school but then we discovered that a small number were being encouraged to lie about it by their parents on the basis that they were otherwise 'missing out'.

I quickened my pace just in case they were on the next road up. The pavement was thick with parents, buggies, and children of various ages and so I said, ''Scuse me, 'scuse me,' as I made my way through them.

It suddenly felt imperative that I found them, and I began to run as the pavement became emptier. I turned the corner into the road at the top and almost collided with a man who was leaning against the wall there and making a phone call.

Of course, it was him.

Tyler was standing next to him, kicking at a stone with a scrunched brow of concentration.

Lee Bennett's eyes widened, and he moved away from the wall with a fluid push from his foot.

'Call you back,' he said, then, more aggressively, 'You looking for someone?'

'No, I, er . . .' My brain went blank. I couldn't think of a thing to say and my cheeks flushed with embarrassment. 'I'm just . . .' I waved my hand ineffectually as I fought for sensible words. 'I needed to give a message to a . . . another parent.'

Bennett swept his arm around in an exaggerated gesture. 'No one else here, mate,' he said.

I decided I had nothing to lose. 'No car today?'

He frowned and pulled his head back a little. 'What's it to you?'

'Nothing,' I said. 'Nothing at all.'

Face still burning, I turned away and could hear him say to Tyler, 'You stay away from him. I don't like him.'

ELLIOTT

Anya was late home that evening and I used the time to finish writing up a report for Jackie on what had happened with Bennett. I left out our uncomfortable exchange earlier that day because I had no idea how to explain what I had been doing.

I kept thinking about Tyler's sad crumpled socks and pasty ankles. It made me wonder how I would have presented to the world at that age.

After the invitation to come in for cottage pie, Mrs Mack invited me in once or twice a week. She usually invented some sort of task that needed doing; replacing light bulbs or taking her rubbish down to the big bins at the back of the flats. But I didn't mind.

She used to make me eat fruit when I went round there but there were usually plenty of biscuits too, or she'd made some sort of homemade cake. This was an entirely new experience for me and one I thoroughly approved of. One evening I brought back some scones for Mum but I got a bit of a strange reaction from her. At the time I concluded she was jealous of the time I spent next door. With my adult eye I can see that it was probably a lot more complicated than that. Maybe Mum felt that Mrs Mack was doing some of my mothering, whether she liked it or not.

Mrs Mack had her own son, a bloke called Douglas who lived in America and worked in a bank. She would show me pictures of him with his smiley, white-toothed wife and boast about how well he was doing. Douglas seemed fairly alien to me but even at that age I found it a bit sad that he never seemed to come and visit her.

One afternoon after school, she asked me to get something down from the top of her wardrobe. It was too high even for me, so I stood on a stool and reached over the tightly packed clothes that smelled flowery and old, just like she did. She was after a tin of photos.

'Do you mean this one?' I said and pulled out a wooden box about the size of a shoebox.

'No!' she said, sharply. 'Put that one back right now!'

'Why should I?' I said, because I was stung, and it made me bolshie and mean.

'Because I said so, young man.' Mrs Mack's voice was ice cold.

I, on the other hand, had flaming cheeks as I put it back and fumbled for the one next to it, a tartan tin with a picture of a Highland stag on it.

She must have seen my expression because her tone softened then. 'Thank you, Elliott,' she said, taking the tin from my hands. 'I didn't mean to snap. That one is just very private.'

I mumbled that it was okay, but it wasn't really. You carry those sort of slights as bright, bitter humiliations at that age. You might be one and a half times the size of the other person, yet they still have the ability to cut you in two with their sharp words.

We went back through to the living room and she sat down in her favourite armchair. She had been intending to show me some of the photos, but I didn't feel like it now.

She opened the lid of the tin with an expression of intense concentration and then noticed I was hovering by the door.

'Are you just going to stand there like a long streak of bacon?' she said. I would have smiled at another of her weird expressions under normal circumstances. They were often Scottish and nonsensical, like 'Hold your wheesht.' But something made me want to punish her a bit today for shouting at me. So I just shrugged.

She frowned.

'Look,' she took off her glasses, sighed and pinched the bridge of her nose. Her voice was tight when she spoke again. 'Has your mother no' got anything she likes to keep away from prying eyes?'

I thought about Mum's photo albums of her childhood and baby pictures of me, neatly stacked on the shelf by the telly. Anyone could look at those if they wanted and Mum wouldn't care.

And then I got an almost physical thump of understanding. Mrs Mack meant valuable things. Jewellery, or money. I pictured a pirate's treasure box, filled with gleaming gold coins and thick chains like the ones rappers wore, even though I knew it was more likely old lady jewellery or bank notes in there. The answer then was obvious.

'No,' I said. 'We haven't got anything like that.'

Mrs Mack made a dubious face and began to take out the pictures, placing them in a pile next to her on the sofa.

'Well, I doubt that,' she said, 'but if you're staying, come and sit down here. You're giving me neck ache up there looking at you.'

I hesitated and then sat down. It was the only time I'd ever experienced a bit of tension in this house and I was glad to be given a way out.

Plus, I thought, later as I went home, I was flattered.

I had been allowed into her confidence.

ELLIOTT

When Anya came in the front door, it was evident she'd been caught in the sudden rain shower that was flinging itself dramatically at the windows. Her hair was slicked to her head so her light brown eyes looked huge in her face, like a beautiful manga creation.

She grimaced and took off her thin jacket, which was wringing wet.

'Hey!' I laughed. 'How come you got so wet when you only had to come out of the station and hop into the car?'

She grimaced and began to head upstairs. 'Really hammering, though,' she called down. 'And I got to the car then couldn't find my bloody keys for ages.'

I laughed and started browning the chicken in the hot fat. After a while she came into the kitchen and wrapped her arms around me from behind, placing her head against my back. I could feel her trembling.

'Hey,' I said, 'you're freezing! Come here.' I lowered the gas under the wok and turned around, wrapping her in my arms. She burrowed in and I kissed the top of her head, smelling her coconut shampoo mixed with rain and the unmistakable smoky smell of travelling on the Underground. 'You really got soaked through, didn't you?'

She nodded and clung onto me. I rubbed her arms until I felt the shivering subside.

'Why don't you have a quick shower to warm up before dinner?' I said, and she drew back.

'Nah, I'll be alright,' she said. 'I think a drink should do it.' She went to the wine rack and pulled out a bottle of Shiraz. I cocked an eyebrow at her. After a fairly drunken summer, we'd vaguely made a plan to cut out drinking Monday through to Thursday nights. But after the day I'd had, I could really do with one.

Alcohol and me had a complicated relationship. The 'topic' caused a mental chafing I tried to ignore. My father had been a nasty drunk, from all accounts. I liked a drink and so did Anya, but I would have two to her one. Sometimes I'd have three. I didn't always know when to stop, as events at the festival had shown.

However, I really did want a glass of wine.

'Ah, go on then.'

There was a heightened energy about her tonight, as if she had absorbed some of the storm outside and was carrying it in her skin.

Much later, we were watching a tacky reality show we liked on Netflix for a few minutes in companionable silence when Anya suddenly spoke.

'Ell?' she said, her voice low. 'Do you ever think about running away?'

I turned to look at her. 'What?' I said. 'What do you mean, *running away*?'

She registered my expression and laughed, before hitting me on the arm. 'Not away from you, you big ninny.' It was pathetic how sweet the feeling of relief was at this. She went on. 'I mean the two of us,' she said. 'Just leaving our jobs and going travelling or something.'

I took a mouthful of food, chewing while I thought, and

then shrugged. 'Not really, if I'm honest.' I paused. 'And anyway, haven't you been there, done that, got the T-shirt?'

Anya went off for a year travelling after university. I often said things about how great it would be to do this together. But if I was honest, it was only in the way that I thought space travel might be interesting. I didn't have much of an appetite for roughing it in some of the flea-bitten hostels Anya waxed lyrical about when she talked of that time. I didn't know. Maybe when you have grown up having foreign holidays in luxury hotels, the idea of a bit of squalor has more appeal. Me, I liked to travel in comfort. There was no way we could afford to travel the way I would want to.

And what about our jobs?

She looked at me with an expression that I couldn't read. Then she made a moue and took another swig of her wine. I realized I'd finished mine and I refilled both of our glasses. I'd somehow finished my plate of stir fry without even noticing but Anya had only had about a third of hers.

'I don't know,' she said after a moment. 'Weren't you the one who was just talking about how shit your job is?'

I put my plate onto the coffee table a little too hard, so it rattled against the wood and my fork clanged.

'That's not what I was saying at all,' I said, aware I was breathing heavily now. 'I just had a bad day.'

Look, I complained bitterly like most teachers, but actually, I loved my job and I loved kids. The untrammelled, shiny-eyed joy, the all-consuming misery when your best friend is being a little sod, or you've bumped your head, the infectious giggling, the constant miasma of farting.

I probably didn't seem all that ambitious to some people. When a couple of Anya's friends found out that not only had I not gone to Oxbridge, Durham, or Bristol, but I'd done my degree through Open University while working in a Virgin Media call centre, they had looked genuinely baffled about what to say next. It was as though I'd just admitted to having herpes or enjoying taxidermy as a hobby.

I'd half wanted to tell them that where I came from, not serving time or being dead from a range of unnatural causes was an achievement in itself. But I'd kept quiet, not wanting to frighten the horses too much; sensitive thoroughbreds that they were.

Anya started out studying medicine at Cambridge, then, after not getting on with the course, moved to Bristol where she took Biology. She worked for a company that specialized in software packages for the NHS and health organizations around the world.

She earned much more money than me. That was just the way it was.

She looked at the telly now and I could feel some sort of unnamed worry begin to squirm inside me. It was like she was trying to pick a fight tonight. I thought about her being asked what her bloke did at work and the moment of surprise when she said, 'Primary school teacher.' I knew it happened. I'd seen it, right there.

Turning back to me, she smiled, but there was a distance in her eyes. 'I just wonder what it would be like sometimes,' she said, 'to up and go. Make a fresh start somewhere else, you know?'

I made a non-committal sound.

The wine tasted bitter in my mouth now as I finished the glass. It felt like the thing I've always dreaded – that she would get sick of me, that I wouldn't be enough – was prowling outside our door.

IRENE

'Oh dear, Mrs Copeland, did you burn yourself? Let me get you a cloth!'

Rowan's voice seemed to come from far away. Irene blinked hard and stared down at the pale brown stain spreading across the beige material of her trousers. She wasn't hurt; the tea was lukewarm now. If anything, the unpleasant wetness was helping to ground her. She focused on it until her breathing began to slow down. The act of spilling the tea felt lost to her. This was what scared her most about being old; that she would disappear into a warren of moments just like these and not be able to find her way out again.

'I'm quite alright,' she said but Rowan was bustling back into the room with a wet sponge and a bunched rosette of kitchen towel. She got closer to her legs than Irene would have liked before she managed to retrieve the items from her. With a stiff 'Thanks,' she dabbed at the stain.

Rowan, sitting opposite, gazed at Irene with her big, damp eyes.

'I'm so sorry if I've upset you,' she said, then, 'Did you not know?'

Irene merely managed, 'Well . . .'

It wasn't the first time she had heard this, no. But Michael himself told her that he had looked into Liam's . . . connections and had to accept that there was nothing to find. Irene had been under no illusions that her youngest son had had his share of trouble and mixing with the wrong people. His caution for a minor shoplifting offence when he was still in his teens had caused the most terrible scene between Liam and his father.

Irene became aware that Rowan was still staring at her. She looked down at the damp cloths in her hand and then placed them carefully on a magazine lying on the table in front of her. She could hear a car revving outside and a clock thunked loudly from the mantelpiece. The perfumed room and the heat were beginning to make her head ache.

'Mrs Copeland,' said Rowan. 'I didn't mean to upset you. I'm sorry.'

Irene attempted a stiff smile. She longed to get up and leave. But she needed to know what Michael had got himself into.

'It's alright, really,' she said. 'I know he had theories about this. But he didn't have anything to go on and the police weren't really all that interested.' She sighed and forced herself to meet Rowan's concerned frown. 'Do you know what, well, what set this off?'

Rowan shook her head. One of the snaky masses held back by her scarf fell over her face and she pushed it back.

'I'm so sorry,' she said. 'He didn't tell me anything other than he felt that he was finally about to uncover, well, what really happened to Liam.'

Irene couldn't help wincing at these words, so easily tossed into the room.

Then something came to her.

'Rowan,' she said, 'do you have a key to his flat?'

Rowan looked down at her stubby hands, which were knobbly with silver rings, and shook her head again. 'I'm afraid not,' she said. 'We spent a lot of time in here. More comfortable, you know.' Rowan nodded towards what was presumably a bedroom.

'Right,' said Irene quickly, in case the other woman elaborated further. Her chest ached with the fruitlessness of her task. She shuffled forward to begin the process of leaving this sagging sofa. 'I suppose in that case I'd better—'

'Look, Mrs Copeland . . .' Rowan was leaning forward again, her hands now clasped between her knees. 'I hope this won't seem out of order, but I'm worried too. I'm not sure we really have good reason to go to the police – not yet – but, well, what would you think about me helping you gain access to his room?'

Irene stared back at the other woman. The oddly formal words – 'gain access' – immediately semaphored some kind of underhand means. She thought for a moment. If Michael came back and found them breaking into his room, he might take such grave offence that it could damage their relationship for good. Her heart rate speeded up uncomfortably. But what other option did she have?

'Yes alright,' she said. 'What do you intend to do?'

It took three-quarters of an hour for Rowan's son to arrive. He was a ratty-faced youth in his twenties, wearing a red and yellow top with the DHL delivery company logo on it. He was unsmiling as he came into the room, dragging deeply on a cigarette, and regarded Irene without much curiosity.

'This is Michael's mum, Dex,' said Rowan. 'She's worried about him, too, and we think it might be a good idea if we could have a little . . . peek in his room.'

'Yeah,' replied the boy. 'You said.'

He didn't look impressed with this plan and Irene wished powerfully that she hadn't agreed to it. What if he came back at a later date and robbed Michael? It would be all her fault. A panicky feeling was growing inside her, but it felt too late to do anything now. The boy – man, she should say – stubbed out his cigarette in a saucer on the table in the manner of someone used to this space, and said, 'Come on, then. But there'd better not be no repercussions for me.'

Rowan put her hand on his upper arm and gave a sugary smile. 'There won't be, darling, I promise,' she said.

They trooped out of Rowan's flat and climbed to the next floor. Someone was cooking a curry in the building and it smelled quite appealing, but Irene's heart was thumping too hard for her to focus. She had never done anything illegal before. Whatever the justifications she might have for being involved in this, there was no doubt it was a criminal offence.

Rowan and Dex looked around and then Irene nodded assent. Irene expected him to produce some manner of complex device, spiky with lock-picking tools, but he merely produced a long, bent hair pin and got down on his knees, and then began to fiddle and poke about in the hole.

It seemed like only moments later that he was shoving the door and saying, 'There you go.' Was it really that easy? Irene feared she would never be safe again.

Rowan pulled him towards her and kissed him on the cheek. He received it without any sign of either pleasure or displeasure and said, 'Right, I've got a job over in Huntingdon and need to get going. You should be able to pull it locked after you're done.'

'Thank you, sweetie,' said Rowan, 'see you Friday?' She seemed to glow a little around the edges now. *What a funny thing to take pride in*, Irene thought, *that your son knew how to break into other people's properties.* Then the irony of this – *her* taking a superior stance on sons – curdled in her stomach.

Dex grunted his goodbye and clattered down the stairs.

Rowan's cheeks were pink now. Irene had the uncomfortable feeling that she was enjoying this too much.

'You want to go in first?' said Rowan.

Irene nodded and headed into the dimly lit room. A sweet-rotten smell hit the back of her throat and for a dizzying moment she was suffused with primal horror. She forced herself to slap at the wall by the door for a light switch and, as the room filled with a sickly white glow from a single overhead bulb, she saw with a flood of relief that there was no one here. Her son hadn't been left like some old rubbish, alone. Dead.

'Ugh, smells shitty in here,' said Rowan, going over to a small kitchen area and lifting the lid on a bin. She pulled out a bin bag. Flies emerged from it in a small cloud. Swearing to herself, she tied a knot in it and then slung it out into the corridor.

Irene looked around the room. There was an unmade bed with greying sheets swirled on the top, and a cheap, MDF bedside table holding a clock radio and a glass of water with dust on the top. The only other furniture was a small television set on a crate in the corner, and a white wooden wardrobe of the sort a child might have. One of those multi-plug, circular extension devices sat in an awkward place on the floor, and several cables trailed dangerously into it.

Irene opened the wardrobe and looked at the clothes stuffed in there; polo shorts she recognized and several hanging pairs of the light-coloured chinos her son favoured.

It looked like such a small life, contained in these grubby walls, and sadness clutched at Irene's throat. For the first time she was glad that Michael had been liaising with this Rowan woman. It was too much to bear to think about him being alone in this dump, with no comforts at all.

'I can't see anything that helpful, can you?' said Rowan now and Irene mumbled a response. 'He's obviously taken his laptop with him.' She paused before continuing. 'Why don't you have a mooch about and I'll tidy up a bit,' she said, 'make it nice for when he gets back, eh?'

Irene, touched by the kindness of this, gave Rowan a small,

grateful smile before beginning to look around the room. There were a couple of receipts on the bedside table, next to a scrunched-up tissue.

Irene picked up the receipts. One was from a café in a place called Casterbourne. Billy Joe's. Michael had had a tuna sandwich and a coffee in there. Another was from a newsagent with the address of The Old Wall, Casterbourne, for items that came to three pounds seventy-five. The final one was a cash point receipt, showing that he had withdrawn fifty pounds from an ATM.

'What you got there?' said Rowan, suddenly at her shoulder. Irene could hear her heavy breathing. She showed her the receipts and Rowan took them from her fingers.

'I know where that is,' she said. 'It's in Kent. My friend goes to the Lathebridge book festival sometimes, which isn't all that far from there. She AirBnBs in Casterbourne because it's cheaper.'

'Did my son ever mention that place to you?' said Irene.

'Not that I can remember,' said Rowan. The other woman had put down the receipts and was now spraying a bleachy cleaner over the kitchen counter with vigour. Irene thought guiltily about her earlier assumption about the woman's cleanliness. She had been nothing but helpful, even if she had rather unconventional methods.

'If I were you, Mrs Copeland,' Rowan said, 'I'd take a trip down to this Casterbourne place, just in case.' She put her head to one side, eyes brightening. 'I could come with you,' she said.

'It's okay,' said Irene hastily. 'I might just leave it for a day or two. Maybe Michael has taken a trip, you know, to . . . clear his head. I'll hang on a bit.'

Rowan made a doubtful face, clearly disappointed.

She had been kind, but Irene had a resolve now, having broken into her son's room. Whatever he had got himself into, she was going to find him. And something told her she needed to do this alone.

ELLIOTT

I slept badly again and had a dull headache the next morning. Anya looked pale. We didn't say much as we carried out our dance around each other getting ready for work.

As she was leaving, she came over and kissed me full on the mouth. I reached for her and she leaned into me, resting her head against my chest. Despite my gritty-eyed, throbbing-headed tiredness, I felt more at peace with the world than I had for days. *This* was what was important, right here. If she wanted to talk about going off travelling, I'd do it, I decided. Being together was what mattered, even if people were putting bricks through the window and frightening the shit out of us. I needed to deal with this situation, because it wasn't going away.

I got two strong cups of coffee down me and managed to get into school early enough that the gates were only just opening.

I made conversation with Barry, our caretaker, who had been at the school about as long as I'd been alive. He was a grizzled old Kentish boy who Zoe and I had long agreed would be our first choice of companion come the zombie apocalypse, such were his impressive array of practical skills. 'Conversation' was largely limited to, 'Getting a bit colder in the mornings,' and 'That it is,' it must be said, but I pretended to take an interest in the work he was doing to a broken section of fence near the gates, so I could keep an eye out for the arrival of Tyler.

Children were now streaming into the playground, mostly trailing mothers who waved them off or chased after them with forgotten lunchboxes and book bags.

No sign of Tyler.

It was an assembly morning, so the children got into their class lines for outside registration. My own class was gradually forming across the playground, a ragtag multi-limbed beast that jostled, wriggled, and yelled.

I checked my watch. I needed to get over there to register them, but there was no avoiding this conversation. I hadn't exactly planned what I was going to say. But it was going to basically involve trying not to put my stick any further into the wasps' nest.

It was a bright morning with the first autumnal chill. I squinted against the onslaught of the light. My head hurt, my injured hand hurt, and my back hurt. The thought of the day ahead made me want to groan as I darted glances between my class line, which was even less straight than it had been a few minutes ago, and then the gates.

I gave up after a few more moments, and hurried over with a shout of, 'Come on, you horrible lot, get in line,' before the bell went. I registered all the names and, as the classes began to stream inside, I spied the figure of Tyler coming alone towards the gate, looking like he was in no particular rush to get here. Clare had already taken his class inside.

His nose was running a snail trail down onto his lip and he snorted into the sleeve of his – non-regulation – hoodie as he eyed me with the air of a cat whose tail had just been trodden on.

'Come on, Tyler,' I said with faux cheerfulness. 'If you're quick you won't be marked late for registration.' He grunted in a way that boded excellently for his later communication methods as a teenager, and we walked awkwardly into the main entrance together.

'No dad this morning?' I said, before I could stop myself.

Tyler shot me a glowering look and mumbled something indecipherable.

'What's that, buddy?' I said as we reached the assembly hall together. I stopped and he did too. I had to lean down to hear what he said.

'He was too tired,' said Tyler. 'Maggie dropped me on the corner.'

Was he, now . . .

My heart kicked a little in my chest. I had no idea who Maggie was but that was not the important thing here.

'Been having late nights, eh?' I said as casually as I could muster. I had a strong desire – worryingly strong – to grab the boy by the shoulder and question him about what time his father had come home the night before last. But I'd lost him now; he ignored me and ran off into the hall. As I came in I saw that Jackie Dawson was watching me, her forehead creased into a frown.

I finished my account of what had happened with Bennett at lunchtime and emailed it to Jackie, leaving out what had been going on outside school.

I found Zoe in the staffroom, looking unreasonably fresh and awake in a bright orange printed dress. As I slumped into a seat next to her, I said, 'Got any shades I can borrow?'

She nudged me, a bit painfully. She had sharp elbows.

'Are you being rude about my dress, you bloody Philistine?' she said.

'No, just got a headache,' I said, then quickly, 'and no, before you say it, I'm not hungover.' That wasn't really true. But I had good reason to drink a little too much, with everything going on right now.

'You do look a bit crap,' she said. I laughed, despite myself.

'You really know how to make me feel like a million dollars, Zo.'

'Come on,' she said with a grin, 'you know I'm not one to sugar-coat the shit. What's going on?'

I told her everything. I could almost feel my muscles unknotting with the relief of unburdening myself. Anya wasn't a teacher and so she didn't completely get what this had felt like. Zoe made horrified or sympathetic noises in all the right places, as I described the stupid non-row with Bennett; being forced off my bike. Then what happened the night before last.

'God, do you think you should go to the police?' she said once I'd exhausted myself. I took a swig of lukewarm instant coffee.

'I'm wondering about that,' I said. 'But I feel like I ought to speak to Jackie about it once she's read my report on what happened.'

'Well,' said Zoe as she began to retrieve the pile of exercise books she'd been marking from the table in front of us. 'I'd get on with it. This all seems to be escalating a bit quickly, doesn't it?'

Jackie was not one to hang about, as it happened. I was summoned to come and talk to her at the end of the day.

I made my way down to her office, in the relatively new part of the school that had been added just last year. Even the carpets were better here, and I could smell proper coffee coming from her assistant Elaine's office.

'Elliott!' said Elaine, a friendly, smiley woman in her early sixties. 'You've got a meeting with Jackie, yes?'

'Yep.' I took a seat in one of the armed chairs just inside the door. Even though I was a thirty-two-year-old married teacher, sitting here still had the effect of making me feel like I was about to get a massive bollocking from a grown-up.

Which, as it turned out, wasn't a million miles away from what happened.

Jackie didn't beat about the bush. She told me straight away that she was 'very concerned' to see me talking to Tyler that morning and wanted a full account of what had been said to him.

I hesitated, and the moment seemed to stretch for ages between us.

Once I explained about the possible intimidation I'd been experiencing, she'd surely see I had good reason to ask about his dad's whereabouts. But it was still not really on for me to question an eight-year-old child when he was at the centre of a complaint against me. How could I avoid it, though?

For the second time that day, I found myself relating the story of being forced off my bike, and then the brick through the window.

I was clenching my fist as I related the final bit, shaking a little with the indignation of it all, and the memory of Anya's terrified face in the moonlit bedroom.

Jackie sat back in her chair and let out a deep sigh when I finished. She was twisting a Biro in her fingers, her expression sombre.

'Elliott . . .' she said quickly, then stopped. Then, 'You still haven't answered my question. What did you say to Tyler on the way into assembly this morning?'

For a moment I felt myself flailing. Heat crept up my neck and stained my cheeks. I felt about ten years old in that moment.

'I just . . .' I started and had to swallow the saliva that flooded my mouth, 'I asked him where his dad was today. His dad usually drops him at school.'

Jackie's face was set as she looked back at me. 'And you think it was a good idea to ask about that when you are currently in dispute with his father?'

I was suddenly awash with outrage.

'I'm not the one *having a dispute*!' I said, far too loud, and I saw Jackie wince. 'He has completely fabricated an argument and might, right now, be waging a campaign of intimidation against me! Or did you miss that part?'

I knew as soon as I'd spoken that I'd handled this all wrong. Jackie was now looking at me with an expression I'd never seen before on her face; a cold mix of anger and something else – sorrow? Disappointment?

'Look,' she said, with a sigh, leaning back in her chair. 'If you really think Mr Bennett is behind anything that has happened to you outside of the school, then you must go to the police and report this. All I'm concerned about is what happens on school premises and the health and safety of my pupils, and yes,' she raised a hand to block me from saying what I was about to say '. . . my staff too. But while this is going on, you absolutely must not speak to Tyler about anything other than school business. You do see that, don't you?'

'Yes,' I said, all the fight having leaked away now. 'Yes, I'm sorry, Jackie. I shouldn't have spoken to him this morning. I'm just finding all this quite stressful.'

She managed something approximating a smile. 'You're a good teacher, Elliott,' she said, 'and you have the makings of an excellent one. Just don't blow it by allowing this whole thing to get out of hand, okay? And make sure you report what has been going on.'

So, I did.

After school I walked to the police station on the other side of town and I reported both the incident on the bike, the brick through the window, and the complaint at school. I was processed by a harassed-looking middle-aged police-woman – who had evidently just spilled coffee on her pale jumper, judging by the angry expression and the cloth she was dabbing ineffectively at the stain the entire time we talked.

She wrote it all down, with the other hand, and told me she would be in touch with any information that she had to pass on. She didn't seem overly interested.

I walked home, the exhaustion of the last few days pooling like sand in my limbs. But once home again I forced myself to take my sad, broken bike down to the bike shop in town to be mended. It wasn't doing anything for my spirits, being without a means of getting around.

By the time I was home for the evening, I'd walked miles and felt both emotionally and physically battered.

I flopped down on the sofa in front of *Pointless* and within minutes my eyelids were getting heavy. I'd just have five minutes . . .

The next thing I knew, my phone was chirruping from somewhere and combining with the *EastEnders* theme tune. My mouth tasted like an old welly and my neck was aching from having slept at an unfamiliar angle.

I grabbed the phone and it fell onto the floor. It stopped ringing and I picked it up to see it was Anya who had been calling.

It rang again and I answered quickly.

'Hey,' I said, 'where are you?'

'I'm at Mum and Dad's.' Her voice sounded thick and muffled, like she was ill.

'You didn't say you were going over.' I couldn't stop the grumpy tone from worming its way into my voice.

'I know,' she said quietly. 'Spur-of-the-moment decision.' There was a pause. 'You're welcome to come too, of course.'

I thought for a minute. I very much did want to be cooked a lovely meal by Julia and not to spend the evening alone. But without the car it was a pain to get to Lathebridge, which she knew. She'd have come all the way back from London on the train, picked up the car from the station, then essentially driven past Casterbourne to get to her parents' house. Without mentioning it.

'What's going on?' I blurted out.

She gasped a laugh on the other end of the phone.

'What do you mean, *what's going on*?'

'I don't know.' I sat up straighter and rubbed a hand through my hair, which was sticking up all over my head. 'I just feel like you're being really weird and distant right now. Things have been strange between us since the festival.'

'For God's sake, Elliott.' She was hissing now, clearly not wanting her parents to hear. 'You get pissed and almost injure me and I've been *ill*! Then we have bricks through the window in the middle of the night, and you accuse me of being *weird* for not wanting to be home! Maybe I feel safer here!'

I was blindsided by this. She'd managed to sidestep the question and make me feel guilty all at once. And she hardly ever used my full name like that. I felt childishly chastised.

'Well,' I said as a huge wave of tiredness hit me. 'Are you staying the night there?'

A heavy sigh on the other end of the phone.

'I think I probably am.'

'Right,' I said briskly. 'I'll see you tomorrow then. Give my love to your mum and dad.'

'Love back from them,' she said, her voice small now. 'See you tomorrow.'

When I came off the phone I sat in the darkening room for a few minutes. It felt like nothing in my life was under control right now. Work was stressful, I had made a weird and inexplicable enemy . . . and now Anya was becoming increasingly distant.

I thought back to the day I got the festival tickets, earlier that summer, I'd sailed down the hill on my bike, bathed in sunshine, feeling like the King of the World. It felt so long ago now.

IRENE

As Irene looked through the window at the thickening jumble of buildings, she tried to remember the last time she had been to London, or even on a train.

Was it when she brought the boys to go to Madame Tussauds all those years ago? It hadn't been an easy day in the end. Liam couldn't stop bouncing excitedly in his seat. There had been his incessant questions ('Will we see Gazza? And Lineker?' 'Will the wax people in the Chamber of Horrors come alive?'). Michael had got annoyed that Liam was kicking his seat and they'd ended up scrapping and knocking over Irene's cup of coffee, so it went all over her magazine and ruined it. She could still recall the disapproving looks from other passengers as she shouted at the boys to behave.

When they got there, the queues had been so long that the boys had bitterly complained about the wait. She couldn't even remember much about the exhibition in the end, beyond Michael teasing Liam about being scared in the Chamber of Horrors and Liam bursting into noisy tears.

She smiled now as she thought about it. Always so noisy and stressful with those kids. She never had a moment to think.

Now that's all she had.

*

Irene had had to get up very early to get the first train into London, then she had to navigate her way across the city on the underground at rush hour to get to Victoria station. As people had shoved and pushed their way onto the trains, she had felt almost suffocated by the sensations, the smells, and the proximity to others. Her heart had felt like it might give out on her with the stress of it all. But when she got to Victoria and bought herself a cup of tea and a toasted teacake for the second journey, she'd experienced a jolt of exhilaration at herself. It was like she had been wrapped in her own net curtains for months, like some sort of insect in a cocoon. She wasn't that old, she told herself now. Look at Helen Mirren. She was the same age as Irene and she didn't sit around watching the hours and the years slip by, did she?

As she took the last bite of her teacake, cool now and soggy, but still a treat, she experienced a pang of guilt at her thoughts. After all, this wasn't a jolly day out to the seaside. She was looking for Michael.

The police hadn't been interested, when she had paid them a visit after going to his flat. As far as they were concerned, a middle-aged man who hadn't checked in with his mother for a couple of weeks was clearly not a cause for concern. She had been quite hot with shame when she exited the police station that morning. She had tried to say to the very young constable that she just *knew* something was wrong, that a mother knows this kind of thing, but his expression had been quite embarrassed at this and she had understood she was shouting into the wind.

When she emerged onto the platform at Casterbourne, the bright clear day was starting to turn. Irene shivered and buttoned up her coat as a cold breeze seemed to envelop her, and then began to make her way out of the station.

She had printed a photo of Michael and intended to show

87

it to people in the places where he had picked up those receipts.

The town centre was busy with people having an early lunch. She made her way, following the map outside the station, to the town square. Seagulls shrieked and wheeled over the war memorial, where litter was scattered about in a most disrespectful way, to Irene's mind.

She located the café first.

Billy Joe's was what Irene thought of as a Greasy Spoon. Garishly coloured pictures of plates of bacon and eggs and pies and mash adorned the walls and the air seemed thick with grease. The clientele was mainly men in work clothes, tucking into huge plates of bacon and eggs, who paid her no attention as she made her way to the counter.

A man with oily hair tied in a ponytail and several rings in his ears was taking orders, while a very overweight woman with unnaturally black, short hair skilfully attended to the bacon that curled and sizzled on the hotplate, along with wobbling, rubbery-looking eggs and brittle fried bread. Irene felt her stomach twist with nausea at all the grease. Nerves were kicking in now.

'Help you, love?' said the man and Irene attempted a reassuring smile. How on earth did she introduce this topic? You saw people doing things like this on telly, but it felt very strange in real life. She hoped he wouldn't laugh. She couldn't bear it if he laughed.

'Yes please,' she said, deciding to just come out with it. 'You see, I'm looking for my son.'

The man frowned and smiled a little as he eyed her and picked up a tea towel, which he used to wipe his hands. His name badge read: 'Keith'.

'Oh yeah?' he said. 'What's he gone and done then?'

He didn't seem to be taking this all that seriously, Irene felt, so she fumbled in her handbag for the photo, which she had printed out onto a sheet of A4 paper. It showed Michael a few years ago when he had bought a new suit for a wedding he was going to with Linda.

He was smiling rather awkwardly in it, but you could see his face quite well, and especially his distinctive colouring.

'I think he might be in trouble,' Irene forced herself to say as she thrust the sheet of paper at the man. He took it from her, frowning now, and she felt a satisfaction that he seemed to have picked up on the gravity of the situation.

'He has a bit less hair now,' Irene said apologetically as the man studied the picture. He turned to the woman who was now plating up food onto several plates at speed. Her name badge read 'Tina' and her pinny was splashed all over with stains. She had small eyes that were close together and greasy with make-up.

'Teen,' he said, holding up the piece of paper. 'Ever seen this guy in here?'

Tina sighed and turned to look before shaking her head. 'No,' she said, 'sorry. Don't know him.'

Irene had known it was a long shot but still the disappointment cut deep as Keith handed back the sheet of paper, with a sympathetic smile.

'Sorry, love,' he said. 'Do you know any more about where he might have gone?'

Irene felt tears stinging her eyes and looked down to hide them as she put the paper back in her handbag.

'Not really,' she said. 'But he had lunch here. I found the receipt.'

'Oh? When was that then?' said Keith and Irene told him the date, which was etched onto her memory from endlessly studying the receipts.

Keith made a face. 'Wish I could help you.' Then, 'Wait a minute.'

He looked past her into the café and suddenly shouted so

loud that Irene flinched and almost dropped her handbag.

'Oi! This nice lady is looking for her son. I'm going to come round and show you all and anyone that can help her gets a free coffee, okay?'

Irene smiled as Keith winked at her and held out his hand for the picture again.

He then made his way round the café showing each of the customers. One by one they looked at the photo, then at Irene, then shook their heads and returned to their lunch.

An old man sitting in the window, which dripped with condensation, was last. He had a yellowish-white beard and thin hair across a pink scalp. There were the remains of a sausage sandwich on the plate in front of him.

He studied the picture for a long time before turning to Irene and speaking.

'I'm not certain, but I think it's him,' he said, in a surprisingly posh voice. 'The one in the paper.'

'The paper?' Irene had stepped forward and had to stop herself from grasping the man's sleeve. 'What do you mean, in the paper?' she said, her voice high-pitched.

He frowned and looked a little sheepish now, darting glances from the newspaper on the seat beside him to Keith before replying.

'The man they found. By the cliffs.'

ELLIOTT

I took a beer from the fridge and drank it quickly while I rooted around for something easy to eat. I ignored the seabass fillets and the vegetables, the bunches of fresh herbs.

Tonight, I wanted fat and salt. In London I'd have called for a takeaway but here there were a limited number of places that delivered, and I had no intention of going outside again.

Carrying a fresh beer, I piled a plate with cheese, ham, thick slices of bread and butter with a whole family-sized bag of balsamic vinegar Kettle Chips. What I was really craving was Monster Munch, but there was little chance of finding those in our cupboards.

Then I slumped down on the sofa and found a football match on Sky Sports. I wasn't really concentrating on the game though. My thoughts kept ping-ponging between Lee Bennett and Anya.

I pictured the scene over at their house. Patrick probably leaving the women to it, knowing that his daughter needed something he couldn't provide tonight.

You and me both, mate, I thought bitterly.

Maybe she was just scared of being here. Of what else might happen in the depths of the night.

I'm not the most macho bloke in the world but there was

something about all this that tapped into a deep, primal place. Like I couldn't protect my woman in our cave. This actually made me snort a laugh through my nose as I imagined the look Anya would have given me had I voiced this thought out loud to her. I'd never have lived it down. Didn't mean it wasn't a little bit true, all the same.

I presumed the police would go around to speak to Bennett, which made my stomach ripple with discomfort. Hard to imagine this was going to lead to a calming of this situation, but it had to be done. I pictured Tyler's round, fearful eyes as he took in the uniformed people on his doorstep.

I knew all too well what that felt like.

I didn't really remember the night my father was finally removed from the house because those nights merged into one: the hard raps on the door, then boots thundering into the house. Tall blue monsters who shouted and knocked things over. That's how it seemed to me.

Our lives were so immeasurably better with Mark Little out of them. That was why I couldn't understand Mum's reaction the day we heard he was dead.

I came in from school to find her whey-faced and red-eyed at the kitchen table.

She asked me to sit down and then told me she had 'some very serious news'.

I remember my first thought was that she had been given only months to live. This was something I'd seen on telly and had spent a lot of time thinking about lately. Then I noticed the official-looking letter on the table and the stamp that said 'HMP Brixton' and iciness wormed its way into my stomach.

'Sit down, Elliott,' she said, and I obeyed, but warily, placing my chair at an angle to the table so I could make a quick getaway.

'What is it then?'

Mum took a deep, shuddery breath before replying. 'It's your dad,' she said. 'I'm very sorry, sweets, but I'm afraid he has been very unwell and . . .' she swallowed '. . . and now he has died.'

I remember an intense wave of heat passed over me. My face felt like it was on fire and I began to shake. I was too young to be able to describe what was happening. I didn't know how I was supposed to react to this. I hated this man, but there was a certain raw shock to hearing your father had died, whatever the circumstances.

'Do you want a cuddle?' said Mum. I shook my head fiercely, registering the slightly hurt look she gave me in response.

'I'm going out to play football,' I said, getting up so abruptly I almost knocked the chair over.

'Elliott!' Mum called as I left the kitchen. 'Come back here, I want to talk to you!'

Reluctantly, I walked back to the doorway of the kitchen and lingered there. Mum was wringing a tissue in her fingers.

'I know this is difficult news, but—'

I cut her off midway through her sentence. 'I don't care! Can't you get that through your thick head? I don't *fucking* care!'

Mum winced as though I'd hit her, and it felt shamefully good. I stomped off down the hallway, and then slammed the door as hard as I could as I left the house. I could hear her calling me as I stood on the doorstep, breathing hard, while I tried to work out what to do next.

'Fucking dead *wanker*,' I said and kicked a crumpled 7 Up can so hard that it clattered a satisfying distance down the walkway, before coming to rest near the top of the stairs.

Mrs Mack's door opened, and she peered out at me.

'What's all that racket?' she said, then, 'Who's rattled your cage, Elliott?'

'No one,' I said sulkily and began to walk down the walkway, away from her.

'Elliott?' she called behind me. 'Do you want to come in for a while? I've made some scones.'

I ignored her and went into the stairwell. But out of sight, I stopped and leaned against the wall, trying to ignore the wee smell that seemed to have been absorbed into the walls here. I wanted to tell her to stuff her scones.

I could feel a sort of poisonous anger burning in me. I wanted to cry and that made me want to punch myself in the face. Why would I feel the need to cry about that man who wasn't even in my life? Who used to beat up my mum? Why was *she* even upset? I hated her, and I hated him, and I hated everyone.

But I was also hungry. I hadn't had a chance to get a snack before I'd stormed off. I had no money and nowhere really to go. I found myself turning back and walking towards Mrs Mack's door before I could talk myself out of it. She'd actually left it on the latch, which half annoyed me further and half made me feel comforted that she knew me so well.

I walked into the flat and she called out from the living room.

'They're in the kitchen, still warm. You know where the butter and jam is.'

She didn't come into the hall, which threw me a bit, so I stood there uselessly for a moment. Then the warm sweet smell drove me into the kitchen and a few minutes later I was piling butter and jam onto the fresh crumbly scones and cramming them into my mouth so fast I almost choked myself.

The combination of sugar and stodge calmed me a bit

anyway and I could feel myself coming down, like I was a helium balloon and someone was yanking on the string.

I went to the doorway of the living room, where Mrs Mack was bent over one of her crossword books, Radio 4 on in the background. She didn't look up as I lurked there, and I was forced to speak first.

'Scones are nice, thanks,' I said grudgingly, and she grunted in response, then looked at me over the tops of her horn-rimmed glasses.

'Want to tell me what's got your goat?' she said. I'd never heard anyone use this expression before knowing Mrs Mack. I shrugged. Then the words just seemed to spill out.

'He's dead,' I said, 'my . . .' I swallowed. 'My . . . father.'

My face began to burn again, from shame using what felt like a poncy word. All I could hear was, 'Luke, I am your father,' in Darth Vader's voice then and I gave a high-pitched, weird laugh.

Mrs Mack frowned and put down the crossword book, before reaching to turn off the radio. She regarded me for several moments in silence before speaking.

'I'm very sorry to hear that, Elliott,' she said, then, 'Shouldn't you and your mum be together right now?'

I shrugged. 'Dunno,' I said. 'Think she wants to be alone.' The lie was so easy. Mrs Mack frowned, and I felt a wash of guilt because I knew she was judging Mum right then.

'Would you like to talk about it?' she said. I shook my head vigorously.

'He didn't mean anything to me,' I said. The phrase felt foreign coming out of my mouth. I was aware I had picked it up from some adult, maybe on telly. I was embarrassed all over again, then angry because I was embarrassed.

'Well, for all that . . .' said Mrs Mack. Then she clapped her hands down on her lap. 'Let's you and me watch some television and have a cup of tea then, shall we?'

She got up. 'I'll go and put the kettle on,' she said. 'Could you go into my bedroom and get my cardigan, please? It's hanging on the chair there.'

I wandered into her bedroom, sighing as though I felt hard done by, and at that moment the doorbell rang. I could hear Mrs Mack go to the front door and begin talking to whoever was there. It sounded like someone collecting for something. Mrs Mack said she wasn't made of money but she wasn't having dead babies on her conscience.

In her bedroom I found the pink knobbly cardigan straight away, and I picked it up. But before I turned to leave the room, it felt as though a magnet was pulling my gaze towards the wardrobe. Mrs Mack was still talking to the person on the doorstep and my heart kicked harder in my chest as I walked over to the wardrobe and opened it carefully, making sure it didn't squeak. My fingers shook as I reached up and took down the wooden box.

I was thinking that I was like my father as I prised open the lid and wrapped a few twenties into my fist, before stuffing them into my pocket.

My heart seemed to be banging audibly as I went back into the living room with the cardigan.

She bustled about in the kitchen and I could hear her humming softly to herself. Then she came into the living room with a tray of tea, more scones nestled on a plate, along with the butter and the jam.

'I imagine you've probably got room for another one or two of those scones, am I right?' she said with a smile and placed the tray on the coffee table.

I didn't reply but went to put the telly on. I stared at *Byker Grove*, my eyes wide and stinging. I felt like I was going to be sick. I wanted to press rewind, right back to when I got home from school. I wanted to do it all differently.

The money seemed to pulse hotly inside my pocket and I wondered if I could take it out and somehow leave it on the floor, for her to find.

But I didn't.

To this day I can't explain why I did it. I remember being a ball of anger and lacking the ability to unpick why I felt so bad. I hurt, and I was sad, and I wanted to do something bad, something extreme. I was angry with my dead father for being such a loser and I was angry with Mum for minding that he was dead. I was angry with Mrs Mack just because she was there.

The match seemed to have finished and the room was dark now. I got up slowly from the sofa and went to the kitchen to find another beer. Leaning into the light of the fridge, I felt sadness and regret throb through me. I reached for one beer, and then changed my mind. I closed the fridge and went to the freezer where we kept the gin.

I sloshed a large measure into a glass and drank it in one go, wincing at the burn as it went down. Then I poured another and took the bottle and glass through to the living room.

Pictures were scrolling across my mind's eye in a way I couldn't seem to control.

I squeezed my eyes tightly shut, trying to block them out. I wished Anya was here.

Looking down, I realized my glass was empty again.

I poured myself another drink.

And then I rooted in a drawer for a cab company card that we'd never used before and rang the number.

I didn't want to be alone tonight.

ELLIOTT

The cab driver tried to start a conversation but I was burrowing into a bittersweet place of self-pity, and so, after a few grunted replies from me, he gave up and we drove in silence along the coastal road.

Peering out to my left, I could just make out the lights of a large ship puncturing the deep blackness. Such a lonely sight. The sheer weight of open space pressed in on me so I turned away, focusing instead on the yellow car freshener in the shape of a winking emoji that swayed from the driver's mirror. It made me feel a bit sick and I suddenly became aware of how much I'd had to drink.

Self-doubt began to crowd in. Would they mind me just turning up? Would Anya be embarrassed that I was . . . not drunk, but not completely sober?

But the thought of going back to the empty house was even worse. I was, reasonably, confident that the worst that would happen would be 'What are you like?' from Anya and friendly hospitality from her parents.

The Rylands' house was up a narrow road that cut into the cliff and wound round to their property, which offered a stunning view of the bay from large windows. In the summer that room was flooded with golden light and I thought now about the times the four of us had gathered there around the table, drinking good wine and laughing, some of Patrick's beloved jazz noodling and tinkling away in the background.

I remembered last Christmas and a pleasant warm feeling spread through me. Carols from King's Choir in the background against the comforting, hypnotic crackle of the open fire. The air sweet with pine resin and the orange-spiced candle flickering on the hearth. White stars winking tastefully from the tree. No garish, coloured fairy lights in that room. No tinsel there. I thought about the Christmas me and Mum shared a Fray Bentos pie on Christmas Day because we hadn't had enough money for a chicken or a turkey roast.

A different world.

'I said, that would be sixteen pounds eighty, mate?'

The taxi driver's irritated voice made me start. I must have begun drifting off to sleep. Fumbling for cash, I ended up giving him a four-pound tip just because I wanted to get out into the fresh air.

I could hear the sea from here as I gazed up at the many windows of the tall, pale house in the moonlight. It was only ten thirty but there weren't that many lights on. I wavered, unsure about the etiquette now I was here.

But weren't they forever telling me I was family too?

I rang the doorbell and waited, pulling my jacket around me against the wind that was knifing into me now. Nothing happened and I rang it again.

A few moments later I saw movement and a light snapped on in the hallway, visible through the large, stained-glass door. The bulky shape of Patrick appeared there and seemed to pause for a second or two, before dipping and then reaching for various bolts. They were very security conscious, Patrick and Julia. But who wouldn't be in that lovely house?

He peered out at me from the doorway, scrunching his

eyes – the same light brown as his daughter's. A cautious smile that was half-frown appeared on his weathered face.

'Elliott, what's wrong, son?' he said. He didn't immediately beckon me over the threshold. This was so unfamiliar and strange I was robbed for a moment of my speech.

'I thought I'd come over,' I managed at last. He stared back at me as if I had made an outrageous statement. I felt a flash of annoyance now.

'Is it inconvenient?' I said. His demeanour changed then and he made a blustery sort of 'of course not' sound. But as he began to move to let me in, Julia appeared at his shoulder.

She usually looked so elegant, but without make-up her face was puffy. Her dark hair was scraped back into a pony-tail. Despite her weak smile she was now standing in the space opened by Patrick, blocking the threshold of their house.

'Elliott, darling,' she said in a low voice. 'It's so lovely to see you but I'm afraid Anya is sleeping and we wouldn't want to wake her, would we?'

This was so bizarre I let out a laugh, which proved to be ill-judged because her face immediately seemed to shut down further.

'Have you had too much to drink, Elliott?' she said and Patrick interjected with, 'Julia' in a warning tone.

'I think you'll find I haven't had quite enough,' I said. It had sounded softer, wittier, in my mind and I instantly regretted it.

The next thing I knew, Patrick was grabbing a coat and car keys and saying he would drive me home 'in a jiffy'. Then I was somehow inside Patrick's big, new-smelling car and we were driving along in silence.

What on earth had just happened? I didn't know where to start.

After a while, the weirdness became too much for me. I

turned and looked at his face, lit by the whitish glow from the dashboard, his eyes fixed on the road ahead.

'Look, Patrick,' I said, 'I'm sorry if I did the wrong thing in coming over . . .' I left the sentence open, ready for his assurance that I hadn't at all behaved out of turn, and that some extenuating circumstance I couldn't quite imagine was the real reason for all this oddness. But all he did was say, 'Don't worry about it, son,' and resume his silent driving again. These five words managed to make me feel very much worse.

But things at the party haven't gone the way she hoped. First, her best friend Yasemin's mum rang to say she couldn't come because her granny had died.

'Why?' she asked her mother. 'Why does that mean Yasemin can't still come?' Mum had explained that Yasemin probably felt too sad for music and games and laughing. She had mused on that for a while before replying that Yasemin was being 'self-centred', an expression she had heard the grown-ups use before.

Then she decided that she didn't like THE dress chosen for the party, even though she had loved it in John Lewis the week before. It just looked 'wrong' now the day had finally arrived when she would wear it.

When the party had hardly been going for any time, Adela from her class accidentally pulled down the grass skirt from the side of the table so it looked just like a regular old table.

Now Lottie keeps showing off about winning a special medal for her karate, which she is always boasting about.

Her brother, whose name is Dylan, sits in a corner and eats crisps, even though all the food is safe for him. She heard some of the mums saying that his mum shouldn't just leave other people to be in charge of him all the time, because it wasn't just 'the nut thing' but that something was 'a bit wrong there'.

Lottie is getting louder and louder but for some reason no one else seems to mind. Then she notices that her dad is laughing and pretending to do karate chops that Lottie is warding off with high kicks that show her knickers under her dress. Mum comes into the room and laughs too. Like Lottie is special.

No one says anything when she goes off to be alone for a while.

IRENE

'Oh love, love, are you alright?'

'Should we call for an ambulance?'

'I think she just needs a minute, give her some space.'

Irene was aware of voices snapping and popping around her head like bubbles. Everything felt far away, and she could hear her own heavy breathing thundering in her ears.

She reached for the newspaper she had dropped on the table with trembling hands and forced herself to look again at the front page and its terrible, awful information.

'That's him,' she said, and her voice felt like such a fragile thing, she wasn't sure anyone else could hear it until there was a too-loud reply right next to her.

'Your son? Are you saying *that's* your son, love?'

The woman's excessive perfume seemed like an odd thing to register at this time, but Irene's nose puckered with the sweet musky smell enveloping her. Three people stood over her: the man from behind the counter, this blowsy woman who seemed to have come from who knew where, and the old man who had said he thought he recognized Michael in the first place.

He had a tatty copy of the local paper on the seat next to him and, when he held it up to show Irene, she had let out a strangled sort of cry and felt the room tip.

Then she was being ushered onto a seat and people were fussing all around her. She accepted the cup of hot sweet tea that had magically appeared from nowhere in front of her and took a couple of quick sips. *Have to get myself together, for Michael*, she thought, bracing herself to read the words in the story.

'Critical condition' and 'head injury' swam in front of her eyes but there was another word that seemed to be blotting them out.

'Suicide'.

It was a known suicide spot.

Was that what he had come here to do? Irene felt a wave of grief thump into her chest and her eyes filled with hot tears. She fumbled in her handbag for a clean tissue and, when she located one, blew her nose twice into it, then dabbed under her eyes.

But it made no sense. Michael had always hated heights. If, heaven forbid, he had been meaning to do that, she was sure he would have found a gentler, more benign way. Pills, perhaps. Irene still recalled the way Liam would tease his older brother for not wanting to climb high on the monkey bars. So for him to deliberately throw himself off a cliff? This series of thoughts, so logical, tore a gasp from her lips.

'You sit there and have a moment, love, alright?' said the man who worked there as a couple of mothers with prams came into the café, laughing and talking noisily. The sound of their bright conversation was offensive to Irene's ears. She wanted to say, 'How can you laugh, when my son is lying in a hospital?'

'Can I do anything to help you?' said the old man in a quiet voice and Irene looked at him. He had a nice way of speaking: well-modulated. Now she saw that he was perhaps her own age.

She was both grateful for his offer and relieved the other

gawkers had melted away, drama apparently over and nothing more to get their teeth into.

'Could you tell me the best way to get to that hospital?' she said.

'Do you have a car?' said the man, frowning. 'It's a few miles from here.'

Irene shook her head. 'I can get a taxi though,' she said.

The man shook his head and drained the last dregs of whatever he had in his mug.

'I wouldn't hear of it,' he said. 'Let me drive you there.'

Irene had hesitated for only a moment. He didn't seem like someone who might wish her harm and she wanted to get to Michael as soon as she could. Beggars couldn't always be choosers.

Now she was sitting in the passenger seat of the immaculate car as the old man – Frank, he said his name was – drove onto a costal road. Colin would have known what kind it was; one of those classic ones that men got excited about. Irene tried to distract herself with thoughts like these as she looked out at the sea, which was sparkly silver in the afternoon sunshine. The thought of her Michael crashing into that cold, unforgiving water and being swept away was causing a panic to swell inside that threatened to choke her.

'How long is it since you saw your son?' asked Frank, breaking her thoughts.

'Just a couple of weeks,' she said and then looked sharply at his profile. 'It's not what you're thinking.' She hadn't meant it to come out so harshly, but he remained impassive, pausing before he replied.

'I'm not meaning anything, I promise you. I was merely making conversation.'

'We're actually very close,' said Irene hurriedly and he

indicated a strange kind of agreement by nodding his head and closing his eyes momentarily.

Fumbling with the little leather tag on her handbag in an attempt to absorb the tremors still running through her, Irene cleared her throat.

'I don't think he was trying to kill himself,' she said and felt Frank turn to her. But even as she said the words, she wasn't entirely convinced by them.

Maybe things really had reached that stage? Logic seemed to unfurl as a series of stepping stones in her mind now. Michael had one of his mad theories about finding Liam. It led him to this area. Then he discovered that it was all a waste of time. He looked around at his life, his redundancy, his failed relationship with Linda . . .

Perhaps he concluded that he had little to live for?

But what about his mother? she thought. *What about me?*

ELLIOTT

As I was gathering my stuff to get ready to leave, Zoe put her head round the door.

'Hey,' she said. 'Shall we get together to talk about Charney Point?'

There was a moment of confusion and then the meaning of her words sunk in and I went cold all over. I had completely forgotten about the trip. By now I should have filled in the risk assessment forms and booked the coaches for the day.

Zoe frowned. 'What?' she said. 'What's the problem?'

'I forgot about it,' I said in a small voice. Zoe's eyebrows shot up towards her hairline.

'*What?*' She came in and closed the classroom door. 'Tell me you're joking, Elliott,' she said quietly. 'Tell me.'

'I'm not joking.'

'Shit!' Zoe slapped her hand on the table between us. 'You do realize it might be too late now to do the forms in time?'

'It might not be?' I hated my own wheedling tone.

'Oh, don't be a twat,' she said, and I flinched. 'You know what has to be done for these trips. And you also know how excited the kids are about it.'

I couldn't think of anything to say.

People who don't work in schools have no idea of the

work that goes into organizing trips like this. The difficulty of lining all those ducks in a row is one of the reasons they don't happen as much as kids would no doubt like. There was no way the trip could just be sorted for another date that easily. It could be months before it worked with both the school calendar and the schedule of the museum itself.

I sank back into my chair and put my head in my hands.

'Shit,' I said, my voice mangled. 'I've really badly fucked up.'

When I looked up, I had hoped, expected maybe, to see a softening in Zoe's expression. She was my friend. Surely, she would forgive me for a simple mistake like this, even if it did mean she would have to cope with a few disappointed tears?

But her eyes were cool as they met mine.

'I'm going to let you tell Elaine then,' she said. 'And she's not going to be pleased.'

Elaine dealt with the school calendar. My error was almost certainly going to be passed on to Jackie, because Elaine was her assistant and they would naturally talk.

And I was in enough trouble with Jackie as it was.

'Zoe,' I said, and she gave me a wary look.

'What?'

'It sickens me to ask this but—'

'No, no, no,' she interrupted, voice rising and taking a step back with her hands raised, palms towards me.

'But I'm already in the shit!' I hissed. 'Because of that parent, Lee Bennett! Jackie's really on my case about it.'

'Bloody hell, Elliott.' I almost winced at the heat in her voice. 'Why should I take the blame for something that is your mistake? Tell me that?'

'Please, Zo,' I said. 'I honestly wouldn't normally ask. I really am in the doghouse right now and I don't know what Jackie's going to do if she finds out that I've fucked this up too.'

Zoe regarded me for a moment then let out a huge sigh of resignation.

'God, you're a pain in the arse,' she said, then, to the sweetest relief, 'If I do this then you owe me something pretty sodding big, alright?'

'I'd hug you right now,' I said, 'but I'm not clear on whether you might punch me in the face.'

'Hmm,' said Zoe. 'Neither am I.'

I tried ringing Anya on my way home as I went to collect my bike, but it went straight to voicemail.

Then I sent a text.

Had worst day. Can't wait to see you. I'll cook. X

The reply came quickly.

Sweetie, I'm under the weather and Mum persuaded me to stay another night. So sorry. See you tomorrow for sure. Will make it up to you X

I swore, then dialled her number. It went straight to voice-mail.

'Anya,' I said, struggling not to sound as irritated as I felt. 'Call me back, okay?'

This was getting ridiculous.

Anya was a grown woman. Was it normal to go running to your parents like this when you felt ill?

Sometimes I wondered if the connection between the three of them was entirely normal.

Anya once told me a story about an aunt – Julia's sister – who they had seen a lot of when she was small. I never learned her name but, apparently, she caused a scene at a family event by getting drunk and saying that Patrick and Julia spoiled their only daughter.

Anya told this story as if it were quite funny, the fact that her aunt would leave tearful messages on the answering machine apologizing for what she had said.

But she was never allowed back into the Ryland fold.

I woke at five with a thumping head, roiling stomach, and mouth that felt like a dirty sock had been stuffed inside it all night. I'd done it again: got into a sorry state. I'd even finished the best part of a bottle of whisky we had been given as a present by someone. I didn't even like whisky that much.

Reaching for my phone, I saw that Anya had left me a message late the night before.

Sorry for silence. Feeling much better and going into work in the am. See you tomorrow night. Really miss you xxx

That was something. But as I groaned and turned my face into the pillow, I decided there was no way I was going into school today. I hadn't had a day off sick in a long time. I wasn't even sure I'd ever had one, now I thought about it.

I called the automated number and logged that I would be off that day.

I slept, more heavily than I had for days, and when I next woke, it was nine o'clock and sunlight was gently warming my face through the open curtains. I got up in slow, experimental increments, and was surprised to find that I felt quite human. I wasn't feeling sick and I had an almost pleasant spacy, light feeling in my limbs.

I had a long, hot shower and, by the time I emerged, I was hungry. I made toast and peanut butter and ate it along with two cups of strong tea, coffee still feeling like a bridge too far.

I went into the living room and idly switched on the television. I flicked through options on Netflix and Amazon, but the prospect of an afternoon's self-indulgent box set bingeing, which would ordinarily be so appealing, held no pleasure. It wasn't the same without Anya.

As I stared at the telly without taking anything in, an idea bloomed in my mind so suddenly that I sat upright, my heart beating harder.

I couldn't do it. Could I? What if I was seen by someone from school?

But even as all the very valid objections were scrolling across my mind's eye, a powerful instinct was tugging me to my feet and over to my phone to look up train times.

I could go to London for the afternoon. If I was lucky with trains, I'd be in town in plenty of time to meet Anya at one, when she took her lunch hour, regular as clockwork. I could surprise her; take her out for lunch. Hadn't she just been saying she was sick of me being predictable? Well, not exactly, but that's what it had sounded like to me. It couldn't hurt to show her that I could play hooky from school and do something spontaneous. I'd just be careful, that's all. I'd get a cab over to Ashington and catch the fast train.

Staying in the house on my own all day wasn't an option. I needed to clear my head, get some perspective on everything that had been happening. Reconnect with Anya and stop all this paranoid stuff once and for all.

IRENE

Irene's hand was sweaty and beginning to cramp but she didn't feel she could move it. What if he was aware that she was here, just as the nurse had said might be possible? What if he thought she was abandoning him if she let go?

A sob spasmed through her from nowhere, like a cough she couldn't suppress, and she pressed her free wrist hard against her mouth in an attempt to keep the emotion inside. Crying was not going to help Michael. It took her a few moments of deep, ragged breaths before she was able to lower her hand again.

He looked smaller than she remembered, lying in that bed and hooked up to all those machines. The big blue one snaking into his mouth was helping him to breathe, she knew that. But it looked so obtrusive and she had a strange urge to yank it out.

He seemed old. Her son *old*. How could that be true? His skin was waxy and pale where it wasn't patchworked with livid blue and yellow bruising.

What had made him do this?

When she had arrived at the hospital, that kind man, Frank, had insisted he come in with her to help her locate the right department. She had been grateful in an abstract way but was too distracted to thank him properly when she had finally been directed to the Intensive Care Unit. As she'd rubbed the alcohol gel into her shaking hands, he had written his phone number on a scrap of paper and gently popped it into the top of her handbag, 'Just in case,' he'd said. In case of what, she couldn't really think, but it had been nice not to feel so alone for a moment. In fact, an impulsive urge meant she almost blurted out a request to come into the ICU with her. Two visitors were allowed, she had been told that by the doctor, a softly spoken West Indian lady who had explained Michael's injuries. There were too many for Irene to take in – broken this and ruptured that . . . but the head injury part was the only one that really mattered. Irene understood that Michael had been put into an induced coma in an effort to stop swelling on his brain but knowing it was deliberate didn't make it any easier to see.

She had asked about the circumstances of where he was found, and the doctor had hesitated for only a moment before asking Irene if she knew whether her son had been depressed? All she could do was shake her head and mumble that she didn't really know.

Then the doctor asked if she would like to see the hospital chaplain. That hadn't seemed like a very comforting question and it had taken quite an effort of will not to tell this woman with her serious, kind manner that she and God had parted ways some years ago, thank you very much.

Her eyes were scratchy with fatigue now and she was desperate for a cup of tea and something to eat. But she wasn't allowed to take a drink into the ICU and she hadn't wanted to waste any more time that could be spent with Michael.

Oh Michael, she thought. *What have you done?*

She hadn't spoken out loud but, in that moment, Michael

moved, as though reacting to her thoughts. Irene almost shot out of her chair and for about a second more a starburst of bright hope filled her with light. But then she saw that he was convulsing, and an alarm was sounding. Then blue-uniformed bodies were rushing into the room and everything was happening at once.

ELLIOTT

As the landscape changed and buildings began to clot into larger and larger configurations, I felt a certain energy creeping into me, making me sit up straighter.

Dirty old town. How I'd missed you.

It had been ages since I had last been here. It was funny, but I'd been sure I was ready to leave when we got married. Anya suggested we move back to where she grew up and it made sense, especially as we wouldn't have had a hope in hell of buying anywhere in London.

But now, as the train made its way towards Victoria, I had the oddest feeling that I would be able to breathe properly here. As though I was literally returning to my element.

I got onto the Victoria Line at Victoria, feeling a bit of a country mouse. The sheer number of bodies felt oddly surprising. When I moved away everyone had been full of plans to come and stay with us, and for the first few months we had a good number of weekends with friends, mainly mine.

But when people discovered that it wasn't exactly Brighton, or even Lathebridge, the visits began to peter out. It was also, partly, just life. A couple of friends moved abroad, and my oldest crowd were in such a different place, and already deep in family life.

I changed onto the Northern Line at Euston and travelled a few stops to Angel, where Anya's office was based. Looking around the carriage I was struck by the sheer diversity here; something I had never even thought about before. There were at least four different ethnic groups around me. What a contrast to Casterbourne. The mixed-race part of me wasn't really that obvious. I just looked like a bloke with dark hair and a reasonable propensity to catch the sun. But it was something I thought about, living where I did now.

I emerged from the station. The sky was a deep, cloudless blue and the air had a crisp nip of autumn. I was a bit early to meet Anya, so I had a cup of coffee in Pret a Manger and read a copy of the *Standard* that someone had left behind, enjoying the buzz of energy around me. This was a good idea, I decided. It would help me get some perspective on things.

At 12.30 I decided to head over to her office.

I quickened my pace as I walked down St John's Street towards her building.

McHenry Inc., her company, was based on the top floor of an old factory on the edge of Clerkenwell. They shared the building with an interior design company and a commercial solicitor's office. It was bookended by an artisan coffee shop that had a cycling theme, and a shop that sold ceramics and art at eye-watering prices.

I went into the bright airy reception that served the whole building and a woman with very short, dark hair and bright red lips in a wide smile greeted me cheerily.

'I'm here to see Anya at McHenry,' I said, and she asked me to sign in, while she called via the switchboard.

I signed my name and hovered over the 'From' part of

the visitors' book. I had a childish urge to write something stupid like 'NASA' or 'Hogwarts' and concluded I had been hanging out with small children too much, so I just left it blank.

'Okay, thanks, I'll tell him,' said the receptionist. She turned to me and her smile slipped by the tiniest degree.

'Really sorry,' she said. 'But it seems she isn't in today.'

'What?' I said. 'Are you sure?' It had to be a mistake. I mean, she'd told me she was going to work. If she wasn't here, where was she?

She shrugged. 'That's what they said.' Her expression became cooler. I struggled to remember the names of Anya's colleagues.

'Look, can you ask for Todd Bernstein, please?' Todd was her immediate boss, an intense American man who always shook my hand for a bit too long, as though hoping to sell me something.

The receptionist murmured into the phone, her eyes down. I found myself opening and closing my fists, a nervous habit. I should have been at school, doing the job that was looking a bit shaky right now. Instead I had come all this way on a whim, for nothing. Plus, I had no idea where my own wife was. For a moment, as Todd emerged from the lift, a hesitant smile playing around his lips, humiliation was my uppermost thought and I contemplated feigning that I had just remembered where she was. But no, I needed information, however embarrassing this was.

'Elliott,' said Todd as I held out my hand for the customary over-shake. He didn't disappoint, and I felt conscious of his crisp suit and ice-white shirt, some subtle aftershave wafting off him. 'What can I do for you?'

I laughed, as though all this was a silly mistake. 'Well, I think I got crossed wires with Anya this morning. Thought I would surprise her for lunch. Is she not here?'

Todd regarded me for a second and then gestured at the seated area.

Three chairs in pale leather circled a round table, each one a triumph of style over comfort. They were the kind that tipped you backwards when you sat down and always killed my spine. I perched on the end in a way that must have looked prim and weird and tried to ignore the thrum of anxiety that Todd's strange expression was causing in my stomach.

'Elliott,' said Todd, much in the way of a man who is about to deliver difficult news. 'We didn't know that Anya was feeling up to coming in, so I'm a bit surprised to see you.' We gawped at each other before he coughed into his closed fist, neatly, and continued. 'We were very sorry to hear about your recent bereavement and had hoped to assure Anya that she could have longer off for compassionate leave, if needed.'

My heart was fluttering in my chest and I desperately wanted some water, partly to ease my suddenly parched throat, but partly also to give me something to do while my mind whirred and buzzed and attempted to come up with a coherent sentence.

Bereavement? What bereavement? Why on earth had Anya told her boss that? If I let on that I had no idea what he was talking about I was clearly going to get Anya into trouble.

Todd helped me out by filling the gap. But what he said turned the heat of my awkwardness into something that felt like a cold stone dropping into my guts.

'. . . so if she needs another few days on top of the week she's had, I'm sure we can get round her absence.'

A week. She hadn't been to work for *a week*.

I forced words through lips that felt tight and dry. 'Thanks, Todd, I really appreciate it. I think we got crossed wires this morning and maybe she wasn't as up to coming in as she thought.' The words felt like they were choking me.

We made our awkward goodbyes and I went back out into the bright sunshine. I didn't notice a cyclist who was dismounting right next to me and almost walked into them, barely registering their complaints as I walked across the road.

I felt as though there might be eyes on me from the building I'd just left, so I hurried down a side street, jabbing at my phone and dialling my mysteriously disappeared, *bereaved* wife.

It went straight to voicemail and I swore viciously, making a woman passing me quicken her step.

'Anya,' I said, in a voice that trembled with anger. 'What the fuck is going on? I went to surprise you at work and I hear you haven't been in for a week. What the hell is this crap about a bereavement? Ring me back.'

I started walking, fast, not really paying attention to where I was going. My mind was turning over and over with the same questions.

What was going on with Anya? What was she playing at? And the worst one of all: was she leaving me?

A terrible foreboding settled on me then like a great weight and I checked my phone, pointlessly. I couldn't stop myself from ringing her again, then again, but it kept going to voicemail. I jabbed out a message, just to give myself something to do with all the pent-up feelings.

Where RU? Call me.

No 'x' now. It wasn't the time for kisses. The humiliation of not knowing where she was still cut. I tried not to remember the pity on Todd's face. I was angry at myself now that my first instinct had been to worry about getting her into trouble over her lie. If she was going to cut me out like this, what the hell did she expect? I never even found out who this mythical dead relative was, I thought bitterly.

I looked up, barely aware of my surroundings, to see that I had made my way back towards Angel and Upper Street. I had no idea what to do with myself as I stood by the entrance to the tube station, throngs of purposeful people passing me. I felt entirely lost. I didn't really belong here any more. And I didn't want to go home.

It felt as though my muscles made the decision before my brain as I began to walk back to the crossing and over the main road at the lights.

I walked quickly down Upper Street, hands in my pockets and my gaze cast down, heading for Holloway Road.

Towards, I guess, home. Maybe I never really left.

ELLIOTT

Mrs Mack's money felt like something radioactive, pulsing out signals from the pocket of my jeans. *Dirty little thief . . .* I could almost picture Mrs Mack hissing the words in her crisp, Scottish accent.

When she went to the toilet, I had the opportunity to run back into her room and return the cash. But even though my heart seemed to throb with fear and guilt, I didn't do it.

I didn't move.

If I'd only had the guts, it would have saved her life.

I mumbled excuses to go, the scones like rocks in my guts, and headed towards the shop on the estate.

Despite the bars on the windows and the baseball bat that Mr Ghosh, the owner, kept under the counter, Minimart Food and Wine was regularly robbed.

I'd done it myself on a small scale.

I perhaps haven't mentioned that Mrs Mack's cupboard wasn't the first thieving that I had done, by a very long way. But it had never been personal before. Pocketing a couple of Yorkies and a can of Fanta now and then wasn't the same as taking an old lady's money. Those minor acts of dishonesty had given me an excited buzz, but this, now, was something very different; like the world was spinning too fast around me and I needed to get off.

I grabbed a jumbo bag of crisps, a 1.5 litre bottle of Fanta and two Snickers bars, then made a last-minute decision to include a Peperami. I wasn't even hungry, but I had to spend some of the money to get it away from me.

'You last of the big spenders today, heh?' said Mr Ghosh, in unusually friendly form, but I was too sick with myself to reply.

Outside again, it was raining now, and Robbie Williams's 'Angels' was blasting from someone's open window. To this day I loathe that song.

I walked through the estate and down to where there was a small park. It was a sorry excuse for one, with double swings, one of which was broken, and a roundabout that was so peeled and rusty it would scour the skin off your legs. Dog shit studded the grass and it was often a place where deals were made, and worse. I didn't know where else to go, though. Because the weather was turning bad, at least no one was there.

I sat on a wet bench, hunched against the rain, which was beginning to come down in earnest now. But I welcomed the miserable wet metal under my legs and the chill seeping through me. It felt like a punishment I deserved.

I opened the packet of crisps with hands that shook from cold and forced them into my mouth, feeling one of them scratch my dry throat as it went down. I tried to picture him, Mark Little, lying on the floor of a hospital cell, dying, and I ground the toe of my trainer into a tuft of dirt and grass in front of me, fighting unshed tears that burned and clogged my sinuses.

'What the fuck have we got here then?' said a voice. I looked up, startled, because I hadn't heard anyone coming. There were three of them, all much older than me, probably close to twenty. I recognized Kieran from next door as one of them, a hood pulled high over his head. The third bloke was a black kid I only knew as King. I never found out whether it was his actual name or not.

I gathered up my tragic picnic stuff and hurried to my feet. But I felt a firm hand on my shoulder and looked up into the face of the one who had spoken the first time. I thought he was called Jason. He had short white-blond hair and very dark eyes that were all pupil. His face was cratered with acne scars and, although he wasn't heavily built, he had the bouncy, wired energy of a man who was smacked up.

'Hey,' he said, and his voice was oily with fake concern. 'Bit damp here, innit? What you doing, sitting with your sad little fucking crisps?'

I shrugged and tried to get up again, but he pressed on my shoulder and then slid onto the seat next to me. He reached for the bag of crisps, which I willingly relinquished, and then began to stuff them into his mouth with an intense focus until they were gone, and he emptied the shards of what was left into his open mouth. I watched his pale throat working as he swallowed, his teeth yellow and spotted with decay.

I had a powerful urge to run away but knew, if I did, I would turn a bit of mild sport into something with more purpose, so I found myself fumbling to offer him the chocolate bars. He looked at the Snickers in my outstretched hands and turned to look at his guys. All three of them started laughing at once.

'You're a right little fucking Willy Wonka,' said King.

Jason ruffled my hair. 'Don't mind if I do.' He ripped the paper off one of the Snickers and threw the other to King, who laughed and put it in his pocket. Jason ate the Snickers in two or three bites, while I sat silently, not sure where to look or what to do.

123

The rain stopped and a smear of evening sunshine appeared above the flats.

Jason reached into the pocket of his oversized trackie top and pulled out a bottle of supermarket vodka. He took a mouthful that puffed his cheeks out and then offered it to me.

'Here you go, Willy Wonka, you shared your picnic with me, least I can do.'

I was about to shake my head then stopped. I wasn't going to argue with him. I reached for the bottle and forced myself to take a swig, which burned viciously all the way down and brought on an explosive coughing fit that made the three men laugh uproariously.

I grinned after I'd recovered, eyes streaming, to show that I was in on the joke.

Then Kieran was sitting on the other side of me, harvesting papers and a baggy from his pocket and beginning to skin up on his leg. King sat on the edge of the next bench along and smoked a rollie. There was a weird air of respect as they all waited for Kieran to finish his work.

The joint was passed around and then inevitably came to me. I'd had one toke before now, just the one. It had made me feel sick and I hadn't liked it at all.

But my head was messed up from what had happened today, and I wanted to forget. Maybe this would help me do that. So, I took a drag like a pro, proud that I didn't choke on it. Jason clapped me on the back and said, 'That's the fucking way, Willy Wonka.'

I had one more swig from the bottle and then it was gone, to much swearing and discussion about who had cash. And that was when I reached into my pocket and produced the notes that suddenly seemed meant to be. I held them out to Jason and said, 'I've got this. You can have it if you like.'

Kieran had hooted with laughter and said, 'Fuck me,' as Jason reached out and took the money from my hands.

It had taken me half an hour to walk to my old estate but, lost in toxic memory, I hadn't been paying much attention to my surroundings. A homing pigeon muscle memory had sent me the right way, taking a wrong turning only once, and now I found myself standing opposite the estate and gazing across at a small group of kids playing football outside.

A woman in a burqa pushing a smiling, chatty toddler in a buggy passed me, peering through the mesh grille over her face.

I leaned against the wall behind me and, for the first time in a few years, I could feel my fingers twitching for a cigarette. I'd stopped when I met Anya because all it had taken was the thought of one tiny wrinkle of her nose at my breath for the urge to miraculously pass.

Morningside House looked exactly the same, but the white paint on the windows might have been spruced up in recent times. I couldn't see my old flat from this spot; I'd have had to go into the quadrant to do so. This was close enough. Washing hung outside one of the flats on the walkway; grey limp garments dangled limply, looking like solid masses, as though they had been drying since I was last here, despite a breeze that was whipping up now. An old woman, as round as she was tall, with a weathered Mediterranean face and a black scarf around her hair, was leaning on a balcony and gazing out, but didn't seem aware of my presence. Maybe she was seeing an azure sea and olive groves instead of this concrete wasteland.

I shivered and pinched my canvas jacket closer around the neck, which didn't help much. The air now had a vicious nip to it and the stone-grey sky was heavy with imminent rain. In Casterbourne, the poor weather days still carried their own beauty; silvery sea and gunmetal smudges of cloud suddenly parting to showcase bright blue patches of promise.

Here, though, the slate sky seemed to touch the tops of the faded redbrick buildings; an oppressive blanket that only highlighted the grimness and poverty below.

I got out my phone again to check if Anya had responded, even though I had the volume on its highest setting and would have heard if she had. As I put it back into my pocket, I noticed a boy of about ten, of Somalian heritage perhaps, staring at me.

He was holding onto a bike that looked far too small for him and wearing trainers that, conversely, were far too big.

'Hey, fam, you got an iPhone X?' he said in a reedy little voice. My lips tweaked with amusement, despite my gloomy state.

I waggled my phone at him. 'Nah, mate,' I said, 'only a regular old 6, sorry.'

He looked genuinely crestfallen and I wondered what had made him think I was the sort of high roller who'd have an eight-hundred-pound phone. I didn't look like a drug dealer. Maybe I just looked like I didn't belong here. This was an odd, confusing thought.

'I got an iPhone X,' he said, but his eyes shifted as he spoke. I'd been around enough small children to recognize baseless swagger when I saw it, but I kept my face impassive.

'Wow,' I said, 'you sound like a player.' He jabbed a suspicious look at me, then a slight flush of pleasure darkened his cheeks. I suddenly felt the need to keep the conversation going.

'I used to live here, a long time ago.'

I had an urge to tell him that, once, this place had been the start and end of my world, and that I hadn't felt any hope of escaping it. But I did, and I wanted to tell him that he would too. But how could I possibly promise that?

He didn't look much interested, anyway, and began to pick his nose, eyes darting around as though searching for a better source of conversation.

'Where you at now then, fam?' he said, after a moment.

'I live by the seaside,' I said. 'In Kent.' This information was met without much comprehension, as though I'd said I lived in Antarctica, or Jupiter.

The boy kicked down on the bike pedal then and cycled away without another word, my company evidently not coming up to scratch. I was oddly disappointed to see him go.

I dragged my gaze back to the entrance to the quadrant and pushed off against the wall. Now I'd come all this way, I couldn't keep putting it off.

Seconds later, I was looking over my old walkway. An elderly man, right-angled with scoliosis, made painfully slow process to a flat a couple of doors down from where me and mum had lived. Two black teenage girls were talking in high, excited voices as they exited the one on the far end.

'And she says to me, I ain't doing you no fucking favours, and I go, you don't do nuffing for me, you know what I'm saying?'

A dull ache began to spread beneath my sternum and for a minute I wondered whether I was having a heart attack. There would have been a certain justice if I had.

But I wasn't going to be let off that easily. This pain was one I'd carry for the rest of my life.

I sat there as though my legs were made from concrete, my shoulders bowed with grief; for Mrs Mack, for Mum.

For me.

The buzzing in my pocket at that moment was a welcome distraction. I fumbled for my phone.

Anya.

ELLIOTT

I stabbed at the screen to unlock it, so I could read the full message.

> E, I'm so sorry. I didn't know where to even start so I'm going to try and do it my own way, okay? Mum and dad have a flat. I know I haven't mentioned it before. Sorry. (Again!)
>
> But if you can come to this address Flat 1, 54 Coleton Crescent, N1 1LR everything can be explained properly.
>
> Please come. xxxxA

The final sign off – *Please come* – sent ice water up the back of my neck. Was she frightened? Had she had some sort of breakdown because of the stress of what had been going on with Bennett?

I turned and hurried back to Caledonian Road, frantically searching for Coleton Crescent on Google Maps. A black cab appeared with a shining yellow welcome as though someone was looking out for me and, a few minutes later, I was sitting in the back, gazing at the streets but not really taking anything in, my heart racing. Why had Anya never mentioned that her parents had a flat in Islington before?

Coleton Crescent was tucked into one of the streets the other side of Highbury station. While geographically it was not that far from Morningside House, it might as well have been in another country.

A white stuccoed Victorian terrace, each house was at least three storeys high, with freshly painted wrought iron fences that shone like black tar. Plants I wasn't able to identify tumbled out of window boxes. There was even the gentle tinkling of a piano streaming from a window.

A massive Porsche SUV parked two doors down from number 54. The doors opened and several small, blonde children, in the old-fashioned, neat school uniforms that certain parents pay very good money for, spilled out noisily. An East Asian woman, a nanny perhaps, began to herd them inside the property, reprimanding one of them in a loud voice.

I walked up the white stone steps at the front of the building.

I didn't know what I was going to find in the flat. And that was terrifying.

There was a metal entry system with flats numbered 1 to 3.

I pressed the button for Flat 1 and then stood back, gazing up at the building. There was no response the first time, and my head instantly filled with images of Anya lying in a pool of sick, or in a bath full of bloody water. I pressed again, harder, and this time could hear the sound of it chiming inside.

A loud buzz told me the door was open and I pushed it, entering a black and white tiled hallway. I ran up the three flights of stairs, barely taking a breath, and at the top of the house saw the black painted door of Flat 1.

The door was partly open and, heart beating from worry and exertion, I pressed it to enter another small hallway, painted in the sort of Farrow and Ball colour that was no doubt called something stupid like Sad Pigeon. The same colour as the one in Julia and Patrick's house in Lathebridge.

'In here,' came a thin voice and I walked into a long room with two large bay windows, which must have looked over the street outside.

Anya was sitting with her arms bundled around her knees, dressed in faded yellow pyjamas with ducks printed on them. They looked a little too small for her, as though they were from her childhood or teenage years.

Neither of us spoke for a moment. She was thin and pale-looking, her eyes large. I could see sweet wrappers on the floor by the sofa and an empty box of Celebrations lay on the arm of the chair.

Finally, I broke the silence.

'What the hell is going on, Anya?'

She started to cry.

'I'm so sorry, Ell,' she said as tears poured down her cheeks and a snot bubble burst in her nose. Her next words were so shocking, I couldn't immediately process them and felt as though I had misheard her.

'*What?*'

'I killed him,' she repeated. 'I killed him.'

When she comes back, Daddy has put on some music and 'Move It, Move It' is playing. Almost all of the girls are dancing and even Dylan has been dragged to his feet. He is throwing his arms around wildly and looking a bit silly.

Mummy catches her eye and smiles with a question in her eyes: Where did you go, pumpkin? But she just moves over to the crisp bowl, where she plunges in her hand and chooses a really big one from near the bottom. Then she lets out a whooping cry and starts to dance along to the music.

It takes a little while for people to notice what is happening. Dylan, being a bit overweight, doesn't dance for long and quickly resumes his seat next to the crisps, where he carries on stuffing them down in handfuls.

At first, he just coughs and looks a bit uncomfortable in his seat, moving forwards and then scratching at his chest and neck, which have gone pink. His eyes go wide. Adults race over to him and he starts flapping his hands and making a breathing sound like there is something stuck in his throat. She watches in horrified fascination as her mum shouts, 'Someone call 999!' and runs into the kitchen, before quickly returning with a small plastic device in her hand. She had seen Dylan's mother hand this over earlier but hadn't seen where it had been kept.

Lottie grabs it out of her hand and her mum starts to object but Lottie is too busy jabbing the thing straight into her brother's trousered leg in one quick movement. Within about ten seconds he begins to cry. Lottie is crying even harder. She clings to Dylan until the ambulance arrives.

Later, her mother will come into the kitchen and find the jar of peanut butter. It is a new jar, which came with the delivery the day before. The foil inner lid has been peeled back to reveal a shape that looks like three small fingers have been pushed into the smooth surface.

ELLIOTT

Anya drew her feet in their oversized fluffy socks closer to her body and snaked thin arms around her middle. I felt a strange distance from her. Normally, her looking this vulnerable would make me want to hold her.

But then, maybe I had never seen her like this before.

'What do you mean?' I said, and then, moronically, 'Why haven't you been to work?' As if that was the most important thing right now. Maybe it was because the words she had uttered were too big to process.

Anya rubbed her nose with the heel of her hand, in a quick, hard movement, as though trying to erase her own face.

'Didn't you hear what I *said*?'

'I heard you.'

I sank onto a low red sofa that was scuffed and saggy with use. Did I recognize it? I wasn't sure. It looked like the one that used to be in Anya's old bedroom. The question of why I never knew this flat existed felt like the least pressing one right now.

'Who did you kill?' I said softly, looking into her eyes, which were dry and oddly vacant, as though she had been completely emptied out.

She gave a heavy sigh.

'I think I'd better start at the beginning,' she said.

She began to speak. As the light faded outside the window, I understood how little I really knew her.

His name was Michael Copeland and he was the brother of another man, Liam, who she had gone out with for a time at Cambridge. She said, 'It was mainly a physical relationship. I'm sorry. I know that's not the sort of thing you really want to hear, but there it is. It was about getting off our heads and then, well . . . you get the picture.'

I did. In high definition.

She said it fizzled out after a while and that Liam 'wasn't the important person in this story'. He buggered off somewhere and there was a rumour he got on the wrong side of someone in his shady circle. Anya said, with an attempt at humour, 'We've both watched enough Scandi crime, haven't we, to fill in the blanks?'

Anyway, it was his brother – a real slimeball, according to Anya – who then became obsessed with her. He did really creepy things like turning up to her college with gifts, which went from being stuff like chocolate and perfume to more sinister dead roses. Her mum and dad got a restraining order in the end but the stress became too much, making her leave Cambridge and take a year out before going to Durham.

In truth, much as it was hurting me to think of Anya going through all this, an insistent voice in my mind kept whispering, 'But why am I only learning this *now*?'

Finally, as she was telling me about some of the letters he used to write to her, I blurted out, 'I think you need to tell me what you mean by "I killed him".'

She stopped speaking then and wrung her hands in her lap. It was a strange gesture I had never seen her make before. I knew my wife's stress habits as well as I knew my own: the way she would bite on the side of her little finger or twist her hair at the root. This hand-wringing thing looked oddly mannered, but I dismissed the ungracious thought as quickly as it came to me.

'I'm getting to it!' she exclaimed. 'Let me tell you in my own way, okay?'

'Okay! But get to the point!'

'This is *hard*, Ell!'

I raised my palms in supplication. 'I said, *okay*!'

So Michael Copeland had turned up again.

First, she saw him lurking outside her work and had to hide inside until he went away. Then he came into the office and asked for her by name. She went out into the street to talk to him, even though, she said, 'It made me feel physically sick.'

'What did he want, though?' I asked.

She made an impatient gesture, throwing her hands into the air. 'He wanted to fuck with me! To intimidate me, Elliott!' Her voice cracked, and I felt myself drawing back, aware suddenly that I was making her feel worse. But it felt so hard to understand the point of this kind of obsessive behaviour.

Breathing heavily, Anya continued.

'I threatened him with the police and he left. But then he somehow got hold of my mobile number. It was the day of the festival . . .'

Understanding seemed to flood through me now. That explained her weird behaviour that day. It hadn't all been my fault.

'Anyway, I was trying not to think about it,' she said. 'I was up there on your shoulders, feeling like Queen of the World and attempting to record the Foo Fighters, when a message appeared on my screen. It said "I KNOW WHERE YOU LIVE ANASTASIA", all in capitals.'

Anya gave a quick, bright laugh and wiped her eyes. 'I'm sorry about being sick on your shoes. I liked those shoes.'

'Fuck the shoes,' I said, emotion rising inside me, hot and damp. I almost wanted to cry, but I was angry too. 'I just can't understand why you didn't tell me any of this at the time.'

Anya gazed back at me, her eyes brimming with tears now. Outside someone was shouting in a foreign language and a car alarm was going on off on a different street. It felt surprising, that life was going on out there, as normal.

'Okay,' she said, blowing out air and lifting up her hair, before twisting it and tying it up with the band around her wrist. 'I won't be able to apologize enough and so I'm not even going to try. This is the really hard bit. I know this is going to make you think you haven't been the big protector, or some other patriarchal bullshit. But honestly, I didn't especially want you to know that I cracked up at uni. I didn't want you to change your opinion of me, to see me as someone else.'

'Anya, I can't believe—'

'*Please*, Ell!' she shouted, making me flinch. 'Let me get this out! Just, please, *listen*.'

I sat back in the seat, raising my palms again.

'So, obviously it *was* Copeland,' she continued. 'I told Mum and Dad straight away and they advised me to change my number. I'm sorry . . . I didn't really lose my phone but it seemed easier to say that. Mum and Dad thought that was the best thing . . . '

Mum and Dad. Of course, she went straight to them. I was only her husband, after all.

'The person who knocked you off your bike,' she said in a rush, 'could have been your Psycho Dad character from school, the one who made the phone calls and threw that brick through the window. But I had a strong feeling that

135

was Copeland. Mum and Dad were all up in arms about getting another injunction against him, but I felt deep down that this wasn't really going to stop him. I got angry then. Really angry. So, I did a stupid thing, Ell.'

Cold hands seemed to snake around my neck, then. Now we were getting to the part that changed everything.

'When I was at Mum and Dad's the other night,' she said, 'I contacted him from the old number. I thought if I could just meet him face to face when I was prepared for it, I could make him understand that he was hurting me and that I would never be with him in the way he wanted.'

I was on my feet again, almost without realizing it.

'For fuck's sake! How could you have been so stupid!'

Anya looked down, cheeks red. Her hands started to twist together again in her lap.

'I know,' she said, voice trembling. 'I know how it sounds. And it *was* stupid. Believe me, Mum and Dad have given me hell over it. But it is what it is.'

Anya swore and leaned back against the sofa for a moment, closing her eyes.

'So?' I said, forcing myself not to grab her by the shoulders and yell into her face. 'What happened when you met him?'

She sat up and threaded her hands around her knees again, making herself even smaller on the sofa.

'I arranged to meet him in the car park at Petrel Point.'

'Shit!' I couldn't stop myself from shouting. 'What the hell were you thinking?'

She started to sob now and spoke indistinctly through her tears. 'It's always such a popular spot. It felt like being out in such a wide-open space would be safer than meeting him anywhere else.'

Breathing as heavily as if I had just been running, I said, 'I'm sorry. Tell me the rest. I won't interrupt.'

The words all came out in a rush.

'. . . when his car pulled up and he got out, looking even more creepy and unkempt than I remembered him, I knew straight away that I had made a mistake. His eyes were all glassy and he had really wet lips that he kept licking. He couldn't seem to look at me directly and I thought maybe he was drunk, or high on something. I gave it to him straight: told him that he had almost broken me once before with his unwanted attention. I was so determined to stay strong, but I became emotional, remembering what a terrible time it had been before, and begged him to leave me alone.

'And that was when he lunged at me. He managed to get his arms around me for a split second, but it was long enough to feel his wet lips against my neck and to smell his rank body. All the other cars in the car park had gone and I was alone with him. I thought, *This is it. He's going to rape me then kill me.* I managed to shove him away and I ran down to the coastal path, the one you and I have walked so many times in happier circumstances. You know how we are always saying that they should put a fence along that one section of it that goes close to the cliff edge?'

Anya slipped off the sofa and sat on her knees in front of me. She took my hands in hers and looked into my eyes as she stuttered out the rest of this terrible story. I squeezed her hands, unable to speak for the moment.

'He chased after me and I could hear him gaining,' she said, 'despite the fact that he was older and more unfit. I don't know, you hear about people getting superhuman strength or speed in times of high emotion, don't you?'

A long, ragged breath in and out.

'And maybe that's what saved me,' she said and gave a strangled laugh that turned into a sob. 'He caught hold of my wrist,' she continued. 'I turned and shoved him with both hands, harder than I could have believed possible. And then . . .' she swallowed, a kind of wonder on her face. 'Then he wasn't there any more.'

'Shit,' I said on a drawn-out breath, before leaning back against the chair and releasing her hands.

'I couldn't bring myself to look over the edge of the cliff at first,' she said in a rush. 'Every corny scene where a murderer comes back for another go at the victim played itself out in my head. But I knew I had to look, so after a few moments I took a small step and forced myself to walk to the edge of the cliff, where the spongy dune starts to turn into rock. I couldn't see him from there. I didn't know what to do. I was hyperventilating, Elliott. It was like I was never going to be able to breathe air again for a minute and I honestly thought I might die from panic and shock. But after a few moments the rational part of my brain took over and I forced myself to walk back to the car.'

I sat there for a few moments in stunned silence. None of this felt real.

'Wait,' I said then, 'was this the night you came in soaked from the storm?'

She gave a small nod, her expression wary.

I remembered the way she was that evening; hyped-up and sizzling with some sort of strange energy. A horrible thought flashed into my mind that I pushed away, ashamed for even thinking it. It was just stress, that was all. None of us knew how we might react in times of such intense drama. You hear about people getting the giggles at funerals. So *what* if she had seemed oddly . . . excited, that night? Who knew how I would have reacted in those circumstances?

Then I just felt sick. The easy way she had lied to me, about there being nowhere to park. It felt as though those words had fallen so easily from her lips.

'Say something,' she said.

'I hate that you went through that,' I said, my voice

138

strangled. 'But why didn't you tell *me*? And why didn't you go to the police? It was self-defence for fuck's sake!'

Anya threaded her fingers through her hair and tugged at her scalp as she got to her feet.

'I don't know!' she said and began pacing the room. 'I mean, I was the one who arranged to meet him. Mobile phone records will show he had contact with me, even if his phone is never found. They may even come out as it is. What's to stop a clever prosecution barrister from claiming that I, a local, lured someone who didn't know the area to this dangerous spot and then got rid of him?'

Then, shocking me, 'I think it would probably make for a very nice tabloid story and I don't think either of us want that kind of scrutiny, do we? I know what a disaster it would be if the press found out about your dad, especially because of the job you have now.'

This felt like a low blow. I looked away and stared at the window. It was dark outside but light glowed from the streetlamp outside the house.

She continued in a low voice. 'When we saw the local paper piece asking whether anyone knew him, I almost died from the shock that he was still alive. Mum pretended to be a journalist and called for updates, so we found out, just a few days ago, that he had died.'

'Murder, then,' I murmured, and she shot me a defiant look.

'As I am being totally honest with you,' she said, 'I was relieved to hear this. I'm sorry if that makes you think badly of me. But you don't know what it is like to feel what I felt, that this man was going to rape and kill me.'

There was a long silence before Anya spoke again.

'I love you, Ell. Please never forget that. I did what I thought was right, but I made mistakes. I don't think I deserve to go to prison for them though, do you?'

139

ELLIOTT

My head had started to ache at some point in the last ten minutes. Maybe it was the stuffiness of that room. I only noticed now that the windows were tightly shut, despite the mildness of the day. Maybe it was shock at what I had just heard.

Anya was sitting again now, leaning forwards, so her head was on her knees, her arms wrapped around her legs. She was rocking a little bit.

I couldn't seem to work through everything I was feeling.

My skin prickled with goose pimples and the flat suddenly felt very cold. I pictured Anya running from that man, in blind terror for her life, and squeezed my hands into fists, before jumping up and pacing the room. The toe of my trainer caught the edge of the Chinese rug and I tripped, almost flying face first into the mantelpiece. Adrenaline sparked up my spine and I was breathing heavily as I steadied myself.

'Are you alright?' she said. 'That rug's a death trap. I'm always telling Mum and Dad it needs to go.'

I turned to look at her, incredulous at her easy tone. There were probably all sorts of quirks to this, the secret Ryland family flat. Maybe some rattly pipes, or a tap that didn't quite turn off. I wouldn't know, would I?

'So you've been here? Hiding away from work? From me?'

Her cheeks darkened as she looked up at me and I could see annoyance there.

I knew I was focusing on all the wrong things here. But I couldn't seem to get my derailed emotions onto the correct track.

'I'm sorry, I have to think,' I said as a hot feeling of fury washed over me, stealing my breath in a way that was a bit frightening. I felt like I was having some sort of anxiety attack. I just couldn't believe that all this had happened, and Anya had chosen not to share one single bit of it with me, her husband. I had to get out.

'Elliott!'

I crashed out of the flat and ran down the stairs and out the front door, hearing her call my name again.

I began to walk quickly and mindlessly until I came to an ugly modern pub that was entirely out of character in these quaint streets. Inside it was gloomily lit and a few old men were sitting in corners, staring balefully into their pints. It felt as though the wallpaper had soaked up all the smells of times gone by and a powerful urge for a cigarette hit me in the back of my throat in Pavlovian response.

I ordered a double Jack Daniel's and soda from a taciturn, Scottish barman and went to sit in the corner. My phone began to buzz with a call and I looked down and pressed decline. I had to think. I couldn't talk to her right now.

The drink warmed my throat and I closed my eyes for a moment.

Anya had killed a man. She did it to save her life.

But I couldn't seem to keep hold of these slippery facts. I knew that Anya would be suffering right now, desperate to know that I was not judging her.

I wasn't. Who was *I* to judge anyone?

A man was dead. A man who had terrorized the woman I loved more than anyone in the world. Why couldn't I focus on this, the most serious part of the whole equation? She needed me now.

Now, she needed me.

That was it. That was why I ignored her next call and the texts that pinged onto my screen, one by one.

Where are you, babe?xxxxxx

Please ring me I'm going crazy here wondering what you're thinking.xxxx

Elliott? Please ring I'm freaking out xxxxxxxxxxxxxxx

I'm scared now. What are you doing? Xxxxxxxxxx

I didn't like to think of her being scared; maybe thinking I was going to the police like some moral crusader. What a joke that was. It wasn't enough though; it wasn't enough to make me call her back.

The truth was, a feeling I can only describe as a deep loneliness had wrapped itself around me like a cold shroud. Her panicky entreaties weren't even beginning to penetrate it.

I felt as though all the things Patrick and Julia said about me being part of the family, one of them, really meant nothing. When things got tough, they hunkered down together and only let me in when all the drama had passed.

I pictured them, a war council of three, sitting round the table in Lathebridge, or in that Islington flat they'd kept hidden away. They'd be drinking good red wine and talking calmly about what to do. Did I even figure in the conversation?

Anya needed me now, yes. But she hadn't told me any of

the history with this Michael Copeland. She hadn't come to me when he reappeared in her life and she hadn't come to me when she pushed him off a cliff.

Pushed him off a cliff . . .

A bizarre yelp of twisted mirth erupted from my mouth. I had no idea where it came from. As a couple of heads turned my way with wary expressions, I had the insane urge to laugh like a lunatic at the ridiculous television-drama nature of this event.

'I'm sorry,' I pictured myself saying. 'But my wife pushed her stalker off a cliff and I've only just found out.' I could almost feel the words forming on my lips.

This was no good. I was going a bit mad here. I tapped out a message.

We'll talk when I'm home but I need to get my head together. I do love you. X

I wanted to switch off my phone but first I began to scroll through London friends' numbers.

Jamie and his wife had not long had a baby. I couldn't impose on them.

My oldest school friend, Ant, was, I knew from Facebook, currently working at a school in Vietnam for a charity.

Clare and Stu were a couple I knew from working in a call centre while I did my degree. They lived in South London. I'd lost touch because Anya wasn't that keen on Clare, who came from Newcastle and had a tendency to speak her mind when she'd had a drink.

I mentally scrolled through the friends I'd gone through the later years of school with and realized I hadn't spoken to them in a long time. Didn't that happen in most marriages, especially when you moved away? That you lost touch with your friends? I wasn't even sure some of these numbers were current. People seemed to have fallen away since I met Anya. Had I really felt she was all I needed? When had I become *that* person?

I could feel my plan to keep some distance deflating by the second. Anyway, I had to get to work tomorrow.

I couldn't face going home, but maybe I could go back to Casterbourne.

I braced myself for the tide of disapproval that was about to slap me in the face over skiving from work and rang the woman who owed me no favours at all.

IRENE

She hadn't known who else to call.

Frank was a stranger, someone who had done an old woman a kindness when she had been in need. He wasn't family, or even a friend. But there was no one else here.

Right after it happened, when the nice West Indian doctor came and found her in the corridor and spoke to her very slowly and quietly, Irene hadn't really followed what she said. She'd known, anyway, when everything went crazy in Michael's room. She'd had a mother's instinct that he was lost to her.

They had made her wait to speak to the police; a nice enough young female constable who looked about twelve and a very slightly older male with a big Adam's apple who kept swallowing, as if he was nervous. They had asked about Michael's state of mind too, just as the doctor had.

She'd had to tell them that, yes, he had been made redundant a while back, and yes, he had been prescribed anti-depressants by the doctor. That yes, maybe he had some odd ideas about things sometimes. She hadn't meant it to come out like that, but it felt as though they were guiding her in a certain direction.

It was obvious what they thought. That Michael had chosen this end for his too-short life.

Frank had come quickly when the nurse asked if there was anyone they could call for her. She'd greeted him in a flurry of apologies and all he'd done was bow his head and say he was terribly sorry for her loss and that his 'humble abode' was open to her during this difficult time. She had slept solidly for ten hours, much to her amazement, and hadn't yet had the sort of crying fit that she knew would hollow her out and leave her fit for nothing. Tears had leaked slowly almost constantly but she had made herself act in a dignified way, the humiliation and loneliness of having to rely on a stranger being an effective stopper on her emotions.

Frank lived in a tidy three-storey house not that far from the seafront. Evidence of his late wife was everywhere, from the framed photos of the couple, to the embroidered and knitted items that seemed to cover every surface.

'She liked knitting, my Sylvia,' he'd said as she entered, with a kind of gruff warning that Irene shouldn't criticize. She wouldn't have dreamed of it, never having had any skills in that area herself. He had prepared a ham salad that she didn't eat and then she had taken herself off to a bedroom with a patchwork quilt and swirling dust motes caught in the early evening sun.

She had lain there, flat on the bed, like a statue on an ancient crypt. The pain inside pressed and probed into every part of her body and she felt as though a sudden movement might shatter her into a million fragments. The light bled from the day and still Irene lay there, staring up at the ceiling and thinking that now there was only her. There had been four of them and now there was only her.

Then she had curled into a ball and wept until she almost needed to vomit.

It had been a very long day.

It was Frank, last night, who had asked whether the hospital had talked about his belongings. Irene had told him that Michael had been found without anything that could identify him. As she said it, Irene had suddenly sat upright, realizing how stupid she had been. Where was Michael's car?

Frank had known where impounded cars were kept and insisted on driving her over there. Irene could drive, but hadn't for years, and was in no fit state right now.

Getting it back, though, proved to be a nightmare. Irene had tried to explain the whole thing to a spotty youth who looked totally disinterested and who, at first, had refused to believe she had any right to pick up the car.

There happened to be a copy of the local paper lying crushed and dusty in a corner of the waiting room and Frank had brandished it at the young man and started talking, in a very imposing voice, about how he was distressing a grieving mother and ought to be ashamed of himself.

Eventually, they had been allowed to take the car, which had been found with keys in the ignition when it was towed away from the car park near where Michael met his death.

The inside of the car, an ugly big thing in Irene's view, was filthy, the floor covered in crisp wrappers and takeaway coffee cups. There was a key on a plastic fob that belonged to a boarding house in Casterbourne.

So now Frank was driving her there, without complaint, so she could collect the rest of Michael's things.

'It has to be done, doesn't it?' she said and her voice came out sounding much more clipped than she'd intended. It sounded like the voice of a woman who was in control. This, at least, was a comfort. Then she found herself asking a question she hadn't anticipated.

'Frank,' she said, 'why are you bothering to help me like this? You don't know me.'

He turned from the road and looked at her gravely, before replying.

'I don't know,' he said. 'If you want the honest answer.'

After a while they pulled up in front of a terraced house with a slightly tatty sign that said 'The Squirrels', with a picture of a rather sinister-looking red squirrel scowling from it and a 'Vacancies' notice beneath.

They were high up in the cliffs now and the sea was a dismal grey skein, the sky white and oppressive. It felt as though the air itself was weighted, pressing down on Irene's scalp. She had a headache. She asked Frank to wait in the car then forced her weary limbs to carry her to the front door, where she rang the doorbell.

A few moments later a man in his fifties with a moustache and a military sort of bearing opened the door and frowned at her.

'Are you that man's mother?' he said, in a surprisingly high-pitched voice. Irene was only able to nod. There was clearly going to be no small talk, which was a blessing in its own way. She came into the dim interior of the hallway, where a narrow hall table was covered in a lace runner and a blaze of coloured tourist leaflets, and the man regarded her with droopy, heavy-lidded eyes.

'I'm sorry about it all,' he said, then quickly, 'Anyway, it's this way.'

She was led up some stairs that had a worn carpet runner in faded reds and golds and up to a first-floor landing. The property smelled strongly of sickly pine air freshener that tickled Irene's nose.

The man opened a room on the right of the corridor.

'This is where he was staying,' he said. 'Then he just sort of . . . disappeared. It's lucky we're quiet or we'd have had to get rid of his stuff. I'm sure you understand that we are a business.'

Now he had started speaking he barely seemed able to shut up. Irene suddenly felt very weary and merely mumbled a reply as she looked around the room, which was surprisingly cheerful after the unprepossessing hallway and its owner.

The walls were painted a sunny yellow and the curtains were white with little blue flowers on them. A dresser, a desk and a chest of drawers all matched the pale wood of the single bed, on which there was a small suitcase with items spilling out. Irene immediately recognized a fleecy gilet of Michael's and suddenly found she was sitting on the bed, rather than standing by it, just as though someone had taken her out behind the knees.

'Are you going to be alright?' the man flapped next to her. 'Only my wife is at a hospital appointment and she usually deals with the guests.'

'I'm okay,' said Irene a little breathlessly. 'Maybe you could get me a glass of water, if you could be so kind?'

The man hesitated and then disappeared out the door, leaving her relieved and alone. She made herself stuff a pair of pyjamas and a T-shirt into the case, then pulled out the T-shirt and held it to her nose. It smelled a bit musty and didn't especially make her feel close to her son. Tears were spilling down her cheeks again and she got to her feet, in an attempt to wrest control of herself.

She walked over to the desk where there was a plastic folder, with paper inside. She looked closer and then felt confusion and exhaustion fogging her brain. What did this mean?

Inside the plastic wallet was a sheet of paper – a type of printed form, as far as she could tell. Its heading said 'Expert Detection Services' and there were headings like, 'Scope of works' and 'Findings'. It all seemed to be biographical details about a person called Anastasia Ryland; not a name Irene had ever heard before. It listed her height and weight, her eye colour.

Was it some sort of missing persons report? No . . . Irene understood in a rush that it was something else. It looked like Michael had been trying to find this person.

There was no other information other than details about where she lived – in Casterbourne – and worked – in London, for a company who could have done anything at all, as far as Irene could tell.

It was all very odd.

For a moment it felt as though this really would all be too much for her and she steadied herself with a hand against the table, while she tried to take some deep breaths. There was no one else to do this. Whatever had been going on in Michael's life, he had been trying to work something out, hence this strange mission to the seaside.

She heard someone coming and turned, heart beating and feeling unaccountably guilty. The man came back into the room bearing a small glass of water and a worried expression.

'Here is your water,' he said. 'Are you all done?'

'Yes, and thank you,' she said, taking the glass and sipping from it. The water tasted much more chlorinated here than she was used to, but as he made no move to take the glass back she felt forced to drink it all, knowing it was going to go straight to her bladder.

They went down the stairs in silence, but Irene could almost feel the weight of something the man wanted to say. She felt a strange sympathy for him. He was clearly the sort of man who left all the real communication to the woman in his life and was at sea, having to deal with her. When they reached the front door, she wanted to reassure him that she understood he hadn't meant to seem brisk. She opened her mouth to speak just as he said, 'Look, there is the matter of the bill.'

Embarrassment blazed across her cheeks. She had entirely forgotten that the dusty little room must be paid for. How silly of her.

She fumbled for her purse in a flurry of apologies and the man made a great deal of hunting for a card payment device, when she produced a bank card. The transaction wouldn't go through at first and Irene feared she might go mad in this small, dark hallway, with this fussy, unsympathetic man.

Irene turned her head to the window as Frank started the engine and he must have sensed she didn't want to talk. They drove in silence for a few moments. Irene wanted to be in her own home now, alone, more than anything else in the world.

But that couldn't happen yet.

'Frank,' she said, breaking the silence, 'I don't want to treat you like a taxi driver, but could I impose on your kindness for one more thing?'

'Of course,' he said, turning to look at her.

'Can we go to one more address?'

ELLIOTT

I knew it was going to be hard not to confiding in Zoe about five minutes after I got to her flat. She let me in with a wry expression and a greeting of 'Hello, you massive skiver.'

There was no sign of Tabitha, which was a relief because I didn't feel like making conversation with someone I didn't know. I walked into the living room, where the television was showing an episode of *Love Island*, and sat down on the low, squashy sofa that had a tasselled African print throw over it. A book by Kamila Shamsie that Anya had been pressing me to read for ages lay face down on the table. The air smelled pleasantly of something garlicky. I let out an involuntary sigh as the sofa absorbed my weight and felt as though I were breathing properly for the first time today.

All I'd said to Zoe was that I needed a night away from home – just one night – and she hadn't asked any more questions.

But now, as she emerged from the kitchen holding two bottles of Asahi beer, she had an expression that was going to brook no excuses.

'Here,' she said, handing me a bottle. 'So . . . trouble in paradise then?'

I grimaced and took a long drink of the beer, which felt

so crisp and reviving I almost sighed with pleasure. I closed my eyes for a moment, trying to remember why I'd thought coming here was a good idea. Some part of me desperately wanted to offload the burden of what I had learned today. But I couldn't tell her. It was simply too much to bring to her door.

In that moment, something came to me like it had been perfectly gift-wrapped. 'It's just that . . .' I took another swig. 'You know we're trying for a baby and everything . . .'

'Yeah, go on,' said Zoe, curling her legs up underneath her on the chair opposite me.

'. . . well I think I'm having doubts about it.'

Zoe let out a long sigh and sat back in the chair.

'Fuck,' she said and took a sip of her beer. 'And Anya feels differently, I take it?'

It was scary how quickly this was all coming to me now. Maybe it wasn't a lie.

'Well, I think she guessed,' I said, extemporizing wildly. 'We had a few words last night and I just think some time away from each other will be a good thing.' There was a silence and then I added, a bit lamely, 'Thanks again for putting me up.'

Zoe was frowning now and pulling on her bottom lip – a habit when she was deep in thought.

'Was it . . .' she said after a few moments, 'a *really* bad fight? I mean, she didn't . . .' She bit off the end of her sentence and took a swig of her beer, her cheeks darkening with what I assumed to be embarrassment, judging by the way she was avoiding my eyes.

'Didn't what?' I said, with an awkward laugh.

She put her beer down on the table and then looked at me, an unreadable expression on her face.

'It's just that . . . she can be a bit . . . fierce?' She laughed again but it sounded fake.

'What do you mean?' Annoyance cut in quickly, just as I was starting to relax.

'Well . . .' she took another sip of her beer, then spoke quickly. 'I saw her really lose her temper at the festival that day. You weren't there. I didn't see what happened, but I think someone knocked into her. When I looked over, she was really mouthing off to whoever it was. I wasn't sure whether to be impressed or terrified.'

I sighed and laid my head back on the sofa.

'Yep,' I said. 'And she did tell me about that. She wasn't feeling well that day, as you know. She's not normally like that.'

This was true. Anya didn't generally have what you would call a hot temper. But this still felt like uncomfortable territory after what I had learned earlier that day.

I needed time to unpack my feelings about everything but, right now, all I wanted to do was veg out and watch television until I became numb.

'Look, Zo,' I said, 'is it okay if we move on? Can we just chill out together tonight?'

She looked a little surprised, I think, but she agreed. I hoped that I could make it up by supplying a Chinese take-away and some booze.

So, we had a few drinks, ate our food, and watched a *Mission Impossible* movie Zoe had recorded. It was pleasant, mind-numbing stuff, and by the time I was bedding down on the sofa, I was hopeful that I could sink into sleep. Guilt about skiving from school was nipping at me underneath the other, more dominant emotions, and I was determined to go in full of enthusiasm in the morning.

But as soon as I closed my eyes, all I could see was Anya, scrambling up that cliff path as she feared for her life. My heart began to pound in my chest and I had to sit up, untangling myself from the thin, single duvet that barely covered half my body. I grabbed my phone, its light bathing my face in the dark room, I looked at my last exchange with Anya. I had expected a barrage of messages and, although I was relieved to have been given the space I'd asked for, her silence was nonetheless discomfiting.

I went to the kitchen and got myself a glass of water. I needed to stop drinking so much. Zoe had stopped at two bottles of beer, but I'd then drunk most of the bottle of red I'd brought with me. It hadn't seemed to affect me at all but now I could feel the dry mouth and inklings of a headache waiting in the wings for the morning.

I lay there, mind churning with pictures of Anya, Mrs Mack, Michael Copeland and that Islington flat, while my back ached from the inadequate length of the sofa. Finally, as the sound of birdsong began to seep into the room and grey dawn crept over the dark shapes of the furniture, I slept.

I was groggy the next morning when Zoe woke me with a strong cup of coffee but dragged myself into the shower and let the hot water pound me awake, before putting on my borderline-smelly clothes from the day before and hoping for the best.

I would normally wear a shirt and smart trousers to work. Now I had on a T-shirt and grey cotton trousers – thank God I hadn't worn my jeans the day before, which really would have been frowned upon by Jackie.

Zoe offered me an iron but we were running late. I'd have to do.

As we walked together to work, Zoe talked about Tabitha and how she was a little clingier than was comfortable. I was listening intently, chipping in advice from my limited pool when I could. I wouldn't have noticed that Lee and Tyler Bennett were crossing the road just in front of us if Zoe hadn't abruptly changed topic.

'Ay-up,' she said sotto voce now. 'Aggressive twat sighting at two o'clock.'

A strange embarrassment hit me as my head jerked up to see them. I was so sure it had been Bennett who was harassing me. I cringed at the memory of going to the police station. I was sure, now, that it was Copeland, Michael Copeland, all along. I almost felt a weird sort of nostalgia for the time before Anya's revelation.

Michael Copeland.

Murdered Michael Copeland.

'Elliott.' Zoe's elbow was sharp in my ribcage. 'Stop being weird . . . you're glaring at him.'

'What . . . ?'

Bennett was looking at me now, warily, and Tyler was staring at me too, his cheeks flushed. Flustered, I turned my head. 'I wasn't meaning to,' I said. 'I was just miles away for a minute.'

We were inside the gates now. Zoe gave my arm a quick squeeze as we parted ways.

'Don't give that wanker any more fuel, okay?' she murmured before hurrying off down the corridor. Feeling even more ashamed of myself, I slunk off to my class.

The day passed uneventfully, and I forced myself to engage properly despite the tiredness dragging at me, and the worries about everything. I saw Jackie at break and knew I wasn't imagining the way her eyes swept lightly over my less than smart attire. I gave her a weak grin, which she didn't return. It felt like something had shifted at school and I didn't really know how to get it back.

But skiving off and then turning up in last night's clothes wasn't, I knew very well, the way to go about it.

Shame was proving to be the theme of the day, it seemed.

As the morning went on, I began to regret my decision to stay out the night before. Anya was probably going through hell. She had laid out what was perhaps one of the worst experiences of her life in front of me, and what had I done? I'd been unable to hack it and had run away to lick my wounds about being 'left out', like the giant man baby I am.

I couldn't wait for the end of the day, so I could take her in my arms and reassure her it was all going to be okay.

IRENE

'Are you quite sure you are up to doing this?' said Frank, yet again. Irene swallowed back an unexpectedly sharp feeling of irritation and forced herself to give him a thin smile.

'If not now, when?' she said. Frank murmured that this was a fair point and drove down the big hill towards the direction of the sea. The sun had peeked out briefly and the firefly speckles of light moving across its surface were soothing but not quite enough to quell the nervous feeling dancing in her stomach.

Three minutes later they pulled into a street that was a few rows back from the seafront. Neat, terraced houses of the two-up-two-down sort that had been her and Colin's first home together. For a moment she allowed the memory to sweep in of her climbing those steep stairs, her round belly and extra weight making her huff with the effort. Then . . . sitting up in bed with her tiny son in her arms, while Colin fussed about, seeming to levitate a few inches off the ground with pride.

Cold desolation twisted in her stomach now and she gripped the handle of her handbag until her knuckles blanched. There would be plenty of time – too much time

– to grieve when she got home. She would never come back to this town again but thank goodness for the kindness of this stranger who was willing to help her.

The car slowed and pulled into the nearest parking space, behind a blue people carrier. The house she wanted, number 15, was a few doors up.

'This is us,' said Frank, and she felt a little touched at the way he was including himself in this strange sequence of events. 'I'll come with you, shall I?'

'*No*.'

She hadn't meant to say it so sharply, and could almost feel him drawing back, a little wounded.

'Sorry, I don't even know if this a wild goose chase,' she said. 'I just want to ask, that's all. And then we can go.'

Frank said, 'It's up to you,' but didn't meet her eyes and she could tell he was offended. She had pushed her luck too far. This needed to be done and then she could get a train back to her own home, somewhere she longed to be now with an intensity that was almost painful.

With a weary sigh, she opened the door and heaved herself out onto the pavement. The sun had been swallowed by cloud again and a chill wind wrapped itself around her. She had forgotten how vicious a sea breeze could be.

She walked warily towards number 15, which had a jaunty red front door and a front garden that looked as though no one ever gave it any attention.

There was no point trying to rehearse what she was going to say; it was all too bizarre. So instead she made herself stride up the path and press the doorbell before she could lose courage and run back to the relative security of Frank's car.

There was no response to her first press of the doorbell, but she saw movement from the corner of her eye at the bay window to her left. Someone was home, alright. They were just avoiding answering the door.

Hot indignation now helpfully replaced her jitters and Irene rang the bell then rapped hard on the painted red wood with her knuckles.

Still nothing.

Almost before she knew she was going to do it, Irene lowered her face to the level of the letterbox and flipped it up with a finger.

'Can you help me?' she said. 'I'm looking for a woman called Anastasia?' Then, 'I know someone is in there!' Her own voice sounded shrill and elderly to her ears and suddenly she felt so tired and sad she feared she would just sit down on the pavement and never get up again. She rapped once more on the door and pressed the doorbell and then the door flew open so violently she almost fell inside and onto the young woman on the threshold.

Irene was so startled that she simply stared for a moment. The girl was tall, slim, and very pretty, with thick red hair piled on top of her head. It was the same sort of colour as Liam's, oddly. The eyes too – that unusual caramel-brown – currently glaring from a pale, heart-shaped face. Her eyes were a bit red round the rims. She was wearing what looked like a man's shirt over a pair of black leggings and her feet were bare, toes varnished with blue polish.

When she spoke her voice came out almost as a growl.

'Yes? What do you want?'

'I'm . . . I'm . . .' Irene's heart was beating uncomfortably hard and she felt a little dizzy. Why hadn't she practised what she would say?

'I'm Michael's mother,' was all she managed to blurt out. The effect of these words on the other woman was shocking. Her face seemed to blanch right in front of Irene and her eyes widened. She opened her mouth, then closed it, then licked her lips. Then she spoke again.

'Who?' Her eyes were changing; from angry to something

else now. Cold. As though she had brought down shutters over her face.

'I can tell you know his name!' Irene felt her voice crack, but she needed to be in control just for a little while longer. 'Please?' she said. 'He's dead and there was some sort of report in his room with your name and address on it.'

The woman, Anastasia surely, was fiddling with her long hair, twisting it around her finger and almost yanking it in a way that looked uncomfortable. Irene suddenly felt a dizzying surge of adrenaline that made her want to take a step back. She had the oddest feeling of wanting to protect herself. Her instinct was to flee. But she knew she had to stay strong.

'Look,' she said, 'please can you just spare a few minutes? That's all I ask.'

'I'm closing the door now.'

Irene forced herself forward until her foot was in the doorway. She had never done anything like this in her life before. This strong young woman towered over her and fear pulsed through her in a way she couldn't entirely justify.

Then Anastasia did something that shocked Irene more than any violence could have done. She smiled.

It was a dazzling smile, like something from a toothpaste advertisement. Her eyes positively shone. Irene, confused, felt her own face beginning to respond in kind but this was all wrong.

'Would you mind?'

Irene looked down and found herself removing her foot.

When she looked back up, the young woman's face was a mask of stone.

She leaned a little closer, so Irene could smell something bad on her breath, and in a low voice said, 'Get your fat arse off my doorstep. I don't know anything about any fucking Michael Copeland.'

161

The door was slammed with such force that Irene felt the draught of it gusting against her face. A strange kind of triumph was cutting through the shock of the encounter though, and she banged her fist against the wood again.

'I never told you our surname!' she shouted. 'You *did* know him!'

Irene began to shout up at the window.

'My son hated heights! Why would he go to that cliff if he hated heights! You know something about this, I know you do!' She couldn't seem to stop.

She became aware then that two people were standing near her on the pavement. One of them was Frank, whose expression was one of total horror at her yelling like a fish-wife in the street. Her cheeks burned, and she cast her eyes to the other person, a tall, thin young man with messy dark curls and a complexion that could have been Mediterranean. He had soft brown eyes and a neat beard and was looking equally horrified.

'What's going on here?' he said, his voice low. 'Why are you shouting at my house?'

Why indeed? Irene cleared her throat and patted her hair at the back. She couldn't really get her breath.

'My son is *dead*,' she said. Her voice fractured as she felt her knees sag from under her, then there were two sets of arms holding her up.

'Let's go, Irene, come on,' said Frank. 'We'll get you back to the car. I think we're finished here.'

'Look, is she alright?' said the young man. He sounded genuinely concerned, which made Irene twist her head to stare at him, despite the fact that her whole body appeared to be made from jelly. His eyes were kind.

'Please,' she managed to say through lips that felt a little numb. 'Ask that woman if she knows why Michael did what he did. He didn't like heights, you see.'

The young man flinched and stepped back abruptly, and Frank led her to the car.

Once she had been bundled inside, she accepted the bottle of water proffered by Frank and took a long drink, despite her shaking hand.

The man was looking back over his shoulder and turning a key in the lock, his expression troubled. He met Irene's eye again and quickly looked away, before disappearing inside.

Irene wondered how much he really knew about the person who shared his house. She'd never met anyone – in all her seventy-three years – who had given her such a chilling feeling as that woman.

ELLIOTT

The air in the hallway felt cold and I could smell something 'off' from the bin in the kitchen. There was also another, sour smell that I recognized as sick.

'Anya?' I yelled and quickly began to look in each room. There was no sign of her and I had the ridiculous notion that she was hiding from that old lady in a cupboard or something. I was shaking from seeing her – Michael Copeland's mother, for sure – on our doorstep and couldn't imagine how Anya must be feeling.

I heard a faint sound from upstairs, and took the stairs two at once, calling her name the whole time.

I found her slumped in front of the toilet, her skin pale and covered with a sheen of sweat. Her eyes were brimming, and her fringe clung to her damp forehead.

She began to cry, pitifully, as she gazed up at me from the cold, tiled floor.

'Oh God,' she sobbed, 'did you see that? Did you hear it?'

I crouched down and put my arms around her, saying, 'Hey, hey,' in a soothing voice as she began to cry in more earnest. She clung to my neck as I helped her to her feet and she buried her face into my neck until I could feel her tears beginning to seep inside the top of my T-shirt.

'Let me brush my teeth,' she said finally, in a muffled, snotty voice. 'Feel disgusting.'

She brushed her teeth and used mouthwash, avoiding my eye the whole time. Her eyes were glassy now and she seemed far away.

'I'm just going to lie down for a bit, Ells,' she said, her voice croaky. 'I've been feeling really shit all day and then that mad woman turned up at our door.'

I simply nodded and went through with her to the bedroom. 'Mad woman' seemed a bit harsh, in the circumstances. What I'd seen was someone who looked absolutely hollowed out from grief and confusion. And we knew things she didn't and never could.

I led Anya through to our bedroom and helped her to get onto the bed, then pulled down the blind. She was shivering, and I put a fleece blanket over her.

'Look,' I said, 'you lie down for a bit and we'll talk later, okay?'

I was walking out of the room when she said, 'Ells,' in a small voice.

'Yeah?'

Her face looked very pale in the late afternoon light edging the blackout blind.

'You know I had no choice, don't you?'

'Yes, of course,' I said, a bit too fast. 'Have a bit of kip now, okay? I'll see you in a while.'

I gently closed the bedroom door and went back downstairs.

For the next hour I busied myself with tidying up the house, which was looking dirty and unloved.

Once the house was a bit more like home, I made vegetable soup from stuff in the freezer. I figured it might be something Anya could eat if she was feeling fragile, plus my body felt so wrecked and unhealthy after recent sleepless nights and

165

too much drinking that I wished I could just take some vitamins intravenously.

As I stirred the lentils and vegetables around in gentle circles I thought about what I had seen on the doorstep.

It worried me that Michael had shared his Anya connection with other people. She'd had no choice to do what she did, but she should have told the police.

And there was something else too.

Ever since that terrible sequence of events back when I was a kid, I had an overly developed conscience when it came to old ladies. It was as though smiling at them in Tesco, or helping them get out of parking spaces, would somehow make up for the evil I had brought about. Utter bullshit, obviously. Nothing could make up for that.

I shouldn't forget this woman's son terrorized my wife, I told myself. There are plenty of mothers like that: refusing to acknowledge they've given birth to a monster.

The fact that we still hadn't spoken about Anya's revelation pressed down on me and I found myself impatient for her to get up again and come downstairs.

Another half hour or so later I heard the thump and gurgle of the water pipes that signified she was taking a shower.

After a little while she came into the kitchen, wearing just my tatty *Breaking Bad* T-shirt. It was too big for me and came down to the top of her thighs. Her wet hair was in a ponytail high on her head and her face looked scrubbed and fresh.

A wholly inappropriate bolt of desire shot through me, so much so that I had to turn back to the stove and make myself concentrate on stirring for a moment or two. I realized then how much I had missed her. I missed the smell of her, the feel of her skin, her voice. The last weeks had been so strange, it felt like all we had done lately was dodge incoming missiles.

'Can you manage a bit of soup?' I said.

She came up behind me on silent feet, taking me by surprise, then wrapped her arms around my waist and held on tightly, leaning her head against my back. I could feel her breasts soft against one and I closed my eyes for a moment. Then, to my surprised pleasure, her hand snaked down and began to undo my zip.

'Ah, you noticed then,' I said in a slightly strangled voice, but she shushed me as she took me in her cool, soft hand, making me gasp.

I turned, dropping the wooden spoon into the soup pan and taking hold of her face, hungrily finding her lips.

'Are you sure you're well enough?' But it was a moot point because she was leading me towards the edge of the kitchen table, where she jumped up and then pulled me into her.

Even the smell of burning soup wasn't a deterrent and for the next few minutes we were lost.

Afterwards she rested her forehead against mine and we both started laughing.

'I've missed you,' she said.

'I've missed you too,' I said.

I was happy that she accepted a bowl of soup and we sat together in the kitchen and began to eat. It was dusk now. I had put on just the under-lights of the cupboards, so the room felt cosy.

'I was scared when you didn't come home last night,' she said, her head lowered towards her bowl. 'I thought I'd lost you.'

I reached over and grabbed hold of her hand. When she looked up at me I expected to see that she was tearful again but her eyes were dry.

'It was just a shock, Anya,' I said. 'I couldn't understand

why you hadn't told me any of this. It . . .' I shrugged and ate another spoonful of soup. 'Well, it hurt, to be honest. I felt really excluded. That you didn't trust me.'

Her spoon clanged in the bowl as she dropped it.

'It was not that I didn't trust you,' she said. 'You have to believe that.' She seemed to suck in her breath, and her eyes lowered. Then she met mine.

'It's just . . .' she said. 'That family . . . honestly. There is something seriously wrong with all of them. I didn't tell you this, but the guy . . .' she hesitated, and then the words came out all in a rush '. . . the one I had a fling with, Michael's brother . . . Liam, he was obsessive too. I think they're all fucking nuts. I don't know where he is now, but I never want to see him again. The very thought makes my skin crawl.'

'Right,' I said.

There was a drawn-out, uncomfortable pause.

Anya leaned across the table and put her hand over mine, her eyes intense.

'Nuts, the lot of them.' She paused and then made a face. 'I wish he hadn't died like that, Ell, but I've got to tell you I'm relieved those horrible people are out of my life now.'

'Well,' I said. 'Let's hope they are.'

SPRING 2003

LIAM

He's not really in the mood tonight. But he has certain obligations.

Liam takes one last glance at the mirror and lets out a sigh. He looks exhausted. Who could guess just how tiring it was being bored out of your skull all day?

He is on a training scheme in the Robert Sayle, working in the hi-fi and television department, and it feels like every day a small piece of him is dying. Everyone is in a state about the whole shop moving site next year and Liam has to pretend to be interested. As if he will still be doing this next year! He's only there to keep the government off his back because he's beyond the period in which he can claim benefits.

Liam pockets a small wodge of plastic baggies, his wallet and his silver iPod. Michael can't seem to shut up about the latter. If he's not going on about him destroying his hearing, he's making snide little comments about how Liam can afford 'tech like that' when he's on a training scheme that pays sixty quid a week.

He doesn't understand anything, not really. But Liam knows his brother can be like a Jack Russell when it comes to sniffing out information. Dad has been giving him some looks lately too, but Liam is all about avoiding conflict right now. It won't be long until he has enough cash to move out of this claustrophobic house, with its air fresheners, its doilies and the constant questions about what he's doing, where he's going, what he's fucking thinking.

His family would never understand how low-level this is. He's such a small cog in a very big wheel and he's only going to do this for long enough to get a bit of cash behind him. Then it will be white sand and turquoise sea.

Thailand, he thinks. He's always wanted to go there.

Liam thumbs the wheel to click on the White Stripes. 'Seven Nation Army' begins to thump in his ears, and he feels the music filling his bloodstream. Unlike his clients (that word gives him a tiny buzz), he doesn't need chemical help to enjoy a good tune on a night out. But thank God for the ones who do, the Jessicas and the Henrys, who have basically been imprisoned by their pushy parents until now, when they're given this intoxicating new freedom.

Liam has worked hard at carving his niche. Generally, the student body keeps its drug use within its privileged walls, with the students themselves dealing the odd bit here and there. Since that girl died, literally frothing at the mouth, at the Junction a couple of years back, some of the colleges have been taking more notice. The press made a lot of the nastiness of how she died. That was a bad business, but the stuff she took was one and a half times the normal strength. Liam is careful.

He knows how to strike the right note between offering these twats a walk on what they see as the wild side, and offering reassurance, telling them that this stuff isn't cut with any of the 'rubbish' you get from other sources. He also knows students tend to like powder too, so has become adept at crushing pills. Won't be long until it's coke they'll be hoovering up like snow ploughs once they start working in their City jobs. But Liam doesn't deal coke that often.

He's almost out the front door when he feels a hand on his arm.

He yanks out his earphones and sighs.

'What is it? I'm going out.'

His dad is in his customary eveningwear of vest, trackie bottoms and glowering eyebrows.

'Didn't you hear your mum calling just now?' he says.

'Looks like I didn't.'

A muscle twitches in his father's cheek. He prides himself on being some sort of tower of patience, but really, he's always on a rolling boil.

'Well,' his father says with exaggerated patience, 'she wanted to know if you would like some apple crumble. She shouted about ten times.'

Liam can sense that Mum is hovering just inside the kitchen door; not wanting to inflame a situation but eager to be involved.

'Tell you what, Ma,' he says, loudly, 'will you save me a bit for later? I'll have it when I get back tonight.'

'Okay, lovey,' he hears from the kitchen and he gives Dad a look that says, 'See? No biggie.' He knows Mum doesn't mind being 'Ma' but for some reason it irritates his father.

'So where are you going tonight?' Getting to the point at last.

'I'm almost twenty years old, Dad,' Liam says as pleasantly as he can. 'See you.'

He pulls open the front door and walks out to the strains of a familiar tune. It's the one that goes, 'While you're living under our roof, you play by our rules,' and Liam hasn't got the time for it.

It's one am and the Junction is heaving. Liam downs half a pint of lager and scans the dance floor. It's packed with bodies, dancing and writhing to the music – currently Oscar

G. & Ralph Falcon, 'Dark Beat' – and his gaze lands on a girl, whose boyfriend he served earlier.

The bloke – a posh dickhead with swept back hair and a big nose – had bought a baggie from him after asking in a way so awkward and comical that Liam had almost kept it going just for the laughs. Now he watches said dickhead being comprehensively ignored by the very hot red-haired girl and wonders whether maybe he isn't the boyfriend at all.

Liam doesn't usually dance – too sweaty – but as this girl throws back her head, exposing a pale, slim neck, Liam gets a mental picture of biting her there, just gently, enough to make her squirm, and feels a stirring.

She's wearing a baggy vest top with the Joy Division *Unknown Pleasures* image on it and a pair of shorts. Her red bra is visible through the arm holes of the top and she weaves her slim arms in the air, twisting and turning them.

Sweat gleams on her skin and Liam finds himself hoping she has been drinking water, then laughs inwardly. Fine dealer he's going to be, if he starts thinking like his mum about his clients.

Still, maybe this will be a way of talking to her.

Armed with a bottle of mineral water, he makes his way down onto the dance floor until he is next to where the girl and Lord Chumpington are dancing. She is ignoring the other guy, who seems to be looking at her in much the same way a Labrador eyes someone's dinner.

Liam hovers, moving slowly to the music and avoiding looking at the girl until he is aware she is turning his way. Her eyes are open and glassy and he grins, then holds out the bottle, removing the lid first.

She takes it and has a long drink, throat muscles working, her neck shimmering with the lights bouncing around the dance floor. Handing it back, she gives him a cheeky smile and says, 'Well. Aren't *you* pretty?'

AUTUMN 2018
ELLIOTT

We moved into the living room and curled up to watch some telly after that, both exhausted by the traumas of our respective days.

I couldn't concentrate, though. I was staring at our latest crime drama obsession but completely unable to take in what was happening. So many things were going through my mind. That woman earlier – her whole body radiating a sort of hopeless grief – didn't seem mad or obsessed to me. The truth was, she reminded me uncomfortably of Mrs Mack, which was sending little hot shards of disquiet into me like poisoned darts. We both kept secrets from each other, it seemed. Although, arguably, Anya hadn't really done anything wrong. I wished I could say the same.

Even though I was exhausted, I didn't get the sleep I craved.

Anya didn't stop moving in the bed all night. If she wasn't going to the toilet and blasting light across the hallway, she was throwing off the covers with heavy sighs, or endlessly turning over.

I kept dipping into shallow, shadowy sleep that was filled with scattered images. I dreamed of schools . . . not just Beverley Park, but the school I went to, finding myself walking the grimy corridors as my adult self, searching for something.

In the morning we were both groggy and uncommunicative and parted ways with barely more than a few grunts between us. I had a headache that was pressing on my temples and we had run out of painkillers. I cycled in, longing for the weekend, and so I wasn't really paying attention on playground duty that morning.

A cold wind was whipping around as the kids were coming in. A couple said, 'Morning, sir,' and I attempted a greeting in return, but I knew today was going to be a bit of a struggle.

When I saw the bullet-head of Lee Bennett coming towards me I looked away, determined to keep off his radar.

But, it transpired, that was not to be. He clearly had something to say.

'A word?' he said as Tyler glanced anxiously between us.

I sighed but forced my face into the most unhostile demeanour I could manage and replied, 'Yes, Mr Bennett, what can I do for you?'

His face sort of twisted, as though I had said something unreasonable.

'Do for me?' He gave a mean sort of laugh and looked around, as though appealing for witnesses. 'I can't believe what you have already done, mate.'

I stared at him. 'Sorry, what do you mean exactly?' It sounded stupid, but with all the other stuff that had been going on, I genuinely hadn't given him a thought since Anya's revelations. Now, the fact that I had reported him to the police came crashing into my head and I felt my face heat.

He was staring at me and then, in a very low voice, began to speak.

'I watched a friend get blown to bits in Iraq, right in front of me. I've made some mistakes, fair enough, but you don't understand a thing about me.'

174

To my absolute horror, I thought he was going to cry. His voice was low and a bit menacing but his eyes were glittering.

'Look, Mr—' but he cut me off, his voice savage now.

'People like you think that you're better than me. I'm doing the best I can for my kid but to you, I'm just an ex-con, that's it.'

By now a couple of parents were lingering nearby, quite clearly listening and pretending not to. I put my hand up in a gesture of placation, but he moved back, making it look as though I was being aggressive. A massive wave of irritation burned through me. Alright, I'd made a mistake in reporting this guy, but I really would have been happy to never see him again.

'Mr Bennett,' I said, 'I don't think anything like that. I don't even, uh,' I flailed, 'know about any of that. I'm very sorry about the . . .' I faltered again, looking for the right word '. . . the *report* but at the time I was being harassed by an unknown person and it seemed a reasonable assumption that it might be you.'

As soon as I said the words, I knew how spectacularly I had messed up. His eyes widened, and he went, 'Woah . . .' taking another step back.

'A *reasonable assumption*?' he said. 'Is that what it was?'

This was ridiculous. I wanted to tell him that I wasn't what he thought, some middle-class teacher who thought he was better. But was he really wrong?

Maybe I did think I was better than him, because he represented the sort of man I had worked hard in my life to get away from?

It was such a strange and complex set of emotions, which I had no way of sharing with him. Frustration at everything, and the sheer irony that he could think that of me. I don't know why my brain sent that particular, highly inappropriate signal to my face.

But I let out a strange bark of a laugh. And as if it was somehow out of my control, I said, 'For fuck's sake . . .'

'Don't swear in front of my child!' Bennett's voice was loud. I heard a murmur from the woman standing to my right.

I knew that I had made a terrible mistake by the triumphant gleam in Bennett's eyes. He had me, at last. That's what he was thinking. Tyler wasn't even in earshot, not really. He was kicking a ball with some other kids a few feet away. But that didn't matter.

'I'm sorry,' I said, my voice low and placatory – or so I hoped. 'I've been having some issues at home and I'm very tired.' I rubbed a hand over my face. 'Look, Mr Bennett, can we maybe move on from this now?'

'You and her – you deserve each other!' he said. The effect was like a slap.

'What did you say?'

His face was all narrowed eyes and curled lip, but he kept his voice low. 'Your missus, or girlfriend or whatever. I saw you at that festival together. She mouthed off at me over nothing.'

I remembered the strange mood Anya had been in when I came back with the drinks. I had forgotten all about the altercation she'd had. For a moment I stared at him, fighting with my own curiosity. But I had to know.

'What exactly happened?' I asked, hating that he knew and I didn't. Hating having to ask him.

'I accidentally knocked her with my arm as I walked by,' he said. 'I apologized, but do you know what she said?'

I swallowed, my mouth suddenly dry. 'No,' I said.

He laughed unkindly. 'Well, I'm not going to repeat the word she used, not with kiddies around. But I will say something . . .' He leaned in close, a nasty little smile playing around his lips. 'No wonder you're like you are, living with that psycho bitch.'

Now, I'd spent my childhood and teenage years avoiding violence. I'd seen enough, growing up. And yes, I didn't want to know what I was capable of, if pushed far enough. An act of anger on my part had resulted in the worst thing that had ever happened to me, after all. What if Mark Little's dark legacy really was just biding its time?

But that day I felt something ugly and delicious all at once flex inside and, before my brain could stop my hands, I had a handful of his T-shirt in my fist and was forcing my face into his. It shames me how gratifying it was to see a brief flash of fear in that ex-soldier's eyes. Packed with muscle he might be, but he was shorter than me.

'Don't you ever speak about my wife again,' I hissed, a fleck of spit hitting his face before he wrenched himself back from my grip.

'You total wanker!'

Shit. What the hell was I doing?

'Mr *Little*!' The sharp voice of Jackie rang out across the playground.

I cycled home, feeling numb.

Suspended. And I was to see the doctor about having time off for my 'stress issues'.

She'd presented me with the *full* list of my misdemeanours, from 'harassing' Bennett when he was on a night out, to turning up for work smelling of alcohol and failing to 'carry out the admin that is a part of your job'. So she hadn't bought Zoe's story after all. I should have fought back. Told her that wasn't how it happened. Or, the Bennett parts, anyway. But I had no defence for grabbing his T-shirt like that. And the fight had been knocked out of me by recent events.

I apologized, repeatedly, and told her that there had been some things happening at home that had put me off my game lately. She looked almost eager then, hoping, I think for some mitigation that she could work with. A bereavement would have been good, perhaps. Ironic, because there had been a death. But it was one I couldn't begin to tell her about.

I could see her disappointment when I didn't go into detail, but I hoped we would be able to work this out. I would write another full apology to Bennett and accept my punishment.

I couldn't face telling Zoe, who would find out soon enough.

Rain-laced wind stung my face now, like it contained gravel. I thought about my mum and how proud she would have been that I got away from the estate and turned my life in a different direction. But maybe I wasn't cut out for this career I'd wanted so badly. Maybe I wasn't made of the right stuff to be a teacher, after all.

When I got home to the dark, empty house, I dried my head with a towel and then curled onto the bed, where I immediately fell into a deep, dreamless sleep.

IRENE

Irene forced herself to drink the cup of tea. It was the oddest thing, but she couldn't seem to taste anything. She had always been fussy about tea, needing exactly the right strength and amount of milk, but since the funeral on Monday, she had been drinking it black. It all tasted the same. She wasn't eating much, just toast, really, and once the weight loss would have been a source of pleasure, but it didn't really matter in the grand scheme of things.

Various people had been coming over: a couple of friends from the knitting circle brought food she ended up throwing in the bin, and her oldest friend Judith, who was quite infirm now, had been round with her son. Irene went through the motions of making them welcome and assured them she was quite alright, but the effort of talking was exhausting, and she longed for the house to be quiet again so she could be alone with her thoughts.

That woman Rowan had been calling her too. She had, Irene had to admit, been a bit of a godsend at the funeral, organizing sandwiches and talking to people when Irene hadn't felt up to the task. But it wasn't as though they were friends.

For the first time, she was allowing herself to wonder

whether Liam really was dead too. This was something so appalling she could only go at it with tiny pecking motions.

All these years she had been living in a sort of fog of denial and now it seemed both ridiculous and terrible that she could have been such a fool. Why would he never have contacted her? Colin and he had a difficult relationship, sure. But why would he cruelly ignore her for so much time?

Could it be possible that she once had these three people in her life, who she loved more than anything, and now there was just her left?

Irene began to cry within deep within her stomach, pressing the back of her hand against the anguished square of her lips. It wasn't so much that she had periods of crying now. More that the tears came and went for most of the day, and sometimes at night too. She was like a leaky vessel, endlessly being filled with wet sadness.

She had thought about going to church and seeking out Reverend Thomas. She always liked him but had long ago fallen out of the habit of church. She would have liked to know, though, how he might justify that she should be given such horrible luck by God. Would he tell her that Michael had committed a sin in taking his own life? She'd have liked to see him try.

Irene got up and walked into the conservatory, where rain was drumming against the ceiling with a hard, insistent beat. The leaves were beginning to turn on the beech tree at the end of the garden, a sight which normally filled her heart with pleasure.

She sighed and her gaze fell on the box she'd taken from Michael's flat when Rowan had helped her with the terrible task of clearing it out. She hadn't been able to stand the thought of going through it, but now she forced herself to pick it up and bring it to the table.

Inside, there were various papers, ranging from utility bills to a folder of neatly kept bank statements. It felt wrong to look at her son's account, even in these circumstances, and she was surprised to find she wasn't particularly curious. Who cared how he had spent his money?

As she lifted the next file – a collection of tax-related documents – two small passport-sized photos fell onto the table.

They seemed to have been cut from a strip of four. There was Liam, making faces at the camera, and someone who was quite clearly the younger version of that woman, Anastasia. She was laughing widely in one and in another pressing her lips against Liam's cheek, while he grinned cheekily at the camera.

Irene stared at the photo of her gorgeous boy, her hand shaking.

That Anastasia woman was lying through her teeth.

SUMMER 2003

LIAM

Christina Aguilera is warbling away about being beautiful as they mooch about in Woolies. Anastasia pretends to sing along, making her eyes all googly to make him laugh.

She has pocketed a handful of Pick and Mix and now offers him one, with a cheeky smile.

'Fuck off,' he says. 'No one likes the purple one.'

'You're a heathen,' she says, unwrapping the sweet and putting the whole thing into her mouth so it bulges in her cheek. Liam tries to suppress the twinge of irritation, but she sees it and nudges him hard in the side.

'Stop being so sensitive,' she says. He flushes, feeling caught out, as though she can see his thoughts, is laying out his insecurities for all to see. Is it any wonder he feels that way though? Especially after that thing last night.

They've been seeing each other for a few weeks now, on and off, but it feels as though it is always on her terms. She will suggest he turns up at a party, or a certain pub, and at first he thought it was only about buying product from him, but even if he is being a little used, it's hard to care.

Then she had allowed him to come back to her college, which she had a stupid name for – Tit Hall, she called it.

Liam wasn't sure why. They had come through an entrance like something out of the Harry Potter movie, past some snotty-faced blokes – porters, she said – who looked at him like he was something on the bottom of their shoes and eventually into her bedroom.

It hadn't been what Liam was expecting, for a student room. He thought it would be all posters of worthy shit and Che Guevara. But it was just a bed, a desk, and a wardrobe. There were some photos above the desk but, when he went to look, Anastasia steered him away.

After they'd gone to bed, they lay there, getting their breath back, skin slicked with sweat. Moonlight poured down on them through the skylight, bathing their limbs in silver.

Anastasia held up one of her long, pale legs and then pressed it next to his.

'We could be brother and sister, couldn't we? Or twins,' she said, not for the first time.

It was one of the things that seemed to delight her when they met, the shared colouring. Both had dark red hair (although hers had a few streaks of blonde she had dyed into it), the same eye colour, and fair skin. She was obsessed with this.

He rolled over and leaned up on one elbow, looking down at her.

'I'm glad we're not,' he said and began to stroke the inside of her thigh.

She gave a dirty laugh.

'Me too.'

As he bent down and kissed her softly on the lips, he had been lit up inside with a feeling he'd never had before. It made him want to run around the room, sing loud songs, do press-ups. Was this being in love? The daring prospect of telling her had jabbed him inside but it was too risky. Instead he had buried himself in her and tried to make the most of the moment.

He doesn't want to admit he still lives with his mum and dad. It doesn't really go with the 'bad boy' image she seems to have of him, because of the dealing.

Last night she had actually made a point of inviting him along to meet her friends.

He'd been nervous, which had made him pissed off, and so he hadn't really gone into that pub with the best attitude, he knew that.

The Eagle was a big student place and it wasn't somewhere he usually went. It was packed out and hard to hear what anyone was saying. Her friends had been alright, he supposed. Two girls called Lydia and Cam were okay, even though Cam clearly had the hots for him and seemed to stare at him all night, turning on a full-beam smile whenever he caught her. There was a bloke called Brynn, who was one of those men who camped it up and fooled all the girls into thinking he was gay, so by the time he made his move, they were too surprised to resist him.

It was the one called Robert who had really got up Liam's nose though. He had handed Liam a bottle of Sol and then said something about how it was exciting to imagine Watson and Crick drinking in this very pub.

Liam had said, 'Who?' and for a moment there had been a silence in which he'd caught Anastasia's expression. She was embarrassed.

He'd looked on the way out at the blue plaque on the wall. Yeah, okay, maybe the people who'd invented DNA or whatever were not exactly on his cultural radar. But it didn't mean he was somehow less than the rest of them.

'Come on,' says Anastasia now, 'let's get our pictures taken.'

She is looking towards the photo booth at the back of the shop. He starts to laugh.

'Seriously?' It's the kind of thing he did when he was twelve, thirteen.

'Don't be a spoilsport!'

There's a mother and a very overweight kid using it right now, clearly getting passport photos for the kid, who is whining.

When the mother isn't looking, Anastasia makes a gun of her fingers and pretends to shoot the kid in the back of the head. Liam laughs, but is a little shocked all the same, despite himself. The boy's only about seven, after all. But she does make him laugh, even if sometimes her edginess takes him by surprise.

Soon it is their turn and she pulls him into the photo booth, wrenching the curtain across so savagely it screeches on the runners.

He sits down and she turns and straddles him on the seat, so he gasps and says, 'We can't, not here,' and she sighs and calls him a spoilsport again, climbing off.

She sits demurely on his lap the right way round but they both crack up laughing because it's not exactly comfortable for either of them, thanks to her behaviour a moment before, and they are still laughing when the camera goes pop, pop, pop, pop and takes their pictures.

AUTUMN 2018

ELLIOTT

It was early October. So far on my enforced absence from work, I'd mended a squeaky wardrobe door, sorted out some boxes that hadn't been opened since we moved in, cooked a range of new dishes (with varying degrees of success) and been running every day.

The worst time was around four pm when I would normally be leaving school and I'd see and hear local kids arriving home. It was hours until Anya would be back. It was the time of day, now autumn was kicking in, when the walls seemed to close in.

I had written my apology to Bennett and was waiting for a formal hearing in a week's time to find out what was ultimately going to happen. Anya and I'd had several late-night conversations about what I would do if things didn't go my way, which usually ended up with her suggesting we borrow money from Julia and Patrick so I could 'retrain'.

As what? I only wanted to be a teacher. And the thought of living off my in-laws for the foreseeable future made me want to gnaw off my own arm in frustration. Anya claimed not to understand this attitude and called it 'macho bullshit', at which point I would usually sulk in a different room for a while until we made up again.

So things were strange at home. We hadn't yet worked out the new shape of our life together after it had been thrown into the air and scattered in pieces.

The letterbox clanged and, keen to avoid my run on what was turning out to be a cold day, I went into the hall to collect the post.

There was a Visa bill for me, and what looked like a card. It wasn't either of our birthdays.

I turned it over and saw it was handwritten just to 'Anastasia'. There was one of those small stickers on the back and it said: 'Irene Copeland', then an address in Cambridge.

My heart jolted and I walked into the kitchen, holding the envelope like it was radioactive.

I sat down at the table and stared at it for about three seconds, during which I debated whether it was right to open someone else's post, then concluded that this was only going to upset my wife and I needed to intercept it.

I tore the manila envelope open with trembling hands and one sheet of writing paper and a piece of A4 paper fell out. I opened the A4 sheet first and saw that it appeared to be a clumsy copy of some photographs, the originals of which had clearly been Sellotaped to paper.

My mouth went dry as I looked down at Anya, about ten years younger or more, with shorter hair in its natural curls, rather than straightened as it was now. The person with her was a man who was, I had to admit, strikingly good looking. He had similarly pale skin from what I could see and his hair was sort of curly and floppy on the top. He looked like the heartthrob from an indie band of the nineties.

With a grimace, I put the sheet down on the table and opened the letter.

The handwriting was very neat and small, and it looked as though the words had been written very carefully. I read them, and my stomach began to churn.

Dear Anastasia,

I am sorry to bother you but you would not talk to me when I came to your house and I feel that I need to try again to talk to you.

You see my son Michael had your name in his possession and also these photographs of my son Liam his brother who I haven't seen since he left home in 2003. It seems very clear to me that you knew Liam and I think this is what lead Michael to track you down.

I have no idea why he would want to hurt himself in the way he did and the fact is that I now have neither of my boys at my side and if you could give me any context at all for what has happened, it would help me greatly in the greaving process.

Michael had a friend called Rowan who is talking about going to the police about it all and insisting they investigate it all a bit more carefully. For now I think that getting together and having a conversation would be the best thing.

I can come to you, or you can come to me. If you would prefer to meet in London or some-where else I'm sure that will be fine too.

I don't wish you any harm. I just need to find some answers so I can begin to properly greave for my son whatever he was to you. I'm sure you will understand and I hope you will do the right thing.

You can write back or call me on my mobile phone. The number is above.

Yours sincerely,
Irene Copeland (Mrs)

I don't know if it was the spelling and grammar mistakes, or the way it all seemed to have been vomited out onto the page in a rush of grief. But her words hit me squarely in the solar plexus. I pictured this old lady, sitting in her house unable to understand what had happened to her.

Surely it would be better if she had an answer, even if it was a painful one?

The idea felt toxic as it began to form in my mind, so much so that it actually nauseated me and sent me rushing to get a glass of water, which I poured with shaking hands.

I was going to try and put an end to this whole business. For her, but mainly for Anya and for me.

I picked up my phone and tapped out a reply.

IRENE

Irene had never had such a lot of messages as she had in these last couple of weeks, so when her phone had vibrated on the coffee table, she almost ignored it at first.

It seemed that all sorts of people were getting in touch with her, which was nice, of course. A few weeks ago she would have been delighted to hear from old friends in that way. But now she had little inclination to see or speak to any of them.

This was a bad attitude though, she knew that. It was the kind of thinking that sent you into an early grave. Not that this held much fear for her any more, not now.

So with a slight groan she made herself lean forward and pick up the phone.

When she read the message a bolt of surprise pierced her so keenly that she let out a little gasp.

Mrs Copeland, I will talk to you if you think it will help you come to terms with the death of your son. I will come to you, or you can suggest a place to meet. If this sounds acceptable please text back where and when we should meet.
   Anastasia Ryland.

Irene hadn't replied straight away. She was too flustered. She contemplated asking Rowan's advice but knew that the other woman would insist she was there for the meeting.

Irene wondered, now, as she hoovered every inch of the house, what on earth she had been thinking in sending that letter. Did she really want to meet this young woman? There had been something so cold in her eyes when Irene had tried to speak to her on the doorstep. There was no sympathy at all for the terrible thing that had happened to Michael.

Irene turned off the Hoover and carefully carried it down the stairs, breathing heavily as she did so. She needed to eat something, before this meeting. It wouldn't do to go all wobbly when she was trying to be strong.

An hour later, Irene was sitting on her sofa, her hands twisted together in an attempt to stop them from shaking. They felt damp, and she wiped them on her skirt – one of her best. It felt important that she presented a smart face to this woman, however she had been connected to her sons.

Irene picked up the photos she had found in Michael's possessions again, grateful that she had the idea of getting them photocopied to send with that letter. She would never have seen them again otherwise, she was sure of that.

Her chest cramped as she stared down at her son. Liam seemed to gleam with life. Didn't they say that mothers knew when their child died?

Irene couldn't believe, now, that she had managed to get through all these years in such a deluded state. Liam must surely be dead too? What on earth would make him stay away from her for so long?

She thought about crime dramas she had watched on television, where witnesses to crimes had been given new identities. They weren't allowed to get in touch with their families, were they?

A well of pain inside threatened to take her breath away

and then the sharp ring of the doorbell pulled her back to herself. She stood up and smoothed down her skirt before forcing her feet to move towards the front door.

But when she opened it, the person on the doorstep was not who she expected to see at all. For a moment she was confused, thinking this was perhaps a delivery of some kind, but the tall, slim bearded man was familiar to her and with an exhaled, 'Oh,' she realized, with disappointment, who it was.

ELLIOTT

For a horrible moment, I thought she was frightened of me, and it struck me, rather belatedly, how this might look, me turning up instead of Anya.

'Oh,' she said.

'Mrs Copeland,' I said, 'I'm afraid Anya had to back out of coming because she isn't well today, so I hope you'll forgive me for turning up instead. She really wanted me to talk to you. I'm Elliott, her husband.'

Two lies, right there. The first of several I had planned for this strange morning.

I'd made up a reason why I needed the car that day – claiming I wanted to drive to the big DIY superstore in the next town. Anya had a work event and wouldn't be home early, so I had plenty of time to drive to Cambridge.

I'd never been there before. I think I must have been expecting to see some dreaming spires as I followed the satnav route from the M11, but I was directed around the northern edge of the city, past suburbs that looked much like anywhere else. If I had ever given Cambridge University any thought at all, I pictured the likes of Sebastian Flyte, all cricket jumpers, teddy bears, and lying around on mint-green grass in the sunshine. But because Anya had given it up and gone on to Durham, she spoke about it almost never.

Irene lived in a northern suburb of the city called King's Hedges, just down the road from a driving range and a couple of tech company premises, in a neat bungalow with hanging baskets outside that looked dry and neglected.

She was staring at me now, chewing her bottom lip. I was conscious of towering over her. I kept well back from the front door and attempted to radiate as much friendliness as I could, in the circumstances.

'If you like,' I said, 'I could maybe buy you a cup of tea or coffee if you want to go to a café?'

She looked at me as though I had made the most ridiculous suggestion she had ever heard before replying. She wore no make-up and her curly, iron-grey hair was short and cut in a no-nonsense style.

'Why would we pay for tea when I have perfectly good tea inside?' she said and then beckoned me in.

'Go on through,' she said. 'But I want you to know that my friend Rowan is just next door and she will call the police if she thinks I am in any trouble.'

Her voice shook a little as she said this and it made me feel even worse about what I was doing here.

'I promise you,' I said as I went into a living room filled with patterned sofas and smelling of pot-pourri, 'I wouldn't dream of causing you any trouble. I just want to talk, that's all.'

She made a harrumphing sort of noise and then said, 'Tea?' in a way that didn't brook much disagreement.

I thanked her and sat down as instructed.

The stone mantelpiece contained a number of photographs and I got up again and quietly went over to have a look. There were two school photographs of the kind my school no longer went in for, preferring instead to attempt arty shots of pupils in groups. One showed a boy with dark red hair, grinning cutely at the camera with two missing teeth. This was obviously the younger son, the one in the picture with Anya.

The other picture was then surely Michael. His brother had evidently been blessed with all the looks as the picture showed a round-faced boy with ginger hair and small eyes, barely smiling at all.

Other photos showed the boys on beaches or playing in sandpits and smiling at the camera.

A more recent one of Michael made me lean closer for a better look.

He was wearing a suit and shaking the hand of another man. It looked like he was being given some sort of promotion or work-related reward. Still very overweight, he was quite short too. I pictured him thinking he had the right to frighten my wife, and pure revulsion and rage sent me back to the sofa to breathe slowly for a moment or two.

I had to remember I was dealing with a grieving mother here, I told myself. Even if her son had been a nasty piece of work.

Irene came into the room holding a tray of tea things a bit precariously, and I jumped up to help, taking it from her and placing it on the table.

There were two cups, a teapot, a jug of milk, sugar, and a plate of digestive biscuits. I distracted myself from the sick feeling inside me by accepting tea gratefully and setting it down on the mat next to me, which had a picture of a poodle on it.

Irene wasn't looking at me, but staring down at her own cup, which she was holding in her lap. Evidently, neither of us really knew how to start.

'Mrs Copeland,' I began, just as she said, 'So, Elliott.'

We both gave polite little laughs and it felt as though the atmosphere had thawed the tiniest bit.

'You go first,' she said.

I paused before speaking.

'Can I just say before anything else, that I am so deeply sorry about your son?'

She gave a tight little nod and then looked up at me, her eyes blurry now.

'I just want to understand, you see,' she said.

'I know,' I said, nodding with as much sympathy as I could. 'I want to tell you, on Anya's behalf, what happened.'

I began to speak, reeling out the carefully constructed story I had been working on since I received the letter.

She didn't interrupt, merely stared at me as I spoke with a set expression on her face, ignoring the teacup cooling in her lap.

I told her that Anya had briefly gone out with her other son while she was a student, but when they broke up, Michael had wanted to go out with her and wouldn't accept her gentle rebuffs. Her face tightened at this and she lifted the cup to her lips, then seemed to change her mind, lowering it again with a slightly shaking hand.

I told her what Anya had told me, that Michael had tracked her down and been harassing her. It was one of the hardest things I've ever had to say. Each word against her son seemed to strike her, so I began to wonder whether this was immensely cruel of me to be doing this.

But she had to know. And she had to be misdirected from the way it ended.

'. . . I think,' I said, 'and I'm so *so* sorry to have to say these difficult things to you, that when Michael finally began to accept that Anya has her own life – has me – and that she was never really interested in him . . . I think that was what led him to take his own life.'

196

She stared at me, her lip trembling, and she hurriedly put her cup and saucer onto the table with a clatter and pulled out a tissue.

'But where is Liam then?' she said, voice shaking. 'Where did *he* go?'

I opened and closed my mouth uselessly for a second before I found my words.

'I don't know, Mrs Copeland. I don't know and neither does Anya. She was just a casual girlfriend of his but she—' I bit off the end of the sentence. How much pain could I pile on this poor woman? But she noticed, leaning forwards in her seat.

'What?' she said. 'Tell me.'

'This isn't easy to say.'

She slammed her hand against her knee with such force that I flinched. 'For God's sake,' she said, 'do you not think I've had time to already think the worst? It has been fifteen years!'

Breathing heavily now, she closed her eyes for a moment and then levelled them on me, calmer now.

'Right,' I said hurriedly, 'right, of course.' I swallowed. This was one of the strangest conversations I'd ever had. The smell of lavender seemed to be filling my nose now and the patterned walls were closing in. I wanted to get out of here.

'Well, I don't know if you were aware that Liam had been . . .' God, this was hard to say to her face '. . . been supplying drugs to students at the university?'

Evidently, she wasn't. Her face sort of crumpled and she pulled a man-sized tissue from a box under the coffee table and buried her face in it.

'Mrs Copeland?' I said. 'Are you alright?' I contemplated getting up and putting an arm around her before thinking about how inappropriate that would be.

But it was horrible to see her distress. I wished I could

have told her the whole truth now, about how Michael had been trying to hurt Anya and how he had fallen to his death. That had to stay secret though. Better, surely, to think her son had been depressed, than that he had been potentially a rapist, or worse?

After a few moments, she blew her nose with real delicacy and waved a hand at me. 'Go on then,' she said.

'And,' I took a breath, 'Anya thinks he knew some quite bad people and that it's possible he got into trouble in some way after they split up.'

'Trouble?' said Irene in a voice that was bubbly with tears. 'What sort of trouble?'

'Well . . . I mean, if he owed them money or something, and he couldn't pay it back.' Then, in a rush, I said once again, 'I'm so sorry to have to say all these difficult things.'

She nodded briskly, eyes tightly shut, then said, 'Does your wife know any names for these people?'

The slight hope on her face now was hard to look at so, coward that I am, I glanced down at my lap.

'No,' I said, 'I'm afraid not. She didn't really . . .'

'. . . didn't generally mix in those sorts of circles,' she said quietly. 'Of course not.'

There was a deep silence then, and the ticking of a clock in the hallway seemed to crash in my ears. I picked up my teacup and forced down the cold drink. It seemed rude to leave it there when she had gone to all that trouble.

Irene nodded and muttered, 'Right, well, okay,' and then got up, walking over to a sideboard that was filled with various figurines and trinkets, including a glass bell that said 'World's Best Mum'.

She came back brandishing a faded news cutting, which she handed to me.

'Does this mean anything to you?' she said. 'I wanted to show it your wife but she didn't exactly give me the chance.'

Puzzled, I took the piece of paper from her and studied what it said.

TRAIN DEATH AT WATERBEACH
15th August 2003

A woman struck by a train at Waterbeach Station on Friday night has been identified as Alice Adebayo, 48, a midwife and mother of two. Mrs Adebayo died at the scene from her injuries. She leaves behind a husband, Ekow, 51, and two teenage boys, Kojo and Xoese. Friends and well-wishers have paid tribute, laying flowers and cards at the entrance to the station concourse. She had worked at The Rosie Hospital since it opened in 1983 and was described by colleague Helen Mills, a Senior Consultant in Obstetrics and Gynaecology, as 'one of the most positive, warm people I have ever met. She touched the lives of the people she worked with and every patient was treated with the utmost professionalism, care and devotion. We at The Rosie are absolutely devastated to lose her.'

I looked up at Irene, who was standing over me.

'We used to live right by that station,' she said, 'I remembered when it happened. Terrible tragedy it was. But I don't understand why my son had this cutting in his possession.'

'I'm really sorry,' I said, with a frown. 'This has nothing to do with us.'

I tried to hand it back and she thrust it towards me again.

'Just ask her,' she said, a steely note in her voice that was new to me.

I found myself taking the cutting and putting it into my pocket.

Who was this Alice Adebayo woman? What did she have to do with Anya? And, presumably, with Michael or Liam?

Irene sighed deeply and sat down heavily on the sofa.

I glanced up at the photos on the mantelpiece again; at her two lost sons. She didn't seem like the kind of mother you would want to abandon so cruelly. The chances were that Liam was dead too. Then there was Michael: overweight, unappealing Michael who had become fixated on beautiful Anya and, when he couldn't have her, brought about his own death.

Because he did. The detail of what had happened on that cliff didn't really matter now. At least this old lady could try to move on with her life a bit.

'Elliott,' she said now, her voice very quiet.

'Yes?'

'I don't know you and I don't know your wife . . . this Anastasia, or Anya as you call her. I didn't get a very good impression of her, I'm afraid to say, but I suppose now I have to accept that it may have been a shock, me turning up like that. Especially if my son had been . . .' she visibly swallowed '. . . been bothering her. But you seem like a nice young man.' She paused again. 'Do you honestly think that my son killed himself?'

I looked her directly in the eye.

'Yes, Irene,' I said softly. 'I'm so sorry.'

She closed her eyes for several moments.

Nausea was rippling inside me now. The pot-pourri smell seemed overpowering and it was yanking me back-back-back. I lowered my head to look at the floor, trying to turn off the memories of being twelve, in Mrs Mack's neat front room, on the cusp of doing the worst thing I have ever done. I'd betrayed one old lady and now I was doing the same thing to another. I had to get out of here.

But despite all those bad feelings pumping through me, despite all my guilt, my work there that afternoon wasn't quite done. Because, staring down at the floor, I noticed something just under the coffee table near my shoe.

The originals of the photo-booth pictures that we had received in the post.

Irene was still gathering herself, dabbing at her nose with a tissue. I did it before I could talk myself out of it; pretended to reach down to scratch my ankle and enclosed the worn rectangle of paper in my fist. I kept it in my palm and then slipped it into my pocket.

We said awkward goodbyes at the front door. I wished her luck and told her again how sorry I was. She did something strange then. She reached up and touched my cheek, gently.

'I think you're a kind man,' she said. 'It wasn't easy for you to come here. Thank you.'

As the front door closed I began to run. I managed to get round the corner before throwing up all over the pavement, watched by an elderly man in a flat cap who was mowing his lawn.

ELLIOTT

On the M11 I had to force myself over into the slow lane after a lorry driver suddenly seemed to come from nowhere, blaring his horn at me and sending adrenaline through me like hot acid.

Shaking, I made myself focus on the road ahead, as rain began to fall. Soon the conditions were terrible, with spray bouncing off the lorries and causing a lethal mist that made me cling to the tail-lights of the car in front that glowed like hot coals.

There really had been something of Mrs Mack about Irene Copeland. Maybe it was the grey curls and the glasses, or the look over the top of them that seemed to go through to your soul.

The final part of that terrible story began to play out in my mind again, just as it did on a semi-regular basis, usually when I couldn't sleep.

Kieran hadn't hung about.

I'd dragged myself into school the next morning with my first bad hangover.

It had been a rough night, coming home in the state I'd been in, and Mum frantic with worry. We'd rowed – I couldn't even remember the content of it the next morning when I woke with a splitting headache, and a pool of sick on my bed. I had to throw the pillow away in a bin round the back of the flats, before Mum handed me a bucket of cleaning products, her face grim.

I remember glancing at Mrs Mack's closed front door that morning and convincing myself that everything would be okay. No harm done.

Mum ranted as I cleaned up, about how living in this place was sending me in a bad direction, and how inconsiderate people were in general. I was only half listening and didn't pay any special attention to her saying Mrs Mack's television had been unusually loud the night before. This was something she did sometimes, when she claimed certain people on television 'mumbled'. It didn't register with me at all, then, only later.

When I came home from school the following evening, after playing football, the world was stained with flashing blue lights.

I watched, along with the rest of the floor, as the stretcher was carried out of the flat, Mrs Mack looking smaller than she ever had as queen of her kitchen, baking up a storm.

She survived only until the next morning, when her heart gave out completely.

If she had only let them take it. But that wasn't Mrs Mack's way. So they tied her to a chair and tortured her until she told them where she had hidden the box.

It was because of me that she had moved it, you see. She knew that I had stolen from her and this is something I think about often. About how let down she must have felt, as though her day had already got as bad as it would be. But the real horror was still to come.

They held lit cigarettes against her papery skin, and beat her with the flex of her iron. *Coronation Street* and *The Bill* on top volume hid the sounds of her pain and distress. Her terror.

I didn't go and tell the police about my own likely role in what had happened. I was too scared and sick, especially after seeing Jason the next morning and him giving me a sly smile before quietly miming a cut-throat gesture.

They were caught, anyway. Too stupid and high not to try and fence her other belongings locally. Both men got life imprisonment for murder.

They may have held those burning tips against her fragile skin and whipped her until they broke her, but they couldn't have done it without my help.

So now you really know who you are dealing with.

As I got closer to Casterbourne, I dragged my thoughts back to what I had done today. I had managed to achieve exactly what I had set out to do – convince Irene Copeland that her son had committed suicide and most definitely hadn't been pushed off a cliff by my wife. I had to protect Anya. She was my number one priority. She had been carrying around this nightmare for fifteen years and she was finally free.

And yet. Something was nagging uncomfortably at me and I couldn't quite place its bruised centre.

I decided I was going to tell her everything about today, but I was going to get the whole truth from her in the process. I had looked that woman in the eye and lied to her. I could see how it had broken her heart to hear that Michael had killed himself and, however many times I told myself that was a 'better' truth than that he had been a creepy stalker who fell to his death while in hot pursuit of an innocent young woman, it didn't make me feel any better.

By the time I pulled into Casterbourne the rain was beginning to ease a little but my eyes were aching from the hard drive.

The house was quiet and unlit. I knew Anya wouldn't be home for another couple of hours yet.

I couldn't face cooking and, anyway, I felt disinclined to be the perfect house husband today. I felt like I had done enough.

So I opened a new bottle of wine and took a plate of toast and Marmite through to the sitting room, where I sat in the light from the telly and watched old episodes of *Friends*. I had seen them all before, many times, but the sugary antics in Central Perk seemed to soothe me and I let myself become numb and without thoughts.

When Anya came in, I was almost dozing. She hesitated at the doorway and I gazed through half-shut lids at her shape there, before forcing my eyes open and sitting upright.

'You alright?' she said. 'What's going on?'

Groaning at the ache in my neck, I stretched and then rubbed my face.

'Shall I put the lights on?' she said and I could hear the exhaustion in her voice.

'No,' I said. 'Come sit over here.'

She laughed, surprising me with the bright harshness of the sound in the gloomy room. 'You're being weird, Ell. What's going on? Has someone died?'

For some reason, this felt like precisely the wrong thing to say.

'Well, Michael Copeland died,' I said.

She turned to leave the room.

'Look,' I said, 'come back. I want to talk.'

Anya hesitated for a moment and then came into the room. She sat down on the chair near the door; as far from me as she could. I had the horrible sensation then that she was a little afraid of me.

'I went to Cambridge today..'

The effect was akin to an electric jolt, it seemed. Her

205

whole body seemed to jerk and then she was hunched forward, hands around her knees, staring at me intently.

'Why did you go there?' she said, very carefully.

Her eyes looked large and scared in her pale face and she was wringing her hands together.

When did I start mistrusting her like this?

'I went to see Michael Copeland's mother,' I said and her intake of breath was sharp.

'Ell,' she said quickly, 'what the fuck were you thinking? What on earth *for*?'

I rubbed my hands across my face and let out a big sigh.

'She wrote to you,' I said and I picked up the letter that was next to me on the sofa. I threw it over to Anya, who fumbled and dropped it onto the rug, then scrambled to pick it up. She normally had brilliant hand–eye coordination and this sign of nerves added to my feeling of discomfort that I was being cruel.

I was just sick of being left outside, that was all.

She reached over and snapped on one of the lamps before opening the envelope and retrieving the letter.

'You might like the dark, but I think lighting is important to an interrogation, don't you?' she said tightly.

I didn't reply.

She finished the letter and then looked up at me, a little expectantly.

'There's something else in the envelope,' I said and she frowned, before looking inside and then pulling out the piece of photo strip.

Her face was impassive as she looked down at it, then back up at me.

'Why did you go to Cambridge?' she said again, very quietly.

I got to my feet, suddenly unable to be still a moment longer.

'Because that man is *dead*!' I was shouting now. 'We should have told the police. And you obviously knew this Liam better than you told me you did!' I was becoming so het up that I wasn't even speaking in grammatical sentences now. 'I don't think you've told me the whole story!'

I reached into my pocket and pulled out the piece of printer paper that was folded there. I had easily found the news story from the Cambridge newspaper that Irene had shown me.

I handed it to her.

'And I have a strong feeling it has something to do with this.'

Can you imagine what it was like for a mother?

Seeing those small finger-shaped marks in the peanut butter and understanding what they meant?

It was hours later. Anya was tucked up in bed, exhausted after all the excitement then trauma of her party. All the other parents had left shortly after the ambulance took Dylan away. Patrick and I had almost finished clearing up all the mess from the party.

The sight of that little boy's face – the terrible flushing of his skin and the terror in his eyes as his throat closed over – kept running through my mind. Thank God he got to the hospital in time. I can't even bear to think about . . . if he hadn't.

Anyway, I was desperate for a gin and tonic. The bottle of gin was in the larder, a space used as an over-spill area for storage at the back of the kitchen. The peanut butter jar had been put precariously on a shelf near the door, not in its usual space.

But here's the thing: because I was so worried about any possible contamination, I had locked the larder with the tiny key that we'd never had any reason to use before, just to prevent anyone prowling for any extra snacks that weren't on the approved list.

At the time I'd almost laughed at my own paranoia about it all. In fact, I had been annoyed about the responsibility being foisted upon me, when Dylan wasn't even a friend of my daughter's. His and Lottie's mother was a glamorous and rather flaky woman called Annabel, an actress with a tendency to dump her children on others, even with Dylan's extra needs. I know that my daughter had registered these ungenerous thoughts, spoken aloud over a Pimm's at a summer party. She missed nothing. So I must share some blame.

That's what I have always told myself.

The key was in a ceramic bowl on the kitchen surface. Only the three people who lived in the house knew about the key.

I called Patrick into the kitchen with an agonized sort of cry and he rushed in, believing I had hurt myself. In fact, he almost looked annoyed that I hadn't. I suppose, after a horrible day, it felt like unnecessary drama for me to squawk like that.

I told him I had seen our daughter leave the room, apparently in a mild huff, then come back and plunge her hand into the crisps. I'd registered it as strange at the time, because she had complained that these allergy-free crisps weren't as good as the Hula Hoops she had requested.

It was shortly after then that Dylan had his anaphylactic reaction. I told Patrick that we should have checked the bowl while cleaning up and he looked at me with an expression I had never seen before. It was horrible. Cold. Almost as though he hated me.

He said, 'Julia, you can't be suggesting what I think?'

I told him it was the only explanation. He didn't seem to have another to offer, but simply said, 'Shame on you, Julia. What a thing to say.'

He has always been that way about her. He refuses to accept things, you see.

Patrick's sister Bridget – a no-nonsense bull of a woman – once said of my daughter that she was a 'monster' after some incident with her son when Anya was six. The look in her eyes when she said it was something I never wanted to see again. We decided to cut contact with her after that.

Sometimes I think about those words spoken by Bridget.

Look, you might judge me. But it is only by understanding my daughter – all the complex parts of her – that I can truly keep her safe.

ELLIOTT

Anya's brow creased as she took the piece of paper from my hands, eyes flickering as she quickly scanned it. I think I saw the fleeting flare of shock but couldn't be sure.

'His mother *kept* this?' she said.

I watched her carefully.

'It was with Michael's things,' I said. Fear twisted through me about what was coming. But it wasn't for what she might say. It was for what she might leave out.

'Please don't lie to me,' I blurted, 'not again.'

She began to knead her fist in under her ribs.

'Can you get me some water?' she said in a flat voice. 'I feel a bit sick again.'

Silently, I left the room and poured water from the tap into a glass. My hand was shaking a little.

When I came back in, she was still wearing her coat. Staring down at the carpet, very still, her hands neatly folded in her lap, she looked entirely self-contained. Not for the first time, I had the dizzying sensation that, while I was familiar with the touch, smell, taste, sound, and sight of Anya, what was inside her mind was sometimes unknowable to me.

I turned on the other lamps and sat down opposite her in the chair.

Outside a car went past, rap pumping from the windows, then all we could hear was the hum of the freezer in the kitchen.

When I spoke, my voice seemed too loud for the room.

'So this Liam. Tell me more about him.'

I was aware this wasn't exactly the most important question right now but I felt the need to circle around whatever was contained in that cutting. Somehow, I knew Liam was central to all this and that she had been holding back before.

'What do you want to know?' she said and met my eyes. I worked hard to keep my expression neutral.

'Don't bullshit me,' I said, quietly. 'Just tell me all of it.'

'God,' she said with a heavy, drawn-out sigh. 'It's such a weird . . . horrible story. I honestly wanted to just forget that period of my life.'

She searched my face for a response but I stayed silent. I needed her to vomit this out in one go now. I was so tired of being in the dark.

'I wasn't lying when I said how I met Liam,' she said, her fingers twiddling the silky tassel on the cushion next to her. 'He sold me drugs at a club. I did a lot of drugs then, Ell, more than you think.'

When no response came, she continued.

'We started hanging out a bit,' she said. 'To be honest, it was refreshing to be with someone who wasn't in my college. You've no idea how cliquey and claustrophobic Cambridge can be. You hang out with the same crowd . . . hear the same sort of voices. Liam lived on an estate. I didn't, then, know anyone who'd come from a council estate.'

She had the good grace to blush. I said nothing, but a snatch of 'Common People' by Pulp burst into my mind; the bit about everyone hating tourists. My brain tends to do this, throw out lyrics at inappropriate times, and I mentally swiped the reference away. Anya wasn't like the spoiled princess in the song. At least, she wasn't now.

She continued in a rush, 'I know you think my childhood was one long run through a sunlit meadow, Ell, but there was always so much pressure to be . . . *good*. To be Mum and Dad's golden girl.' She grimaced and looked up at the ceiling. 'I suppose Liam,' she swallowed, 'represented something wildly different. I don't know.'

My impatience and hunger for more information, even if it was going to wound me, felt like a physical pressure in my guts now. But I'd sit here all night if needs be. She had to do it in her own time and I had to hear everything.

'Anyway,' she said, 'after a while I suppose the novelty began to wear off a little. He was possessive, like I told you. I realized I was getting in too deep with him and began to get worried about how I was going to get out from under the relationship.' She stopped again and stared down at her hands, resting on her thighs. She scrunched her hands into fists.

'Things came to a head one evening when I finally went over to his house in . . . whatever that place was called.'

'Waterbeach.' She couldn't really have forgotten. The cutting was right there. I felt myself drawing back against the chair.

'Waterbeach, yeah,' she said and looked down at her hands. 'Anyway, he had some acid . . . I ended up taking it, even though I knew it was a bad idea. He took it too, which he didn't always do, for obvious reasons.'

A deep sigh. A hard rub along her jaw line, eyes distant now.

'We started arguing,' she said. 'I told him I wanted to end things and he got really aggressive about it. I ran out of the house and went to the station, before realizing there was ages before the train back to Cambridge. He followed me there.'

Her hands were now fluttery pale birds in her lap.

'We started rowing again,' she said, voice jerky. 'Really viciously. Both of us were off our heads. We'd thought we were alone but this . . . woman suddenly appeared and asked me if I was okay. A middle-aged, black woman.'

'Alice Adebayo . . .' I murmured. Anya winced and closed her eyes momentarily before nodding.

'Liam started shouting at her to piss off,' she continued in barely a whisper, 'said it was none of her business. But she didn't seem to be cowed at all. She was threatening to call the police. I slunk back because I couldn't cope with it all. I felt like my head was going to explode. The bell started clanging to announce that the crossing was closing and there was an announcement about a non-stopping train. All I could hear was Liam and that woman shouting at each other and I was feeling really sick and then . . .' Anya started to cry, covering her face with her hands. 'I don't think I can do this . . .' she said with a strangled sob.

'You have to,' I said in a low voice. 'I need to know the truth. It's the only way I can support you.'

She nodded miserably, eyes swimming. Taking in a shuddery breath, she carried on. 'Then I heard the warning scream of a train that wasn't stopping at the station. The fast train to London.' Anya was almost hyperventilating now and I could feel my own eyes prickling at her distress. 'That Alice woman was calling Liam all sorts and she even belted him with her handbag.' She made a strange sound that was partway between a laugh and a sob. 'And then he, he . . .' she gasped, 'he . . . *shoved* her, once, twice, and she fell. She fell onto the tracks.'

As she dissolved into sobs I went and sat next to her on the sofa. I took one of her hands, which was icy cold and clammy. She squeezed mine back so hard I could feel the imprint of her nails.

'She was unconscious,' she said through her tears. 'We

were both yelling about how to help her up and I even tried to reach down there, but Liam shouted that it was too late. And then, and then . . .'

'The train came,' I said quietly, closing my eyes.

I didn't want to, God knew, but I could see it, see it all. The woman falling into the tracks and the panic of the moment as the scream of the train began to approach. The whoosh and suck of the air and the impact. The train slamming on brakes and slowing, slowing . . .

I shuddered at the mental pictures suddenly flooding through my mind. The force of that speeding train meeting a soft, human body. It was too terrible to imagine and I tried to jerk my mind's eye away.

We sat without speaking for a few moments. I chafed her cold hands and she cried quietly, head bowed.

'What happened next?' I said finally.

Anya took her hands from mine and rooted in a pocket for a tissue. She gave her nose a loud blow before replying.

'We ran,' she said, and then looked up at me, her face unreadable.

'Why?'

A flash of irritation crossed her face, surprising me. 'Why?'

I stared back at her, utterly nonplussed. She made an exasperated noise in her throat.

'Look, we were tripping off our faces, and a woman had just been torn to bits by a train because of *Liam*. It was terrifying. I swear to God we were just demented with it all. So we ran.'

I still said nothing and this was, rightly, taken as a judgement.

'I was fucking nineteen, Ell!' she cried. 'A kid! Anyway,' she sniffed loudly, 'I thought that once we had the stuff out of our systems that we would go to the police.'

'But you didn't.' It wasn't a question.

'No,' said Anya quietly, 'we didn't. It almost felt like a bad dream the next morning when I woke up in my bed in college. For a little while that morning I convinced myself it hadn't happened. But then I saw it in the local paper.'

She paused, then said, 'I didn't think there was anything further that we could do.'

'But, sweetheart,' I said, exasperated. 'Don't you think that woman's family would have wanted an explanation? They probably think she killed herself.' I laughed, a harsher sound than I intended. 'Guess they have something in common with Michael Copeland's mother.'

Anya didn't respond.

'So,' I said, unbelievably weary all of a sudden, 'what happened to Liam then? Where is he now?'

Anya puffed out her cheeks. 'He came to see me, a week or so after. He was in a proper state about what he'd done. Told me he was going away – for good. I didn't ask where because I didn't want to know.'

We sat quietly for another few moments, both lost in our thoughts.

'How did Michael end up with that cutting, then?' I said. 'Did he know what had happened?'

Anya lowered her head and stared miserably at her feet. 'I don't know,' she said in a tiny voice. 'He didn't say anything about that. I have no idea why he had the cutting. I don't think Liam was very close to him, but maybe Liam kept it for some twisted reason.'

'Christ,' I said, then, 'Where do you think he is now? Liam, I mean?'

Anya shrugged. 'My honest feeling is that he's dead. As I said before, probably an overdose somewhere in southeast Asia.'

Previously she had said he had probably fallen foul of people he knew in the UK but I let it go.

'Wasn't there CCTV or anything then?' I said. 'At the station?'

'No, I guess there wasn't,' she said gently. 'Not everywhere then. I did think about going to the police, you have to believe that. But I was too scared. And anyway . . . Mum and Dad told me not to.'

And there it was, again. Of course they'd known and I hadn't.

Anya looked down at her hands.

A silence fell across the room then. The sounds of next door's television bled through the wall; the tinny strains of *Casualty*.

'Shit,' I said, after a few moments more. 'I can't believe you've never told me any of this stuff before, Anya. Why? Why the hell haven't you?'

'Oh Ell . . .' Anya wrapped her arms around her knees. 'When could I tell you? What would have been a good moment to share all this?'

'I don't fucking know!'

Anya curled herself up into the chair, face pressed into a blue fluffy cushion she'd had since she was a girl, when it was in her bedroom.

'It must be nice to be so perfect,' she said, her voice muffled by new tears and the soft fabric of the cushion. 'Never doing anything wrong.'

'I'm not perfect by a long way,' I said quietly.

'Oh no?' she said, looking up, her voice harsh. 'I'm not sure you know what it feels like to be eaten up by guilt. It's like having something corrode away at your insides. It's like, it's like . . .' she started to cry again. 'It's like cancer.'

'I know exactly what that's like.' A pause. 'There are things you don't know about me. We all have regrets.'

Was this it? The time when I shared what had happened to Mrs Mack? It seemed so.

I found myself letting it out. I told her in just a few sentences about my friendship with the old lady, my tantrum, my betrayal. Funny how it could be expressed in a handful of sentences in the end, this bag of pain that I had carried like a dead weight for all these years.

That expression was back, the unreadable one. She had stopped crying and seemed very calm now.

Was she disgusted? I found that I couldn't meet her gaze so I looked down at my hands until she broke the silence.

'I guess we both had things to hide from each other, didn't we?' was all that she said.

I don't think I had ever felt so exhausted as I did right then. I laid my head back against the sofa and closed my eyes.

'No more secrets?' I said quietly.

'Well . . .'

My eyes were instantly open again, a charge of new worry snapping in my spine. But for the first time in what seemed ages, she was smiling at me, a languid, untroubled smile that surprised me.

'There is just one more,' she said. 'It's what I've wanted to tell you since I got in. But then we got side-tracked by all this shit.'

'What?' I said. 'Tell me what?'

'I'm pregnant, Ell. I'm actually pregnant.'

ELLIOTT

This is where I want to slow right down.

People talk about pregnancy lasting longer than expected. Some think this is nature's way of easing you into it all, a slow run to the seismic changes. But, in the light of what was to come, the thirty-eight weeks of Anya's pregnancy seem to have happened in speeded-up time.

When the morning sickness kicked in, those weeks were certainly long for Anya. 'Morning' sickness. What a misnomer. Anya had it quite hard and I'm sure none of that passed with any speed.

I sometimes look back at that night, with the two of us having supposedly spilled all our worst secrets, and wish I could press the pause button.

We finally went to bed after two am that night, both utterly spent after the evening of revelations. I didn't react as I should, when she told me about the baby. Too many things were competing for space in my head.

That horrible story about Alice Adebayo.

Finally telling her about Mrs Mack.

In fact, when she said she was pregnant, I'd been unable to respond for a couple of seconds until I'd seen her stricken expression and the bright teardrops filming her eyes. Then I'd gathered her into my arms and kissed the top of her head.

It was just too much to take in, while I was still trying to process all this . . . *past*. She'd kept so many secrets from me, both over the history of our relationship and more recently. Two people were dead; both accidental, both from falls that were horrific in their own way. Neither was her fault, exactly. But she hadn't done the right thing, either.

And now she knew the very worst thing about me. The fact that I felt guilty about my part in an old woman's death didn't get me off the hook. I still let it happen.

We existed in a state of polite friendliness for a couple of days and then I found her slumped on the bathroom floor, crying after a bout of sickness, and all distance melted away.

I got through my disciplinary hearing and resolved to do everything I could to regain Jackie's trust in me and get back on with the job I loved.

I managed to make excuses about seeing Patrick and Julia for a while. Endless invitations for lunch arrived, and I made a host of excuses. It hurt Anya, but I couldn't help that.

The fact that they knew everything about what had happened to Anya – both in Cambridge and with Michael Copeland – was an irritation that felt like a stone in my shoe. Particularly the latter. Maybe it was because I had been parentless for so very long, but I couldn't understand it, however hard I tried. We weren't children, running to Mummy and Daddy when things got tough, were we?

So, yes, you could say I was bitter.

But I knew I couldn't put it off for ever.

Patrick rang me one day and suggested we have a beer together.

We decided to meet that evening in Lathebridge, at my suggestion. He had offered to come over to Casterbourne, but I didn't feel that any of our small number of pubs were quite his scene.

He said he'd pick me up and, as I climbed into his red Jaguar, we exchanged brisk, awkward greetings. The seat was low and luxurious and the interior smelled new. I was quickly told that it *was* new. You couldn't resent Patrick's enjoyment of spending his money. He got so much pleasure out of having good things around him, and never seemed to take it for granted. Anya told me her parents donated to lots of charities, which was more than we did beyond the occasional *Big Issue* purchase, so who was I to judge someone showing off about their two-litre four-cylinder turbo-charged diesel whatever?

Patrick kept up a steady stream of chat as we drove to a pub on the seafront in Lathebridge. I nodded and responded in all the right places but was conscious of shifting about in my very low but ergonomically designed seat. I hadn't felt awkward with my father-in-law since the very earliest days of knowing him. I didn't know what to do with this sensation.

Finally, we were sitting in the upmarket gastro joint, me with a pint of Stella, him – being of that generation that's blurry about drink driving – with a large glass of Pinot Noir. There was nowhere to hide.

It was early December now and the pub was festooned with Christmas finery.

We sipped our drinks in silence for a few moments and, finally, Patrick put both of his hands on the table and gave me an imploring look.

'Elliott,' he said and then took a breath. 'I hope you know that me and Julia care about you, well, almost as much as if you were our own son.'

His ruddy face blazed even redder as he said this, as did mine. We usually left the emoting to Julia and Anya. I mumbled something and then took a too-big gulp of my beer, trapping a painful gas bubble in my throat as I did so.

Then he spoke again, his voice low.

'I know Anya has told you about her sister,' he said, 'about our Isabella.'

It was the first time I'd ever heard her mentioned by Patrick or Julia. There was a photograph, just the one, on their piano, along with all the ones of Anya doing ballet, riding horses, or grinning up from sandy beaches and boats.

This one showed Julia looking exhausted but rather beautiful, a bundle in her arms that she held towards the camera. All you can see is the tiny wizened face of the baby who was destined to live for only a week after the photo was taken.

'Julia was a carrier of Strep B, you see,' said Patrick.

I knew this already but nodded, encouraging him to continue. Anya had explained that this common bacteria could, in some women, be passed to babies during delivery. She was going for a test soon, herself.

'We didn't know then, of course.' He paused and stared down at the wine glass in his hand. He was gently twisting the stem, almost as though he was unaware of doing it. 'Bloody unlucky, because most of the time babies survive the infection. But sadly, that wasn't the case for Isabella.'

'It must have been awful,' I said quietly.

Anya had once said, a little guiltily, that she found it hard to connect with the idea of her dead, older sister. Patrick and Julia being who they were, it wasn't something they brought up in passing, so this surprised me. But I could tell where it was heading.

'And then, two years later, our Stasi was born.'

Most of the time, Patrick and Julia called Anya by her preferred name, but now and then they slipped into their childhood nickname for her. Patrick's eyes shone and he cleared his throat, before taking a sip of his drink. Then he raised his eyes to meet my gaze and I was taken aback, a little, by the look in his eyes. They seemed to blaze at me with some sort of purpose.

'The thing is,' he said, leaning forward slightly, 'that when she was born and I looked down at her in my arms, I vowed that I would never, ever let anything bad happen to her.'

I stared back at him. For the strangest moment, I wondered if this was a warning of some kind but then his face broke into its customary warm smile and he said, 'I'm so excited that you two have this wonderful new life ahead of you!'

'Um, yeah, me too,' I said, and drained the last of my drink. It had gone too fast.

'What I'm trying to say, Elliott,' he said, serious again, 'in my usual bull-in-a-china-shop way, is that I can't apologize for my daughter not telling you some of the things you now know. That's business between you and her. But maybe . . .' he paused, frowning '. . . maybe she did it for the very best of reasons. Not because she didn't trust you. But because she was scared that only Julia and I could still love her.'

That, finally, broke through and, a bit too loud, I exclaimed, 'I'll always love her!'

Patrick smiled, and it was an oddly sad smile.

'I know that, Elliott,' he said. 'And she knows too.'

His phone pinged with a text message then and, glancing at it, he sighed.

'Damn,' he said, 'seems I forgot to take my tablet.'

'Does it matter if it is a bit late?' I asked. He pulled a doomy face.

'According to Julia it does, because it will muck up what I have to take later.' He downed the last of his glass of wine and placed it on the table, decisively.

'Right!' he said. 'I hope you don't mind, but I might just

whizz home and take it before I drop you back. That okay with you?'

'Of course,' I said, although inside I wished I could just go straight home. I hadn't banked on seeing Julia quite yet but decided I might as well get the rapprochement with the in-laws over in one evening.

We pulled up in front of the house with the familiar crunch of gravel on the driveway.

I got out of the car and followed Patrick inside. He called out, 'Darling!' in a cheery voice and was met with an, 'In here,' from Julia's study, which was one of the first rooms down the hallway on the right.

'I'll just get that tablet,' said Patrick, heading for the kitchen at the back of the house. 'You go and say hello.'

I poked my head into the open door of Julia's study. She was sitting in warm lamplight on a sofa that took up one end of the room. The dark red walls were covered in various posters of books she had published, plus one large poster for an Oscar-nominated movie called *Loves Me Not*. This had been an international bestseller that ended up being made into a film starring Jake Gyllenhaal and Emma Stone. Julia (or more likely her assistant) had discovered it in what they called the 'slushpile', in her business. That's the constant stream of manuscripts from hopeful, unpublished writers that arrived every day in her inbox.

She had a soft, grey blanket over her knees and her glasses perched on the end of her nose. Her face looked thinner than the last time I had seen her.

'Hi,' I said, a little shyly. She rose from the chair without a word and clasped me in a hug. Her head only came up to my chin. I hugged her back, a bit shocked to smell that her hair wasn't very clean. Apart from the last time I had seen her, that strange night when I had felt unwelcome at the front door, I had almost never seen her anything less than immaculate. It troubled me.

The hug seemed to go on for longer than was usual and, when she pulled away, her eyes were sparkling a little with emotion in the reflected light of the lamp. I could feel my wariness dissolving.

'It's good to see you,' I said. She smiled what seemed a sad, slow smile.

'It's *so* good to see you, Elliott,' she said in her low, perfectly modulated voice. 'We have missed you, you know.'

I didn't know how to respond to this. It was unlike her to say something like this and I was touched, but a little confused.

'Yeah, well . . .' I said, lamely.

'And how is Anya feeling?' she said.

'She's okay,' I replied. I knew for a fact she had spoken to her mother that day, so was unsure why she was asking me.

Her eyes searched my face.

'I mean, about the baby?'

I made a puzzled face. 'I'm not sure what you mean?'

She lowered her voice then, and her eyes flicked to the door, almost nervously.

'I mean, does she seem happy and excited? About the baby coming?'

I gave an embarrassed little laugh. 'Of course,' I said, 'we both are.'

She nodded and then placed a hand on my arm.

'I think this will be a big change for you. It may be that it takes time for her to adjust but if you're ever worried, at any time, I want you to—'

She stopped speaking abruptly then as Patrick called out, 'All sorted! Fancy a drink first, Elliott, or should I run you home?' He appeared in the doorway and clearly knew we'd had an odd exchange because his brow furrowed.

'Everything okay, Julia?' he said, rather pointedly.

She smiled tightly. 'Everything is fine,' she said. 'I was just asking about how Anya was feeling.'

Patrick and his wife exchanged loaded looks and then Patrick was all bluster again.

'Right, right!' he said. 'Anyway, we should probably get you home to our daughter and that bump, shouldn't we?'

'Yep,' I said, and met Julia's eyes. She was staring right at me, her expression flat.

WINTER 2018
ELLIOTT

Despite Julia's odd comment and everything that had happened that autumn, things fell into an uneasy peace as we headed towards Christmas. There was an odd sense that we were living in a permanent held breath; that this was the calm before the storm.

Anya was feeling well now and, as her bump gradually expanded, the distance between us conversely closed over cosy evenings watching telly. She saw surprisingly little of her parents and we hunkered down at home, a unit, a soon-to-be-three.

She never spoke about anything that had happened, recently or in 2003. It was as though a lid had been firmly sealed on the whole topic in a way that I marvelled at. It also scared me a little, how effectively she was able to compartmentalize.

If I ever tried to bring any of it up, she closed things down quickly, becoming distressed and protectively placing both hands on her growing belly.

But I wasn't so good at forgetting.

I often found myself, in quiet moments, trying to work out a series of complex emotional equations.

For example: *Would Irene Copeland rather know her son*

was a stalker who was killed unwillingly? Or is it better to think he was just a lonely man who ultimately took his own life? And here was another one: *Adebayo's family had had fifteen years to heal . . . if you ever really did after such a sudden and violent death of a loved one. Would knowing the truth help, or merely rip open wounds in places where scars had formed?*

Quite the conundrums, these.

They were the thoughts that went round and round my head, often in the middle of the night while Anya gently snored beside me. She had a stuffy nose all the way through the pregnancy and the snoring was something new but kind of endearing all the same.

Then there was the flowers thing.

The Scandi Netflix drama we'd liked in the autumn returned for its second series. We settled in to watch it that evening, and the programme started with a recap of the last series.

The shock of the finale had been that the killer playing cat and mouse with the police detective had turned out to be one of her own team. The final episode had been from the killer's point of view, and we'd seen them buying a large bouquet of flowers, which they then left to die before scattering over the body of the second victim.

Something sparked in my mind and I found myself glancing at Anya, only to find she was staring at me with the oddest expression, her eyes bright. She'd said that Copeland sent her dead roses. She looked away, wordlessly. Maybe this was bringing back painful memories.

A horrible thought thumped into my brain from nowhere. *Is that where you got the idea about the flowers?*

No. It was a coincidence. This sort of thing was always happening in crime dramas, for Christ's sake. Copeland probably got the idea from some equivalent back in 2003.

227

Instantly deeply ashamed, I reached over and rested my hand on Anya's leg. She pressed her foot into my thigh with a satisfied little smile like a cat.

On Christmas Day, we exchanged our own gifts in the morning: a shirt, the Bob Woodward book about Trump I'd asked for and fancy noise-cancelling headphones for me, and for her, a silver bracelet she'd admired in a craft shop in Lathebridge, a cashmere scarf and some perfume. We were due over at Patrick and Julia's at one pm.

As we ate thick slices of panettone and drank tea, we talked about how strange it would be for a brand-new human to share Christmas with us next year.

But as Anya went off to take a shower, I started thinking about Irene Copeland. Maybe she would be eating a sad ready meal in front of the telly while we ate goose-fat roasted potatoes and drank wine that cost at least twenty quid a bottle. I hoped she wouldn't be alone today.

Perhaps it was approaching parenthood, too, which made me think of my childhood Christmases and the inevitable path these thoughts followed.

The nature of guilt, that was what was on my mind. The burdens we have to carry around with us and how each of us does it differently.

After her shower Anya went back to bed for a morning nap, a painful sciatic twinge in her back having affected her sleep the night before.

I decided to go for a walk to clear my head, despite the rain beginning to batter the windows outside. The house suddenly felt small and dark and I craved space, even if it meant getting soaked.

The obvious thing would have been to walk along the seafront, but I found myself getting in the car and, before I almost knew what I was doing, I was driving along the coast road. Rain and wind buffeted the sides of the car as I drove to the turning into Petrel Point. There were several small car parks, rather than one big one, which was always confusing to out-of-towners. I pulled into the nearest.

What was I doing here? I couldn't rationally explain it. A link, I suppose, with everything that was dragging me away from enjoying my Christmas Day. Maybe I felt it would be cathartic to see where Copeland died so I could put it behind me, as Anya clearly had.

No other car was here, unsurprisingly.

I parked up and sat for a moment, watching silvery rivulets of rain chase each other down the windscreen. It was oddly hypnotic and peaceful, but I made myself leave the relative comfort of the car.

I struggled to open the door against the force of the gale but then I was out, pulling up the hood on my waterproof and shoving my gloved hands into the pockets. Head down, I started to climb the path that wound up to the top.

The bitter wind snatched the breath from my lungs. I looked down at the sandy path, which was fringed by semi-frozen dune grass that crunched under my boots. It was a far steeper climb than I had anticipated, and because the air was so unforgivingly icy, I soon felt a little out of breath.

I played the scene over in my mind: Anya running from the man who had been haunting her for all those years, sobs tearing from her, in terror for her life. This thought made me squeeze my hands into fists and, just then, I was glad Michael Copeland was dead. He deserved it. I would have liked to have been there. The violent thought was like a pleasurable shiver in the dark places of my mind. Maybe I really was my father's son.

When I got to the top, I made myself stop and look out at the wild sea, a writhing, angry mass of silver-grey and white. I could feel the raw, salty air scouring my lungs. It was savage and beautiful, but I couldn't enjoy the sheer majesty of it because it was too treacherous there. I stepped further from the edge of the cliff and turned around, back to the wind now.

There was a World War Two lookout at the top, a red-brick building with two open windows that seemed to stare back at me in judgement. I had forgotten that it was there, even though it had significance for us. Anya and I had once had a passionate kiss inside it. It might have turned into something a bit more serious had it not been for a party of children arriving just as clothes were being unzipped and pushed to one side. The memory forced a smile to my frozen cheeks, but just as quickly, I felt it fade.

Thoughts were beginning to clot and take shape in my mind and I couldn't seem to stop them from connecting in a way I didn't want to recognize.

Something wasn't right, as I pictured again the scene that Anya had described.

I couldn't help wondering why Anya hadn't suggested meeting Copeland in a café, somewhere safe and surrounded by other people, rather than here. And that wasn't all.

I kept picturing the obese man who looked so out of condition in that photo.

I was thinking about Irene saying, that day, that he didn't like heights, and that he was in poor health.

And I was picturing my fit, strong wife who went to the gym every day near work. Who could have run up this hill with ease, pre-pregnancy.

Something didn't fit.

Something wasn't true.

I let out a moan and pressed a hand against my forehead, hearing the whip and thwack of my hood as it was almost torn from my head by the wind.

Then it felt like I couldn't stand to be here a moment

longer and I began to run, back down the hill, slowly because the wind was against me, then pounding my feet into the compact frozen surface and sprinting until my lungs were on fire.

It was as though I thought I could outrun it, the sudden absolute conviction that I hadn't been given the true version of this either.

That my wife had lured Michael Copeland to the top of the cliff and then pushed him off.

I sat in the car, breathing heavily and shivering from cold, or shock, or something. Horror, maybe. Disgust.

Fear. Fear that I didn't know what was really inside my wife, what she was capable of doing.

This is the point in the story where I could have made yet another correct moral choice.

Where I went home, confronted my wife and told her that I knew what she'd done. That we could find a way to work it out together; go to the police and confess everything that had happened.

Except, I didn't do any of that.

What I did was think about the child she was carrying – our child – however abstract that still felt. She'd go to prison. Because how could she have explained what happened to Michael Copeland, without also telling them about Liam and what happened in 2003?

I started the engine and drove home.

We were due at Patrick and Julia's in less than an hour.

AUTUMN 2003

LIAM

'Love? Liam? It's actually five o' clock.'

His mother's voice bleeds through his consciousness until he can't ignore it any longer. He's dimly aware this isn't the first time today he has heard it.

There is an apologetic tapping at the door now, which then grows in confidence and he winces, wishing he could disappear into the depths of the bed and never come out.

'I've got you a cuppa here,' she says now. 'Would you like me to bring it in?'

Liam hasn't locked the door and, before he can say anything, she is there, at the entrance, somehow looking sympathetic and annoyed all at once. Then she sees the state of the room and her brow wrinkles.

'I'll just bring it in, shall I?' Then, more decisively, 'I'll bring it in.'

She picks her way through the discarded clothes and junk on the floor with exaggerated patience, as though having to hack her way through thickets of thorny undergrowth, then places the cup of tea next to the bed.

Liam grunts a thank you. Hopefully she may leave now. But she is still standing there, gazing down at him.

'Are you still under the weather?' she says but doesn't

wait for his reply. 'Only, your dad is worried about your work.' She always does this; hides her concerns behind what *he* thinks. Like she has no mind of her own. It's pathetic.

He mumbles something about having 'squared it with Janice,' his line manager. But he hasn't really. Who cares if he goes in?

Who cares about anything?

Finally, Mum takes the hint and leaves the bedroom, sighing theatrically as she goes.

When the door closes, he rolls onto his back and stares up at the ceiling, not seeing the cracked whorls of textured paint.

Every time he hears the clanging of the bell from the station closing the crossing, or any announcement about trains, he thinks he might start screaming and never stop.

His breathing begins to quicken now and he makes himself sit up and glug down a sip of the hot tea, painfully scalding his tongue. His hands are trembling. He shakes all the time now. Maybe it's that thing soldiers get? PTSD?

Their small village had been filled with investigating Transport Police that night, according to his mother, who kept talking about 'that poor, poor woman' and being woken by blue lights and sirens.

But by the time Liam had got home in the morning, shaking, pale and sick from drinking half a bottle of brandy in Anastasia's room, you wouldn't have known what had happened on those tracks.

He can't forget though. If only he could 'un-see' it, just for a little while.

It's like the whole evening is on a constant loop in his brain.

One of his old school friends had been having a party. He lived in a big fuck-off house in Landbeach, a village that was walkable from Liam's house. He'd made the mistake of telling Anastasia that it was near his home and she had gone on and on about seeing where he lived, and cracking jokes about wanting to see his bedroom and all his childhood teddies and posters.

He refused, of course. The thought of Mum's over-polite awkwardness made him squirm. It would be like having a visit from Gwyneth bloody Paltrow or a member of the royal family. He imagined Anastasia being presented with a doilied-up plate of biscuits, or secretly taking a photo of their downstairs loo and its knitted crinoline lady toilet roll holder. No way was he having that.

The plan was that she would meet him at the station and they would drink in the local pub before walking to the party.

But the evening had gone badly. She had been in a strange mood in the pub and they had ended up going to the party too early.

It wasn't his sort of do either, but it was hers, as it turned out. Clearly his friend Matt had changed since he had last seen him. It was all City twats who talked in baying voices and thought they were so edgy because there was coke. Liam stuck to alcohol – there was plenty of that – but Anastasia was in the mood to party now she was here, evidently. She seemed to come back to him then and they went out onto the terrace at the back of the house for some fresh air. It was still early; they had only been there for an hour.

She had pressed him up against the wall and begun to kiss him urgently. He responded as he always did, almost giving way at his knees with the effect she had on him. He ran his hands down her sides and felt her smooth legs where the short dress stopped as she ground her hips against his.

But then, with a sexy little giggle, she had leaned up and whispered into his ear, her breath hot against his skin.

For a moment, he couldn't process what he had heard. She was smiling at him, then going in for another kiss, but no, her words had been clear.

'*I wish I could keep you as my sex slave, even when I meet someone proper.*'

The effect of her words was like someone had driven a blade up between his ribs. It was an actual impact.

He had pushed her away, registering the slightly amused shock on her face. He had almost stumbled through the thickening bodies in the living room and hall and he could hear her calling him from behind, but he didn't turn.

She had run to catch up with him outside, rubbing her arms because she had left her jacket behind, and he marched ahead, ignoring her entreaties that she was 'only kidding' and couldn't he 'take a fucking joke?'

'I'll wait for you to get on the train then I'm going home,' he'd said.

When they reached the station, she had finally lapsed into silence and he could almost feel the sulky weight of her mood pressing against him.

The truth was he couldn't think of a single thing to say. All his energy was taken up with literally moving one foot in front of the other. He hadn't experienced this sort of pain before. There was all that bullshit about the heart and love, but it was more like someone had reached inside him and yanked out all his tender inner organs. His chest actually hurt and he felt brittle, like he might shatter.

The worst thing was that he had always suspected she felt that way but he had – like the fucking idiot he was – allowed himself to imagine they really might have some sort of a future.

They were alone at the station, with fifteen minutes before the next train. The waiting room was closed and Liam sat against the railing that ran along the outside. Anastasia sat near him and he could actually hear her shivering, but he didn't want to touch her. But he couldn't bring himself to go, either.

He was pretending to himself that it was some sort of chivalrous thing, waiting with her at this quiet station, but now there was someone else, a middle-aged black woman, her round body packed into a sturdy coat, on the platform too.

She glanced at them and stood a little further down.

'Liam,' said Anastasia after a moment, in a small voice. 'I didn't mean it, you know. I really didn't expect you to react like this.'

Rage bubbled up, hot and quick, inside, and it helped a little.

'Oh yeah?' he said, aware that his voice was loud in the still night air. 'How the fuck did you expect me to react then?'

He sensed the other woman moving a little further away.

'I don't know,' shouted Anastasia suddenly. 'I didn't expect this big fucking tantrum.'

Liam made a disgusted noise and walked down the platform, away from her. It was childish, but he didn't care about that.

He hated her right now. He loved her. He wasn't going to speak to her.

For the next five minutes, Anastasia tried to engage him in conversation. She hated to be ignored, he knew this. So even when she stuck her face up close to his and said, 'I'm not going to go away until you speak to me. I love you, don't you know that?' and started to cry, he simply turned his head.

Anastasia got up then and began to walk up and down the platform, muttering to herself.

He thought again about leaving, but was acutely aware that, if he did, it would be the end. Wracked with indecision, he was turned the other way when he became aware of raised voices. Anastasia and the woman were now arguing.

He heard Anastasia say, 'What fucking business is it of yours what I do?' and the low murmur of the reply.

Anastasia was walking quite close to the edge of the platform and the woman seemed to be remonstrating about this. She reached for Anastasia's arm and was violently shrugged off with a yell of 'Get your hands off me!'

Liam hurried down the platform.

The other woman was breathing heavily, her eyes bright with outrage behind thick glasses.

'This young lady needs to get home and into bed, I think,' she said in a strong West Indian accent. 'She is putting herself and other people in danger by behaving in this way.'

'I know,' said Liam, in a placatory voice, 'I'm sorry, I'll get her home.'

Anastasia gave a scream of frustrated fury that cut through an automated announcement:

'*Will passengers on platform one please stay clear of the edge. The next train does not stop here.*'

'How dare you fucking speak for me, Liam!'

She slapped him on the cheek. It wasn't that hard, but the shock was great and for a moment he just stared at her.

'I don't think you should—' said the woman and Anastasia turned to her.

'And fuck you too! You all think you can control me!'

She went to hit the woman, who, with surprising speed, quickly caught her hand. Anastasia began to wrestle it out of her grip in a disproportionately aggressive way.

Liam finally came to his senses and physically dragged Anastasia away from the edge of the platform.

The woman backed away too, muttering to herself in anger and fumbling with a mobile phone she had pulled from her pocket.

'Please, calm down a bit!' he said.

Then everything happened so quickly.

They were standing apart from each other. The train was just visible in the distance.

Anastasia gave a sort of high-pitched scream and hurled herself towards the other woman.

And then there were only two of them on the platform. Anastasia had her hands to her cheeks and was peering over into the tracks.

'Shit!' she yelled. 'She's not moving! I didn't mean, I didn't think . . .'

'What the fuck!' He ran over and saw the woman lying at an awkward angle below, her head on one of the rails. She was unconscious.

'We have to get her up!' he yelled and Anastasia was pulling at his arm and screaming that it was too late.

The worst part, the part he wouldn't ever be able to get past, was that he wanted to be as far away as possible from the horror that was about to unfold. So he let Anastasia drag him along the platform and out of sight on the other side of the waiting room as the train came thundering into the station.

Then, the dreadful screaming of the train's brakes that seemed to go on and on.

Liam swipes at his eyes, remembering this now.

Anastasia had been crying hysterically as they ran down the road from the station. He was cocooned in shock, a welcome fleeciness that lasted only as long as the first flood of adrenaline.

'I didn't mean that to happen!' she kept crying over and over again. 'I just felt so angry with you and with her.'

And then, as they reached the main road, finally he had turned to her. For the first time in his life, Liam had wanted to hit a girl.

'You're blaming her?' He actually had to clench his fists. He saw his own spit fly from his mouth and Anastasia flinched as it hit her face. But he didn't care.

'I'm not blaming her! I'm just trying to explain!'

The rest of that night was a blur. Anastasia paid for a taxi all the way back to her room, where they had drunk brandy and cried and gone over everything time and time again.

All Liam could do since was imagine what that train would have done to the woman – Alice Adebayo was her name, he now knew because it was in the local paper.

He kept imagining her shattering into a mess of blood and bone, like someone had detonated her from the inside. This was where the nights took him now. The days were spent endlessly going over what had happened; the nights, when he finally slept, a gruesome slideshow of bodies being torn and ripped apart in different ways.

One night he'd dreamed he had looked over the platform edge but there had been no blood; just a pile of brown limbs like a doll's, with a head sitting neatly on the top.

Liam throws back the covers and gets out of bed. He can't stand being inside his own skin any more. He's going to see her. They're going to the police.

He can't live with this a moment longer.

SUMMER 2019

ELLIOTT

Olivia Rose Little landed in our world like a tiny red-faced missile in the early hours of one June morning.

Anya had quite a long, rough labour. It all feels blurry in my mind and I haven't even got hormonal surges to blame for the bits I can't remember.

Because her waters broke at home early in the whole process, she was told to come in. Then, because of the Strep B, she had to be hooked up to antibiotics throughout. For hours and hours she didn't progress but was in an uncomfortable level of pain.

Anya was, it's fair to say, quite angry about the whole thing. When the pain became bad, she refused an epidural for some reason and I pretty much watched uselessly while she bared her teeth, told the world to 'go fuck itself' several times, and told me she hated me at least three times. Then, finally, a second midwife was rushing into the room. Anya transformed into an astonishing warrior woman then, who pushed out our slippery little daughter with a sound that was almost inhuman, from a deep, animal place inside her that I had never seen before.

My primary emotion was astonishment. Despite the visible evidence that Anya had been growing a small person over those months, the actual sight of her – scrunched, slimy, beautiful – was truly awe-inspiring. I didn't even know I was crying until the midwife said something like, 'Come on, Daddy, blow your nose,' highlighting what a useless spare part I was in that room.

I stumbled out into a pale, drizzly dawn at about five that morning and looked around, wanting to tell someone, anyone, that I'd witnessed a miracle.

I was a dad now.

How did that work, then?

I had no precedent from my own life to show me how to do it. All I could do was think about Patrick, my only blueprint.

Anya needed a couple of stitches but was home by the following afternoon.

Neither of us really knew how to fit the car seat into the car. We hadn't had a practice run, and as I tried to strap it into the seat, the weight of this new responsibility felt heavy round my shoulders.

Anya seemed cheerful, despite the various physical discomforts, and somehow didn't lose patience while I battled to get it sorted out. We drove home at about twenty-five mph, just in case it still wasn't completely safe, and came into the house as three for the first time.

Livi – as we slipped into calling her within days – was asleep and I laid the car seat in the middle of the living room and gazed down at her. Her tiny chin was creased inwards, her lips puckering as she dreamed of suckling.

We met eyes across the room and Anya said, 'What the fuck do we do now then?' and we both started to laugh. It was an exhausted, slightly hysterical sound and in that moment, for the first time, I felt something settling inside me. A peace, despite the fear this new unknown brought. Maybe we really could put all the secrets behind us now. Maybe Anya, me, and Livi would be a self-sufficient unit.

*

But Anya's post-birth happiness only lasted for a couple of days. The health visitor arrived a few days after she came home and found her crying on the sofa, Livi screaming for milk and in a wet nappy upstairs with the bedroom door closed.

I arrived back from the supermarket a little while later. Anya tried to make light of it, saying she had been told that day three or four was classic 'baby blues' time. The health visitor – a young, thin woman with spiky blonde hair, glasses and a gentle country accent – said that it was indeed common to feel like this. But she emphasized that Anya needed to sleep 'when baby slept' and generally try to look after herself.

I'd been trying to feed Anya as much as possible but she claimed she felt sick and only seemed to want Diet Coke and toast. When I voiced this to the health visitor, Anya had given me a look that gave me an unpleasant jolt. There was a hardness there, bordering on dislike, that chilled me a little.

The next two weeks, before I went back to work, passed in a blur of broken nights and meals eaten with one hand, our snuffly little animal pressed into our necks, other hand against her squirmy, delicate back.

One night I woke up suddenly, drenched in shock. I couldn't work out what was wrong until I realized Livi wasn't even making her usual nocturnal grunts and snorts. Anya was so deeply asleep I couldn't sense her breathing. Moonlight edging the curtains in a glowing border gave the room an unearthly feel and my heart was thudding so hard it felt as though it would push its way out of my chest.

Scrambling out of bed, I raced round to Anya's side to the Moses basket on its stand next to her.

Livi was lying with her arms flung back, chest rising and falling quickly. She let out a surprisingly loud fart and I held my breath in case it woke her, but it didn't.

A wave of pure, sweet joy at this funny little girl spread through me.

It was a shock when I looked at Anya and saw her eyes were wide open, the moonlight making them shine oddly.

Then she spoke, in a wide-awake voice that was a bit too loud.

'I'm not sure I want to do it.'

'What?' I whispered, puzzled.

But she turned over then and her breathing told me she was asleep again within seconds.

Just as we were beginning to fall into some sort of new routine as a three, something happened that sent everything spinning once again.

Julia hadn't been round at ours to help with Livi as much as I'd expected, citing a series of bugs that had laid her low. Then, when Livi was three months old, Anya rang me at work in a hysterical state. Julia had been diagnosed with Adult Acute Myeloid Leukaemia – cancer of the blood and bone marrow.

The remission rate for treatment, we learned over that next week, was high, but the relapse rate, in turn, was also high.

When I got home that night, I could hear Livi screaming from outside the house. I let myself in with the key and found our daughter, puce-faced and roaring her outrage from her bouncy chair in the kitchen. I scooped her up and she arched her back and yelled even harder. Shushing and murmuring nonsense words, I took her to the changing table and sorted out the Armageddon in her nappy that had seeped yellow up to her hairline.

I shouted for Anya, but she didn't reply. I could hear movement above though, and once I had cleaned up the baby and myself, I carried her against my shoulder and climbed the stairs. She was only making little grunty sounds now.

Anya was in our bedroom, leaning into the wardrobe. A wheelie case was open on the bed and she turned and threw in tops that she was wrenching out so hard the hangers were bouncing and tinkling together.

'What the hell are you doing? Didn't you hear the baby crying?' I said.

She didn't look at me as she yanked a cardigan down and rolled it into a messy ball before stuffing it into the side of the case.

'She was alright,' she said. 'Mum needs me. I'm going over.'

I was momentarily speechless.

'They need peace and quiet, surely?' I said, trying to keep my voice level. 'You can't take a small baby there.'

'It'll be fine,' she said crisply.

Anger burned, hot and quick then. Here we were again. Anya running 'home'.

'It won't be fine!' I said, trying not to shout, because Livi was stirring at the air of stress in the room and I didn't want to set her off. 'It'll be noisy and unrelaxing and everything Julia doesn't need right now!'

She turned to me, eyes glittering with unshed tears and wired energy.

'What do you know about it?' she snapped. 'I know my mum better than you ever will.'

I sucked in my breath then. I'd never seen her like this before. She had an almost feral air about her, like she would attack if pushed into a corner. It was as though all the usual guy ropes of her reason that tethered her to the ground had been severed.

'I'm only going for a few days, while she has the first round of treatment,' she said, her voice a little more reasonable now.

I stared at her as she went to the chest of drawers and then began throwing balls of paired socks into the open case.

I laid our daughter, who was watching us with her knowing baby eyes through all this, on the small sofa under our window. Anya glanced up at me and turned back to what she was doing. I pushed the lid on the case closed, making Anya turn again with a surprised expression.

'What are you doing?' she said.

'You're not going to stay there,' I said. Her eyebrows shot up and she took a step back, before giving a sharp little laugh.

'Look at you, all macho,' she said. 'And why is that, oh Lord and Master?'

'Because it would be extremely selfish to do that,' I said, keeping my voice even. She glared back at me.

'How's that then?' she said.

'You can't take a small baby into a house where someone needs to rest.'

Anya regarded me then shrugged.

'I'll leave Livi here then,' she said.

'What the fuck, Anya? I'm at work!'

'Take a few days off,' she said flatly. 'Not like you haven't before.'

Maybe the anger was still a leftover from what had happened in the autumn but the next thing I knew was that I was shoving the whole case onto the floor, where it landed upside down, spilling clothes into a slithery pile on the carpet.

'No,' I said through gritted teeth. 'This isn't happening.'

Anya looked at me with wide, shocked eyes. I hated myself then for frightening her. I wished the baby hadn't seen my actions too.

Then my wife's face crumpled and she began to cry, silently at first.

Covering her eyes with her hands, she slid down the wall into a ball on the carpet and I felt something soften inside me. I went round and crouched next to her, pulling her into my arms where she shook and sobbed.

She said something I couldn't decipher and I gently asked her to repeat it.

Anya pulled away and then looked up at me, her eyes pink-tinged and her nose running a glistening line to her top lip.

'I'm being punished, Ell,' she said, bottom lip squaring into another sob. 'It's never going to go away. I'll never be allowed to be happy.'

I hugged her and shushed her, much as I had our baby ten minutes before. I told her she wasn't being punished and that she needed to stop thinking that way.

She murmured something else into my shoulder.

'What's that?'

'She hates me,' she said. 'The baby.'

This chilled me. I had no idea what to say and just hugged her a little harder.

AUTUMN 2003
LIAM

Liam checks his watch as the bus winds its way around the lanes. It's cloudy but hot today and the heat seems to squeeze his already aching head like a giant fist.

A baby is crying at the front of the bus, a piercing sound that drills into his brain while its mother casts defiant, angry looks around at the other passengers, as though daring them to say anything. An old man is mumbling to himself gently in front of Liam and he sighs at how depressing it all is. Lately, all he can think about is white sand and deep blue sky. Something different to this endless grey that feels like it is filling him up from the inside and suffocating him.

Why on earth they had to meet there, he had no idea.

When he had called Anastasia and told her they needed to talk, that this couldn't go on any longer, she had been surprisingly calm on the phone. He'd expected a bit more of a fight but she had quietly told him she agreed, then suggested they go for a walk out towards Chesterton where they could speak freely.

He had complained about this plan but she insisted she needed to build up to telling people and that he shouldn't push her. So he agreed, and now he was on this sick-making bus in the middle of frigging nowhere.

Liam doesn't want to ask the driver where to get off because it feels a bit naff, but it strikes him now he has no real idea where he is going. Thankfully, after another five minutes or so, he sees a sign advertising the adventure trail playground and remembers Anastasia saying to meet him on the opposite side of the woods to there. Near somewhere called Camelot Lake.

He leans over to the middle-aged woman sitting on the seat opposite him and says, "Scuse me, love,' with a grin. Her first flash of suspicion melts away at his easy smile, just as he knew it would, and he keeps it fixed on his face as he asks her how many more stops to the one nearest the lake.

She tells him to get off at the next one and then to head in past the car park. He thanks her, then pings the bell. Giving her another smile as he exits the bus, he feels for his rollie tin in his pocket.

There is a trail leading off from near the bus stop and he lights up the rollie as he makes his way into the trees. It feels gloomy in here, the pale light of this muggy day not penetrating the dense tree cover. But now he has made the decision, he feels a little lighter than he has for the last week or so. He's fully prepared to take the blame for giving Anastasia the drugs. He knows exactly what this means, and what his mother is going to think. But he hopes that one day she will be able to be a little bit proud of him for finally doing the right thing.

When he has smoked the rollie, he crushes the butt underfoot, then gets out his phone to call Anastasia. He'll see if she is here yet. But all he gets is the discordant chime of the 'number no longer in service' message. His spine stiffens at this and he wishes he didn't have the curdle of disappointment in his stomach. What did he expect, after today? That they could still be friends?

Ahead he sees the trees opening out and the blue of a car bonnet.

He steps into the car park and sees Anya leaning up against a car on the other side of the small car park – a black Beamer. She pulls herself away in one fluid motion and Liam swallows down the feeling that swells in his chest at the sight of her, the effect she always has on him.

She gives him a small smile, which he returns, a little uncertainly. He can't quite work out how he is meant to be today; what sort of mood to strike with her. He's fully prepared for a row, almost certainly for tears . . . but he is adamant that he won't be budged now he has reached this major decision.

'Let's have a wander,' she says.

He still hasn't spoken as they head into the trees towards the lake. There is a smell of damp leaves and the white sky makes the bare trees look ominous and spiky. A Canada goose takes flight by the water with a slow crack of wings, almost like a mechanical thing.

There is a neglected-looking bench in long grass at one end of the small lake and Anya heads for there and then sits, drawing her knees up and wrapping her arms around them. Liam steals a glance at her. She's in jeans and a white T-shirt, with battered white Converse on her feet. When she lifts her arm to push back her hair from her face, metal bangles jingle against her creamy skin. Liam feels a stab of pain in his chest, remembering the way they stretched out their arms and compared hand sizes as they lay in that attic room, warm and happy in the after-sex glow.

'So what are we going to do then?' she says after a moment's silence, still looking out at the water.

Liam hesitates.

'I think you know,' he says quietly. 'There's only one thing we *can* do.'

'I'll say you spiked my drink,' she says and he twists to look at her. There's a gap between her easy tone and the content of what she said that he doesn't understand, an unknowable space.

He turns his head back to the water and gets out the rollie tin again, more for something to do than a genuine desire for nicotine.

'You can if you want,' he says easily and it's Anastasia's turn to look at him now. He lights up and turns slightly. Her face is pinched and furious and he recognizes that she has been doing a very good job of pretending to be calm until now.

'I'll deny it,' he continues, 'but even if they don't take my word for it, it's a price I'm willing to pay. I just can't walk around another day knowing what I know.'

Anastasia is silent, then very softly murmurs, 'No . . .' almost on a breath.

An urge to cry washes over Liam now, and he sucks hard on the damp paper of the rollie, drawing the smoke deep into his lungs.

'Why did you do it?' he says now and Anastasia sighs heavily and thumps both feet back down onto the ground at the same time.

'I don't know,' she says. 'I can't really remember. I was just so . . . angry. I wanted you to pay attention and listen. Just to *listen*.'

They meet eyes then, two sets of such similar light brown, like they are twins. The sadness in Liam's chest seems to swell. Something softens in her expression and he feels the creep of her hand reaching for his. They squeeze hands tightly and a kind of relief, a glimpse not of peace, but of a time when it might be on the horizon, steals into his brain.

'I'll explain that it was all about the coke,' he says. 'And that I gave it to you.' His words are coming out too quickly now, in the relief of this being so much easier than he expected. 'I bet it will be worse for me than it will for you at the end of the day.'

Anastasia nods vigorously, eyes shining with tears that are welling there and gets up from the bench.

'No point putting it off any longer then, is there?' she says, and Liam gets up too.

They start to walk back towards the car park and then Liam notices a figure standing just by the start of the path. A middle-aged man, strongly built, who is staring at them oddly.

Anya pushes ahead and Liam wants to call her back because there is something unnerving about this guy. That's when he notices something in his hands, which he is holding lightly behind his back.

It's a golf club.

Fear sparks inside him now and he cries, 'Anastasia!' But she walks up to the man and squeezes his arm. A look passes between them. Anastasia gives a tiny shake of the head and a rueful downturn of the lips before climbing into the black car she was leaning against earlier on.

'What the fuck is going on here?' says Liam and he knows his voice sounds scared and childish, but he can't care about that because, too quickly, the man is raising the golf club over his head and Liam's next sound is a cry of shock and pain.

I think I placed too much hope in the transformative effect of the baby's arrival.

Of course, it is a massive change for the two of them in all the usual ways: the sleepless nights, mess and disruption. That's not what I mean, though.

I believed – and maybe she did too – that some form of alchemy would occur inside her after the birth, something that would turn that baffling, numb place she manages to hide so well into something that beat and pulsed with powerful, all-encompassing emotion.

I know I was changed by my two births in all sorts of ways, good and bad, and I suppose I just assumed she would be the same, even though she marched to a different drum in all sorts of ways.

The pure love I felt when I saw their little faces was a surprise. Where had that been? I couldn't understand where it could have been hiding until then.

I hoped my daughter might find that love too. But I am really not sure she has. And in anyone else, I would just say, 'Wait and see. Let her find it in her own time.' But this is Anastasia. My dear, darling, complicated Anastasia.

When she told us the terrible story about that Alice woman, both Patrick and I cried.

We were devastated that our daughter had been responsible for something so horrific and, yes, I'll admit this, that she had to see it. We were frightened that it would scar her for the rest of her life.

We wanted to blame him, that Liam boy.

I never really asked for details about how Patrick persuaded him to stay away.

But he sounded like the sort of person who would probably do anything for the right price. I'm not too concerned about that, I'm sorry. My daughter is my priority.

Anya remained dry-eyed while she told us about what happened at the station. It was when Patrick left the room that she grabbed both my hands and whispered something I have never forgotten, which chilled me and saddened me to my core.

Her expression was momentarily wild and she hissed, 'There's something missing inside me, Mum. I know I'm meant to feel awful but I just want to forget about it all. Is that normal?'

What on earth could I say to that? Patrick came into the room and she drew back and gave me a warning look about repeating what she had said. I didn't know what to do or say and left it at that. But the next chance I had, I suggested she see a therapist again. She followed my advice, but I am not sure she ever really allowed herself to tell the truth in those sessions.

We couldn't have been happier when she met Elliott. Of course, we were surprised, at first. Their backgrounds were so different and, in the beginning, we thought there may be elements of that other, disastrous, relationship at play. But we quickly fell in love with Elliott too. He has an essential sweetness to him that she needs in a partner. He balances her out. I believed, I really did, that maybe she had grown out of the more problematic aspects of her character.

Then that Michael man came back into her life.

She has no remorse for what happened to him, not really.

For my daughter, it is a little like watching her actions through a screen. She knows they are directly connected to her, yet she is able to tidy them away.

She didn't spend her childhood pulling the wings off insects, if that's what you are thinking. She doesn't, as far as I am concerned, nurse violent urges or have an inability to care about people. My daughter loves me and her father. She loves Elliott.

Patrick doesn't want to hear any of this, as usual. He says it's 'a bit of the baby blues, that's all, nothing to panic about'. He never would truly discuss it. Says now that I need to concentrate my efforts on getting well and to stop panicking about matters that are largely in my head.

He doesn't see things he doesn't want to see.

A couple of days after Olivia was born I went round to the house. I had been keeping my illness from Anya for a while but knew I would have to tell her soon. It terrified me that the one person in the world who truly understood her, and loved her all the same, was on borrowed time. But I was so elated at the birth of my granddaughter that I kept putting it off. Who wants to talk about death when birth is so very much nicer?

Elliott told me Anya was just changing the baby but I could go up, so I climbed the stairs, feeling the effort as though there were three times as many.

I came to the small room they had converted into a nursery with primrose yellow walls and a border of silver moons and stars. My heart lifted as I saw my daughter bending over the wooden changing table, two tiny pink legs waving around near her hand. But the baby wasn't happy about being changed and began to grizzle.

I watched in horror as Anya grabbed one of Olivia's feet, quite roughly, and swore before telling her to 'Stop it.' As if the baby was being disagreeable on purpose!

I rushed in and she started to cry, saying she was just sore and tired and hadn't meant it.

I took over and told her to nap, while I changed the baby's nappy with shaking hands.

I carried Olivia – so very carefully – downstairs. Elliott was making tea, oblivious, in the kitchen. I wondered again about talking to him – really talking to him. But I'd tried before and sounded a bit mad, plus I wasn't sure what he did and didn't know.

I smiled as his whole face lit up at the sight of his baby daughter, swaddled and sleepy now in a yellow crocheted blanket.

He is besotted with Olivia, I think.

Thank goodness.

But he can't be there all the time, can he? And he would never believe me. He thinks she is so much better than he is, that's the trouble. That's why she chose him.

Now she has the baby, it changes everything.

Anya isn't the priority, for the first time ever.

I have to think about Olivia now.

SUMMER 2019

IRENE

The handles of the plastic shopper were biting into her palm so she stopped for a moment to swap hands. Irene could have sworn this bag was now twice as heavy as it had been when she left the shop. She'd only needed a few essentials – eggs, milk, a tin of beans – but everything felt so exhausting these days.

It had been an effort to force herself out and about, as she kept being advised she must do. People had been very kind though, overall, and she had been pleasantly surprised by how many friends she appeared to have. She supposed that was one small silver lining to it all.

Huffing now, she began to trudge up the small incline that would take her to her own corner. It was like having sand-bags attached to her arms and legs all the time. She had forgotten how bone-tiring sadness was. Or maybe it was her age. She was trying not to nap like an old lady, but it was hard when she fell into bed and then her mind seemed to switch on like a bright light that searched all the dark corners for answers she could never find.

As she rounded the corner to her own road, she saw that a police car was parked right outside her house. Her heart seemed to kick in her chest and she felt her breath come faster.

It couldn't be for her, surely? She mentally scanned for any reason her neighbours might have the police round. Cathy at number 14 had that business with her son, Kyle, a while back, but that seemed to be over now and Irene had seen him going off at rush hour in a shirt and tie recently.

A strange thought leaked through her now, one that she didn't quite know what to do with.

Most people got a shock when the police came to visit because they thought it might signify bad news about a loved one.

But Irene didn't have anyone left to lose.

When she was almost alongside the car, both doors opened, and two women in plainclothes got out, both impossibly young-looking.

One may have been Chinese, with a short black bob and glasses over eyes that were peering keenly at Irene. She was small and slim and the other, with a brown ponytail and a straining blue blouse, was smiling, a bit nervously, Irene thought.

'Mrs Copeland?' The Chinese one approached her now. 'I'm Detective Sergeant Amy Jin and this is Detective Constable Katie Morgan. Would it be okay if we came in and had a chat with you?'

Irene realized, afterwards, that she hadn't even offered them a cup of tea.

Her heart was still beating uncomfortably hard, even though she'd had that strange thought before. There was something in their manner – a kind of intense focus – that alerted her to the fact they were here about something serious. Something that directly involved Irene. She brushed away a guilty feeling; she hadn't done anything wrong. Everyone knew this was how the police made you feel.

'Mrs Copeland,' said the one called Jin, leaning forward

in her seat and clasping her hands together in quite a mannish way for such a slip of a girl. 'We are here about the death of your son, Michael.'

The jolt from these words brought Irene's hand to her chest, as though to stop her heart from bursting right through her flowered blouse and onto the carpet.

'Yes,' she said, although it might have been so quiet only she heard it.

'You are aware, Mrs Copeland,' the policewoman continued in a firm, but kind voice, 'that your son's death was believed to be a result of suicide.'

'Yes,' louder now, maybe too loud.

'Well, someone has come forward to say that they believe there may have been foul play involved.'

Foul play.

'What does that mean exactly?' Irene pressed the hand against her chest and tried to get her breath.

'Would you like a glass of water?' said the other police-woman and Irene wanted them to get on with it, to explain why they were here, but she was aware that she might be on the verge of some sort of panic attack again, like when she was in that café. She didn't want to be keeling over, so she said, 'Yes, yes please,' and the policewoman got up quickly.

'Kitchen's through there,' said Irene, wafting her hand in the general direction.

She stared down at her hands, suddenly oddly self-conscious in the silence that remained, with the Chinese lady still looking at her.

'There you go, have a sip of that,' said the other one and she drank down half the glass, grateful for the distraction.

'Are you okay to continue?' said the Chinese one. DS Jin, that was it.

She nodded and mashed her hands together hard in her lap.

'As I was saying, we have had a tip-off about possible—'

'Yes, foul play, you said, already.' Irene was suddenly impatient to hear the rest. 'But what does that mean, exactly?'

DS Jin paused. 'Mrs Copeland, this person claims to know for a fact that Michael was not alone at Petrel Point and that he may have been pushed from the cliff.'

It was funny, now that the words were out there, that Irene didn't faint or cry, or pass out. She was suddenly suffused with a feeling of numb calm. Later, she would understand that it was perhaps a bitter sort of satisfaction that her deepest belief – that Michael wouldn't have done this to her – was correct.

The two policewomen were staring at her intently now, the larger one perched on the edge of the sofa as though she might have to catch Irene in a dead slump.

Irene took a breath in through her nose and let it out slowly.

'I see,' she said. 'And did the person see this happen?'

The two police officers exchanged glances then.

'We are not sure, Mrs Copeland. But we have been told he had an altercation with a woman.'

'A woman?' said Irene, then. 'But why would a woman . . .'

She gasped, breaking off the end of her sentence and both policewomen leaned forwards as though pulled by strings simultaneously. They waited for her to continue but she was staring up at the ceiling now, reliving the look on that Anastasia's face at her front door.

One of them cleared her throat in a deliberate way.

'Mrs Copeland,' she said, 'do you know a young woman called Anastasia Ryland?'

Irene looked back at the Chinese one; the name gone again in all this stress.

And then, a breach occurred like something had been severed inside. She began to sob hard, hot tears that wrenched from so deep within it felt as though her insides were being yanked out.

Later, she leaned her head back against the chair and closed her aching eyes. The policewomen had been very kind, asking if they could ring a friend to be with her, but Irene had wanted only to be left alone to try to process this violent swerve in her life.

She had been hungry for detail, once she had cried and made tea and managed to get a grip on herself, but they weren't able to tell her too much. Irene kept asking, 'Why now?' Why had this supposed witness not done the right thing when they should have, a year ago? But all the officers would say was that this 'individual' had personal reasons for not coming forward at the time, but that their circumstances had changed in a way that made it now possible.

They also said some things Irene didn't understand about there being no other hard evidence at this late stage to prove the story. At the time she hadn't been able to take in why they were emphasizing this so much, but now, she understood with a dropping sensation in her stomach, that they might not have much to go on. If someone – *her*, that Anastasia – had done this to Michael and somehow got off, then she thought she would rather be where she was this morning. In total ignorance. She didn't think she would be able to stand that.

Irene's head was throbbing from her explosive crying episode – funny how she would have felt embarrassed to cry like that in front of strangers a year ago – and she hefted herself up from her chair to get some paracetamol from the cupboard. She didn't like to take medicines on an empty stomach but she felt as though her throat would simply clamp shut if she tried to eat anything.

As she climbed the stairs to get to the bathroom cabinet, she found herself going over, yet again, how that woman could have been connected to Michael. He had been trying to find out something about Liam, and Liam was the connection.

When she had tried to explain this to the policewomen, it had all come out garbled. She'd noticed them exchange looks again when she said that Michael had apparently been on a mission to discover what had happened to his brother. The English policewoman, or at least the non-Chinese one, had written notes rather frantically when she told them her youngest son hadn't been seen by his family since 2003.

They asked the same questions that had come up when he first left.

'Was his passport missing?' Yes.

'Were any clothes missing?' Not really.

'Has there been any contact with him whatsoever since the last time you saw him?' Just that postcard. She was able to show them that and they asked if they could take it with them, which seemed a bit strange.

'Was there any reason to suspect Liam may have been in any trouble?'

Irene had hesitated before she'd said, 'No.' They had noticed it, for sure. But she couldn't bring herself to say that he might have been involved with drugs. Maybe it was because she imagined their expressions might shift; harden. She would go from being the poor bereaved mother of the victim to someone who had criminal elements in the family.

Irene winced and filled the tooth mug with water from the bathroom tap, before swallowing the two painkillers. Each seemed to catch, scratching her throat as it went down.

Despite needing to be alone earlier, she suddenly had a strong desire to tell someone. Quickly dismissing her local friends, kind though they were, her mind settled on Rowan.

She had seen the other woman a few times since Michael's death and rather liked her, despite her odd ways. Yes, she would ask her to come over, especially as Rowan deserved to be told this new information.

Irene made her way down to the telephone in the kitchen and looked for Rowan's number in the address book she kept near it.

Frustratingly, the call went to voicemail and Irene was about to hang up, when she forced herself to speak. She hated these message things.

'Rowan,' she said, aware of how wavering and old she sounded to her own ears. 'It's Irene, here. Irene Copeland. I wondered if you might be able to drop by . . . I . . .' she tried to swallow, her mouth suddenly desert-dry. 'I have something I need to talk to you about,' she said. 'About, about my Michael. Well, thank you. Goodbye.'

She hadn't really known how to sign off – never did on these messages – but the prospect of Rowan's company was welcome. That was, of course, if she got the message and wasn't off on some whale-singing course or something.

She clearly wasn't though, because less than fifteen minutes later Irene heard a soft, tentative knock at the front door. The bell had stopped working some time ago and, without Michael, she hadn't been able to fix it.

Feeling a lightening inside, she got up from the sofa, where she had been trying to watch a little television to take her mind off things, and made her way to the front door. It didn't look like Rowan standing there – someone taller, slimmer, surely?

When she opened the door, it wasn't Rowan. It was a young man, tall and skinny, but with muscled arms coming from a faded yellow T-shirt. He had glasses and the sort of red beard people wore when they were dressing up as comedy

Scotsmen. He was probably one of those homeless people, who sold sponges and whatnot, but casting her gaze around, Irene couldn't seem to see anything other than a large rucksack that was resting by his feet.

Frowning, she peered at him and said, 'Can I help you?'

Then her eyes widened and she let out a sound that was half gasp, half moan. Her hands flew to cup her face for the second time in an afternoon.

'Mum,' said the man in a low voice that cracked, giving the word two syllables.

ELLIOTT

I'd bumped into Lee Bennett that morning.

Since I had formally apologized in that difficult, sweaty meeting back in October, I had kept my head down and tried to throw myself into the job with all I had. Two weeks off for Livi's birth was all I took, just because I was still feeling the last remnants of a cloud over my head from all that happened in the autumn. We'd never known for sure whether it was Copeland who'd tried to run me over or thrown that brick through the window. He was dead. But I felt, deep in my gut, that I had originally accused the wrong man.

I'd somehow managed to avoid Bennett in the playground at the start and end of the day, averting my gaze if we happened to be within ten metres of each other.

The previous day I had shown some of the children in my class pictures of Livi on my iPad. There had been much cooing from the female contingent, and various helpful observations from the boys, ranging from, 'My brother once pooed all the way up to his own head,' to my personal favourite, 'She looks like Noel Fielding from *Bake Off*.'

I was on my way into school. Tyler was, for once, queuing outside and waiting for the gates to be unlocked by Barry, the caretaker. His father was standing with him, smart in a dark grey suit. I couldn't help thinking he looked just like someone on their way to a court hearing, as he kept pulling at the collar of his shirt as though it were choking him.

I nodded quickly and turned away and then heard Bennett say, 'Hey . . . Mr, uh, Mr Little?'

Warily, I turned back to him and tried to arrange my face into something friendly and non-confrontational, remembering I'd had that exact intention before. And look how that all turned out.

'Tyler tells me you have a baby girl,' he grunted and then, while my brain was still trying to catch up, he stuck out his hand. 'Congratulations.'

A little dazed, I took his hand and we shook.

I felt like I could finally trust myself to smile and it not be misunderstood.

'Thank you, Mr Bennett,' I said, 'that's really, really nice of you.'

He knuckled the top of Tyler's head, a slight reddening on his cheeks now, and he avoided my eye.

'You take good care of her,' he said, then, 'Goodbye you, be a good boy.'

I thanked him again as he turned and walked away, head lowered and hand reaching into his pocket for car keys.

'My dad has a company car,' said Tyler in a rush, and I beamed down at him.

'That's absolutely brilliant, mate,' I said. 'Well done, your dad.'

I was warmed through by this for the entire day.

Things had been better at home too, although Anya still seemed a little distant. Julia's treatment had started and she seemed okay. I was really starting to feel as though the horrors of the autumn and the weird adjustment to new parenthood might finally be easing into something better and more stable.

We had a staff meeting at the end of the day and I even found myself volunteering to be the liaison teacher for a French exchange visit with a school in Calais next year, such was my good mood.

Coming out of the gates at about four, I went to check my phone and saw that there were about ten messages and several missed calls from Anya.

The messages started as Ell, I need you home NOW xx through PLEASE COME HOME!!!!!' to WHERE THE FUCK R U????????????

I tried to call her back then but the phone just rang out, so I had no alternative but to jump on my bike and pedal as hard as I could. The car was free now that Anya wasn't working, but I was trying to lose a few pounds put on by the stress-eating a new baby brings.

Sweat poured down my temples as I hammered those pedals and, as I came to where I could see the silver swathe of sea, a memory came back of that other day, last summer, when the End of the Summer tickets were burning a hole in my satchel and the world was a simpler place. When my wife wasn't a murderer.

This thought curdled with all the worries about what could have happened at home. I had visions of Livi accidentally scalded with a pan of boiling water or being snatched from the back garden where Anya occasionally put the bouncy chair.

Funny that it didn't occur to me that what I would see would be a police car.

I used my key and, coming into the house with a knotted stomach, found a scene of calm, despite the frantic nature of Anya's messages. There were two policewomen in the living room, plainclothes, but so obviously coppers to anyone who had grown up where I did. One was East Asian and had the bearing of the more senior of the two, the other a plump brown-haired woman. They were both about my age.

Anya was standing in the middle of the room, burping Livi over her shoulder, rubbing small circles against the yellow terrycloth of the baby's sleepsuit. Her eyes were unnaturally bright, it seemed, but when she spoke, her voice was oddly formal, clipped and polite.

'Elliott, this is DS Jin and DC Morgan.'

I said, 'Hello,' to them and they murmured greetings back with frowns.

'They need me to come down to the station to have a chat, so you need to be here for Livi.'

Anya handed me our daughter, who felt dense and a bit too hot, as though she had been pressed against her mother for some time.

'Mr Ryland—' began the Asian policewoman and Anya interrupted her.

'No,' she said, 'he is Mr Little.'

'Mr Little,' said the woman, with barely suppressed irritation. 'It's not quite a case of asking your wife down for a chat. We have just arrested her on suspicion of murder.'

ELLIOTT

There are moments in your life so strange and shocking that you have no immediate response and all you can do is flounder in a sea of confused emotion. I stood there, mouth opening and closing helplessly.

Arrested?

All three of them were looking at me, Anya with an oddly calm expression which I knew belied the panic underneath. Livi squirmed in my arms and stretched her legs out so her feet pressed into my chest, almost as if she was reminding me she was there. I kissed her downy scalp and saw a look of sorrow wash over Anya's face. She reached out to touch the baby's back, then drew her hand in again and reset her expression.

'How long will this take?' she said in a rather haughty way to the two policewomen, who exchanged loaded glances.

'It will take as long as it takes,' said the one called Jin and Anya nodded, crisply, and spoke to me without meeting my eyes.

'There is some expressed milk in the freezer,' she said, her tone entirely neutral.

Finally, I found my voice.

'On what grounds have you arrested her?' I asked, realizing, far, *far* too late, that this question should have come immediately, along with a passionate defence of my wife's innocence. This thought sent iced water through me. Had I made things worse?

A few minutes later, they were gone. Right on cue, and maybe picking up on both the atmosphere and her mother's absence, Olivia began to cry.

Time seemed to pass at an agonizingly slow rate that afternoon and evening.

Livi cried on and off for an hour and a half, despite all efforts to placate her. It really felt as though she understood what was going on.

I started off with all the basics: checked the nappy, offered milk. But her nappy was dry and, when I presented her with the carefully prepared bottle of Anya's milk, she turned her head angrily and bunched her tiny fists in a way that would have been comical if everything hadn't been so awful. I supposed these weren't the best circumstances in which to introduce bottle feeding for the first time. Anya had been stock-piling milk in the freezer for when she went back to work, but we hadn't quite got round to starting Livi on the bottle.

In the end, it was a combination of me running around the room with her and playing 'Lonely Boy' by The Black Keys at top volume that stunned her into silence. Every time I went, 'Whoah-oh-oh-oh . . .' she blinked hard, finally, when I was sweating with the effort of it all, breaking into a heart-crushing smile.

I slumped onto the sofa with her then and had another go with the bottle. She moaned and turned her head away until I dribbled some of the now-cool milk onto my hand and let her suck at it. The fierce pull of it gave me some indication of why Anya had found breast feeding so painful at first.

This seemed to soothe her until she grudgingly allowed the plastic nipple of the bottle into her mouth for a small suck, before spitting it out again and starting to cry once more.

I didn't dare leave the house in case Anya came back. I wanted to speak to Zoe, just to hear a friendly voice, but what could I have said? That I had no idea why my wife had been arrested? Before she left the house, Anya had made me swear, a ferocious look on her face, that I wouldn't tell her parents yet. This felt wrong on so many levels but I decided I would honour her wishes if she was back within twenty-four hours. Otherwise, they had to be told.

As I began to pace around the house with my increasingly furious baby daughter held against my shoulder, I mentally picked over what might be happening at the police station.

What would Anya say? Might she actually confess? This thought caused a curious sensation of fear and relief at once. It would depend on what they had on her, of course.

Why now? Why arrest her all these months later?

These thoughts played on a loop around my mind. By nine in the evening, Livi had cried herself out and was lying on my chest, spent, while I stared at the television on low volume and tried not to think about how much I wanted to get up and get a drink.

When I heard the sound of an engine outside, I started to move into a more upright position and then the front door opened into the living room.

She looked drained. Her face was chalk-white and she had a milk stain on one side of her white T-shirt where she was leaking.

Without meeting my eye, she just said, 'My tits are like hot rocks. Give . . .' and held out her hands for the baby, who instantly woke and began to grizzle.

Anya sat down opposite me and latched the baby on, with a small wince. Livi instantly began to drink with little happy grunts, one little star of a hand pressed against her mother's neck.

'What happened?' I said, after the silence had dragged on for a couple of moments.

She sighed and laid her head back against the sofa cushion, before closing her eyes.

'Someone says they know,' she said in barely a whisper. She paused, swallowing visibly. 'About him going over.'

'How?' I said. 'Were they there?'

She shrugged. 'Wouldn't say other than that they'd had a tip-off.'

Acidic bile rose in my throat. I could only be there for her through whatever this brought if she told me the truth. But I couldn't confront her when she was so beaten. Knowing her, she would just clamp down and go off to bed without saying another word.

'That why they let you go?' I said. 'Because it's just their word against yours?'

She sighed and transferred the baby to the other side, forgetting to wind her in between. I didn't say anything.

'They have only let me go on police bail, so they can do further investigations. They kept asking me about my "relationship" with Michael Copeland and about that day. I admitted I was there, of course, but I just tried to get across what really happened.'

A silence fell and it made her look at me properly for the first time.

'Why don't you just say what's on your mind, Elliott?' Her voice was loud enough to make Livi jolt all four limbs at once, before she continued sucking.

'I can only try and help if I know the truth, sweetheart,' I said carefully. 'I mean, everything.' Then, 'You know that

I love you and will stand by you, whatever happens, don't you?'

She gave a harsh, short laugh then, and got abruptly to her feet.

'She's only sucking for comfort now. You wind her for me. I'm going to bed.'

And with that she handed me our slightly startled daughter and began to climb the stairs.

SUMMER 2019

LIAM

The lack of sleep, after-effects of yesterday's emotional tsunami, and the jet lag were conspiring to make this motorway drive much harder than it should have been, and it was taking every scrap of his concentration not to end up under the wheels of a juggernaut. The morning sun was high in a bright sky, but the colours were muted in comparison to what he was used to, like a filter over a lens.

It was possibly a good thing, he mused, as he clenched his buttocks in anticipation of overtaking a caravan he was fast approaching in the slow lane. Maybe he needed to spend time outside of his own head before doing whatever it was he was going to do when he got to his destination.

He reached for the bottle of water Mum had prepared for the journey and flipped back the lid with his teeth to take a drink. He gave a small involuntary smile as he noticed the pack of sandwiches she had also made, carefully checking he still liked ham and cheese as she did so.

Standing on the doorstep of his childhood home, hearing the terrible, banal, sounds of the station so nearby, he had been sweating, his head buzzing, and it had almost broken his resolve.

But it wasn't his mother who answered the door. Instead, it was a young woman holding a wriggling toddler in her arms. She told Liam she had a forwarding address somewhere.

Soon he was heading back into Cambridge, weak with relief that he didn't have to stay in Waterbeach.

When he had pulled up at the neat bungalow in King's Hedges he had been eager now to see her. But the aged nature of the woman who opened that door had shocked him, despite the fact that he had tried to prepare himself. At first, she hadn't recognized him, then it had seemed to flood her face, the knowledge of who she was looking at, and they had fallen into each other's arms, both crying.

She was tiny, surely much shorter than she had once been, and he had to lean down to hold her shaking body.

They had sort of staggered back inside the house like a many-limbed creature and she had stood back a little, holding his arms and gazing up at him.

The slap that followed then, not that hard, across his cheek, had been almost welcome, albeit a surprise. Then she had sobbed again and pulled him towards her.

Finally they had been sitting in her tidy living room, Mum holding onto one of his hands as though afraid if she let go, he might disappear again.

'Where have you *been*, Liam?' she'd said. 'Why did you never come back, lovey?' Then she had said, with satisfaction, 'I knew it. I knew you'd come back someday,' before bursting into tears again.

Liam had taken a breath, trying to think about the words he had arranged during the thirty-odd hours he had spent in the air, rabbit-hopping the cheapest way he could get from Bangkok to London. He still hadn't found the right ones. But now he decided there was no point in anything but the bluntest truth.

'I had to go away, Mum,' he said, looking into her eyes, which seemed to be roving all over his face and neck, like she was checking him all over for something.

He thought back to that night, fifteen years ago, when

Anastasia's father had come at him with the golf club. The surprise and shock of it had floored him before he had time to fight back.

The blows had rained down, on his legs, his arms, but never on his head or his back. He only understood why later. This was a beating by someone who knew with almost surgical precision what to do when you wanted someone to be in pain, but not so battered that they might die or need to be hospitalized.

When the beating had stopped, the man, whose name he only later found out was Patrick Ryland, spat on him, the hot froth of it landing on his cheek.

Then Ryland said Irene's full name, his dad's, and Michael's and gave all the details of where they worked and at what hours. He said that if Liam ever talked about what had happened at Waterbeach station, then his family would end up in a ditch with bullets in their brains. Furthermore, he was to get out of the country and not to come back unless he wanted to see his family in a news story.

Anastasia had been sitting in the parked car the whole time this had been taking place. This was something it took many years for him to process. Sometimes he feels he still hasn't. Maybe the journey he is taking today is the proof of that.

Her father had finally stopped. Liam had been able to hear his ragged breaths as he gave him one last, half-hearted kick. He heard the sound of the car starting up then, and soon he was alone, gasping with the pain of drawing air into his lungs as his ribs screamed at him.

A van drew up a few blurry minutes later and, at first, he had been filled with hope. But then two men in balaclavas got out and a brand-new terror had stolen what little space he had to breathe. This was it. He was going to die right there.

But after a savage kick to the hip and some mumbled

words about shutting his mouth, he had been thrown into the back of the van.

Curling into a pile of sheets that smelled of white spirit, he'd cradled his ribs and panted in panicked fear as the van stopped and started, jogging him about painfully against some tins of paint. After the first hour he'd tried a half-hearted attempt to open the doors, but they were locked, and anyway, the van was travelling fast now, maybe on a motorway.

Another hour later, after he'd somehow slept a little, the doors were thrust open with a harsh clang and all he caught was what sounded like the deep, melancholy bellow of a ship foghorn before a punch knocked him unconscious.

He'd woken up inside a shipping container, his passport and five hundred pounds next to him in a carrier bag. The thought that people had broken into his house to get the passport – where his mum might have walked in – made him feel even sicker, once he was able to process it. It was so . . . clinical. And how long would that money last?

There was a plastic trench that became his toilet in one corner, and multi-packs of water and, bizarrely it seemed at the time, boxes of crisps and peanuts in another. To this day he could no longer eat processed, salty snacks without feeling the absolute terror he'd felt in the back of that metal coffin.

It felt like a lifetime but he now knows (easy to find online) it would have been two days later that he arrived in Rotterdam. Here, he was wordlessly bundled into another van and deposited at the airport.

Yes, maybe he'd had a choice at that point. The threat to his family had felt real, though.

For a long time he'd told himself that was his sole reason for staying away. But the truth was, he was glad he had a reason not to go back home. How could he be in that house, hearing the train announcements and the *ding-ding-ding* of the crossing gate without reliving the horror of that night, over and over again?

At first, not contacting home had been hard. But he knew that if he spoke to his mother, he would feel so guilty that he would be on the first flight back. As time moved on, and he went from lying with a needle in his arm in that filthy room in Koh Pha-Ngan, to the life he had now, with Pimchan, it got easier to simply stay away.

But now that there is a chance that he might be a father himself, it sheds a whole new light on what might have been.

As the car shudders with the effect of a huge lorry overtaking him, he feels a pang of pain at the thought of Pimchan. Hard to know when he is going to see her again. Now that they are married, he shouldn't have trouble getting back into the country, but he has no idea what repercussions may flow from him going to the police. He didn't cause that poor woman – Alice Adebayo – to be obliterated by that train, but he had been there and was pretty certain that Anastasia would be able to get the most expensive legal representation behind her to twist the truth.

Reading about Michael's death in a syndicated Kent local news story online was the tipping point that had brought him home at last. His mother was alone now. She needed him. He hadn't known for sure whether he intended to go to the police at that point, but then his mother had told him what she told him, and it had all come together in his mind.

His brother hadn't in fact committed suicide, as he had believed; it was all about Anastasia. That evil bitch had turned up, like broken glass in his skin again after all these years. Liam had had to resist the temptation to smash a fist into the old coffee table, which still bore the marks from when he crashed his trike into it twenty-nine years ago.

His mother had begged him not to get involved, and he had managed to convince her that he would do nothing. But when she went to bed, he had rooted through all the drawers in the dresser for anything that might lead him where he needed to go.

There had been a sheet of paper, what looked like a private investigator's report in there, which gave him a curious mixture of pride and sadness at the ingenuity his brother had showed that led him to his death.

Liam had slipped out early this morning, still jet-lagged and unable to sleep properly, leaving a note that stated he would most definitely be home later that day and that she wasn't to worry. Then he had gone into town and hired a car, thankful that he was able to use his Thai licence because his UK one had long expired, and got on the road to Kent.

It wasn't hard to find the house, using his smartphone GPS.

Nice little place, which reminded him of holidays they'd had in Hunstanton as a kid. Not exactly where he'd imagined her ending up, that was for sure. In his head, he had pictured her living in some riverside apartment over the Thames, or in a massive pile in the country.

When he was informed he had arrived at his destination, Liam sat in the car, listening to the cooling tick of the engine, thinking about what he was going to do.

His hands shook a little and he squeezed them into fists and then flexed them.

Getting out of the car, he stretched his stiff back and began to walk towards number 15.

Liam stood at the gate and hesitated. He could see into a sitting room, where a woman – yes, it was her – was holding a baby to her shoulder and patting its back a bit robotically. She looked like crap, he was gratified to see, although still beautiful.

That's what had fooled him the first time though. He had swallowed the childhood fairy tale lie that monsters were always ugly.

ELLIOTT

'I got croissants and pain-au-chocolat,' I called out, 'so I hope you're hungry, although it's possible I may have eaten some of them on the way back.'

I could hear unhappy cries from upstairs now I was properly inside. My heart seemed to fall in my chest at the thought of a Saturday morning so different from the one I had been hoping for.

My plan was to try and behave normally, to make Anya feel as safe as she possibly could with everything that was happening. But now I had visions of her and the baby both in tears upstairs. So it was a surprise when I heard her call out, 'In here,' from the kitchen. We didn't usually leave Livi to cry.

She came into view first, standing over by the sink, an expression on her face that I couldn't read. I gave a start when I saw we weren't alone in the room.

Maybe on some strange level I knew who it was. I can't really say, because my memory of that day is an odd, fickle thing. There are some moments that are scarred upon my mind for ever more, and I have to live through them in increments that feel even slower than seconds. Other parts, well, they are less clear.

I know that I stared at him, this wiry, bearded man sitting at our kitchen table, and he stared at me, for several seconds, before anyone spoke.

Then Anya said, 'This is Liam.'

Liam gave a bitter laugh, shaking his head slowly then looking from her to me again.

He stood up and completely surprised me by holding out a tanned, knobbly-knuckled hand in greeting. I almost took it, before stopping myself.

Anya snorted and angled her body away to stare out of the kitchen window.

'I know this is a bit weird,' he said in a quiet, deep voice. 'But I'm not here to actively hurt anyone. I just wanted to speak to Anastasia. It's part of my recovery, you see. I know that I didn't behave as I should have back then. I wanted to say sorry.'

Anger flared, bright and bitter; the same horrible thrill scaring Lee Bennett had prompted twitching inside me. This man had almost ruined my wife's life and I hated him right then. Wanted to hurt him.

I looked at her narrow shoulders, hunched in as she stood at the sink, and knew I would do anything to protect her and our daughter.

'Anyway,' he said a little hesitantly, perhaps guessing the direction of my thoughts. 'I've finally had enough and I'm doing what I should have done all those years ago.'

'You're going to tell the police?' I said, trying to sound calm. Maybe his confession would help the current situation in some way? I had no idea.

He nodded. His eyes were an unusual light bright brown and it struck me, unpleasantly, they were oddly like Anya's. They had similar colouring in general: the dark red hair, the pale skin. They could have been related. Was that an attraction, originally? It wasn't something I wanted to dwell upon.

My mouth was dry and I picked up a glass of half-drunk water that was sitting on the kitchen worktop. I didn't know how long it had been there and it tasted stale. Still, I drank it down.

I had absolutely no idea what to do here.

Anya (so strange to hear him calling her Anastasia) and Liam were staring at each other, in silence. It felt weirdly like they were coiled, waiting to see what the other did first before springing into some sort of physical action.

'So,' I said finally, 'you're actually going to confess what you did to that woman?'

Liam turned his gaze to me, a look of amusement on his face now.

'Ah, right,' he said, with a sharp laugh. 'I shouldn't be surprised that's the story she concocted. The trouble is . . . *Elliott*, is it?'

I nodded.

'The trouble is, Elliott, that you have been played for a fool.'

'What the fuck are you—'

'Don't listen to him, Elliott,' said Anya loudly, turning back to look at me, 'he's absolutely full of shit. Of course he's going to deny it.'

'Okay, then,' said Liam. 'Shall I tell you why I haven't seen my family, why I missed my own father's funeral, and then my brother's?' His tone started out even but now his voice was rising and I saw that he was holding back emotion with a visible will. He had tanned, sinewy arms with lots of leather and cloth bracelets on his wrists and he kept clenching and unclenching his fists. I was bigger than him, but he had an energy about him and a wiry strength that meant I wasn't confident about overpowering him if the need arose.

He wiped his hands on his canvas trousers. Nervous sweat? I instinctively moved a little closer to Anya.

'So since the afternoon when *her father*,' he tipped a thumb at Anya, whose jaw was set, her eyes cold now '. . . beat the shit out of me with a golf club then threatened my family, it felt wise for me to stay away. D'you understand what I'm saying?'

He was breathing heavily. I think I had my mouth open now. Patrick had done that? *Patrick?* Or was it all lies?

Livi had gone quiet upstairs, thank God. I didn't want her anywhere near this.

'So why,' he went on, his eyes swimming now, 'why would he have gone to all that trouble if it had been me who pushed that poor woman under a train?'

He roughly wiped his nose with the back of his hand, his composure crumbling. When he spoke again, his voice cracked.

'I can't tell you how many times I've been over it in my mind,' he said in a rush, breathing heavily. 'I nearly killed myself with the guilt of it all, that I didn't stop you . . .'

'Liam—' said Anya in a loud voice but he shouted over her.

'No!' he said. 'You killed her in cold blood and it's time you paid for it!'

Something was beginning to crumble, so painfully, inside my mind.

I turned to look at Anya. Every single atom of my being was resisting what I was hearing. It couldn't be true, it couldn't. It was too horrible. My wife, who I had always believed to be so much better a human being than I could ever be, a double murderer? It couldn't be true, it couldn't be true, it couldn't be . . .

And yet . . .

I knew it, deep in the marrow of my bones.

I knew, finally, that she was capable of this.

When you have lived so long in the dark, the light is a searing, painful thing. I wished I didn't know.

*

Now is the moment that I have gone over, again and again, in the broken, splintered time since.

She could read what I was thinking. Her expression collapsed, a tremor of grief passing over her face, then she somehow smoothed it back into an impassive mask.

Liam stood up and cleared his throat.

'Okay,' he said, sounding flat and weary now. 'I just wanted to come here and look you in the eye. I wanted to say I am sorry that I didn't do the right thing or try and help you to do it. I can only say that when you end up in a prison cell – where you belong – you'll have plenty of time to think about what you have done to two families.'

He stopped and looked at me, his eyes full of pain and regret. 'No, wait,' he said. 'Make that three. Because there's your own, too.'

All I could do was stare, wordlessly, as he moved to the door.

Then Anya cried, 'Wait, Liam!' and came towards him quickly. I thought for a moment she was embracing him, which seemed weird and wrong. But then he made a horrible gasping sound and looked down at himself, his eyes wide.

Anya stood back, panting audibly, and it was only as Liam said, 'Fuck!' and crumpled in half, that I could see the bread knife, slick with blood, she was still holding in her hand.

'Shit! Anya!' I yelled. 'What the hell have you done?'

Liam was now lying on his side on the tiles, gasping and holding onto his abdomen, his T-shirt dark with the spreading stain. Anya just stared down at him. I grabbed a tea towel and got down on my knees to press it against his stomach.

'Call an ambulance!' I shouted. Then, to Liam, 'Keep that pressed as hard as you can. You'll be alright, mate, you'll be alright.' I had no idea if this was true.

Anya barked, 'Elliott!' at me and I looked up to see her standing over me.

She was holding the knife, handle first, her expression unreadable again.

'I need you now,' she said.

'I know!' I said. 'We'll work this out, but ring 999 now!'

'No,' she said quietly. 'You said I should have come to you before. Well now I am coming to you! Finish it. For me.'

I couldn't speak. I couldn't take in what she was asking me to do. I stared at the bloodied knife blade clutched in her fist. It must have been cutting her hand; her blood mixing with Liam's. The wooden handle shook as she thrust it towards me again. Liam was making a horrible gurgling sound and staring at me with terrified, wide eyes.

Did I think about doing it, in that moment, even for one second?

Was I my father's son after all?

'Take it!' she shrieked.

I grabbed it from her hand, jumped to my feet and then threw the blood-slippery knife into the sink.

Because, no.

It turned out that it wasn't true, you see, that I would do anything for Anya.

I didn't have it in me after all. Whatever dark place she had somehow held inside for so long, I couldn't join her there.

I was crying now.

'I love you so much,' I said. 'But it's over, sweetie, don't you see?'

I ripped another towel off the counter behind me and got down on my knees next to Liam again. His face was ashen, and he was breathing in small gasps. I began to press it into the wound, scared I was making it worse because he cried out, pitifully quiet.

All I heard was, 'I'm so sorry, my darling,' before something slammed into the side of my head and my existence became just a starburst of pain.

You probably think I am a monster. Or at least, a coward. I still don't know if I did the right thing in tipping off the police. It felt so sordid.

But now she knows I am dying, I have seen with my own eyes that she has lost interest in Olivia. She tells me she won't be able to cope, that she can't live in the world without me and Patrick side by side, to support and understand her.

People used to comment with envy at what a tight family unit we are. But I wonder whether we got it wrong, whether we made it impossible for Anya to face the world properly on her own.

I don't want to go to my death knowing what I know or leaving my daughter in charge of her own child. It is better that Elliott and Olivia make a new start.

Yes, I know I sound callous. But it is for the best reasons.

And now she is here. Crying and covered in blood. She says, 'I'm sorry but I can't do it any more.'

And I think, not again. Not again.

ELLIOTT

I can't have been out for that long but there was a period of time that was just a hazy hinterland between the two states of being unconscious and being awake. I was almost comfortable, stuck in this not-knowing place.

Sometimes, on the longest days, I wish I could go back there.

It was the feeling of the cold tile against my cheek that first began to feel all wrong, and then the knowledge of what had happened zapped through me like the shock of a Tasering. I scrambled onto my knees, the side of my head throbbing and tender when I gently touched it. I wasn't bleeding, though, and I wasn't very dizzy once the initial swoop of nausea passed.

Liam was lying just behind me, panting very softly, a dark pool of blood spreading across the pale tiles beneath him. I swore and leaned over him and his eyes flicked to me with an animal look of fear in them. He whimpered.

'It's okay, mate,' I said, 'I'm going to get help.' I was scared to touch him, but at that moment there was a thunderous banging on the front door, followed quickly by a splintering, smashing sound and then the kitchen was filled with people in various uniforms.

Radios crackled and two paramedics immediately bent to Liam as I leaned against the sink and held my aching head.

They started throwing around words I'd heard only on television hospital dramas before, about 'resp rates' and 'systolic' and 'cannulating' before they were putting a needle into Liam's arm and an oxygen mask over his face.

A policewoman – DS Jin from yesterday – was suddenly right there and she came to me now.

'Elliott,' she said, 'do you need medical attention?' Then, 'Where is she?'

I'm still ashamed about this part, despite everything, because it was only then that I thought about Livi.

I ran out of the room, almost pushing past one of the paramedics and a uniformed male officer who called out, 'Hey!' as I took the stairs two at a time.

I knew Anya wouldn't hurt Livi but I couldn't bear to think she had been screaming, alone and scared up there. But when I approached the cot and looked down, I saw her peacefully asleep, her little cheeks red and damp. My chest flooded with hot, protective love and I lifted her up in the delicate yellow blanket that Julia had crocheted.

'*Elliott*,' said a sharp voice, and I turned to see the male uniform. Everything was too strange and confused to make sense of but it's only now that I know they didn't suspect me of having stabbed Liam because Liam had been able to gasp out what happened into the phone in his hand. Anya's phone.

I like to think she put it there before she fled. That maybe she didn't really want that third death on her conscience. I don't want to think that she simply dropped it in the panic of everything that was happening.

'Do you or the baby need medical assistance, Elliott?' said the policeman, a burly man with thinning hair across his scalp and large pale eyes.

I shook my head.

'I'll be okay,' I said, 'but we need to find her. We need to find my wife.' I was babbling now, the anaesthetic of shock wearing off and leaving sharp, cold panic in its wake.

I was about to push past him again and he lifted a meaty hand to stop me. 'Do you have any idea where she is, Elliott?' he said, his constant use of my name annoying me now for some reason.

'No, she could be any—' I started, then stopped. It was as though I was in the eye of the storm now; a place of utter stillness and certainty.

I knew exactly where she had gone.

'Her mum and dad,' I said. 'She's gone to them. She always goes to them.'

DS Jin was reluctant to let me come at first, especially with Livi. I yelled that Anya would listen to me and they would only make it worse. After exchanged looks between her and the other plainclothes officer – a man about my age with glasses and a dark beard – she agreed.

We drove through the streets of Casterbourne towards Lathebridge with the siren on in an unmarked car, and two panda cars following. I cradled the baby close to my chest, silently begging her not to cry as she began to grizzle in the back of the car, wishing we could travel faster, even though the motion was making my head hurt even more, and the urge to be sick was almost overwhelming.

Faces on the streets I knew so well turned to us in unison as we sped through the town. As we shot past the road that would lead to school, I imagined being in that building on a weekday and hearing these sirens so close by. The kids would be all of a babble over it. They'd think something cool, something exciting, was happening.

As we came into Lathebridge we drove down the coast

road to the house and I saw our car, parked on the drive, like she had been coming round for Sunday dinner.

DS Jin turned to me, her face severe.

'Elliott, you've to stay here until we tell you, do you understand?'

I nodded miserably, and she and the other officer were out of the car as one, slamming the door behind them and hurrying up the white stone steps to the large black and stained-glass front door. They knocked and shouted that they were police but nothing happened.

One of the policemen appeared from the side of the house that faced the coast, where the big bay window was, and his expression turned my spine to ice as he began yelling and gesticulating, which set off what seemed like an explosion of movement.

And I knew that things had gone from being bad to true horror.

A short, red battering ram was produced and pounded into the beautiful old door, with its distinctive lion-shaped knocker I had seen a million times.

I was out of the car now.

I heard a uniformed officer – I don't even know if it was a man or a woman – call my name from where they were standing at the front of the house, but I ignored them and ran past the broken, open door and into the cool, tiled hallway. I was carrying Livi, which is something that still haunts me. I don't remember if I squeezed too hard, or even if she woke up. I just remember the warm density of her in my arms. That she was there, where she should never have been.

In my memory of it, there are no crackling radios, none of the shouting and urgent activity that must have been taking place. It's as though it happened in a dream state.

All I can hear is my own fearful, rasping breath. I see the heads of the police officers slowly turning towards me and mouthing urgently words I can't hear from angry, frightened faces.

I saw Julia first.

She was lying on their long red sofa, her head back against a cushion as though she had dropped off into a pleasant nap. Her glasses had fallen onto her chest. The top of her head was now a mashed, pulpy mess of pink and white. The shotgun was on her chest.

Patrick was next to her but slumped sideways so I hadn't seen him at first. I wasn't able to see the damage to his head and learned of it only later.

Hands were reaching out for me. I think I screamed; I must have screamed. Then I pushed past the PC standing with an ashen face in the doorway and climbed the stairs two at a time, past another policeman who was just standing there doing nothing and into Anya's childhood bedroom.

Lilac wallpaper, flowered curtains. Bookshelves that still held all the books she had loved as a child: the Jacqueline Wilsons, the Harry Potters, the horsey books. A big arty picture of the three of them, black and white, tumbling about and laughing.

I seemed to see each part of her in stages. First, my wife's feet in her scuffed red Converse, up to her legs in the only jeans she could get into since Livi's birth, then the flowery nursing top that crossed over at the front.

Finally, her face. What was left of it.

Hands were yanking me away then and I was bellowing, 'Anya, Anya,' over and over again, the pain something I won't be able to describe, ever. I was crying and shouting, clawing at my own skin as though trying to escape from being me.

And then gentle but firm hands were taking Olivia from me and saying, 'It's over, Elliott. It's over. Let's go.'

SPRING 2021

IRENE

Irene checks her suitcase for probably the tenth time that morning, then her handbag to make sure she has her tickets and passport.

She isn't being picked up by Frank for another half an hour for the journey to Heathrow. Irene takes a Rennie from the peeling packet in the bottom of her handbag in an attempt to quell the nerves fluttering in her stomach.

It is such a long way. She can't even pronounce the name of the airport in Bangkok – Suvarnabhumi. How on earth is she going to cope if people don't speak English? And what about all that spicy food? She liked the unusual new things that Liam cooked her on his last visit, but they had given her awful indigestion afterwards.

Irene looks at her watch. Twenty minutes until Frank gets here. He is always on time.

She wishes now she hadn't turned down his offer to come with her to Thailand. But maybe next time. Everything is still so new. Having her son back in her life is a blessing she thanks God for every single day – now she has decided to give God a second chance. Having a new friend in the form of Frank is lovely too, but she doesn't want to rush anything, after all.

When Liam had been in the hospital, stabbed in the stomach by that woman whose name she still can't bring herself to say, she thought she might lose him again. It felt like the cruellest, most unfair joke that the world could play on a person, to bring him back into her life and take him away again. But the wound had been 'quite superficial' the doctor explained to her. He was smiling gently as he said it, and Irene had been struck by the difference in doctors, after Michael, when the news was good.

Her eyes flick to the mantelpiece and she looks at the pictures of her boys from a lifetime ago. She blinks back tears as she thinks about the sacrifice Michael made in trying to find his brother. This is something she knows still haunts Liam. She held him when he cried and told her he was so sorry for staying away all that time.

But it is what it is, and they must make the most of what they have now.

Two years ago, she had been alone in the world. A mother with two lost sons. Now one has come back to her, like a wonderful gift. And she has a new friend, Frank, not to mention Rowan, with her wacky baccy and her funny teas and her kindness.

Irene feels a jolt of pleasure at the thought of seeing Liam's beautiful Pimchan and baby Aroon, who is such a big boy now.

She opens her case once again to check she has the Percy Pig sweeties Aroon likes. She knows she shouldn't give them to him because they are bad for his little teeth, but isn't that what grannies are for?

Irene re-zips the case and decides to have one last wee before Frank arrives. He'll be here any minute and she doesn't want to keep him waiting.

ELLIOTT

'Not too high, Liv!'

My words fall on deaf ears. My daughter climbs like a little monkey to the next level of the climbing frame, giggling. I rush over and envelop her in my arms, pulling her away.

She's about to object, but I swing her round and let her lie back, eyes shining as she holds out her arms to the sides, and smiling so all of her small, neat teeth are on show.

'Down! Down, Daddy!' she says, and I place her gently on her feet. She toddles over to the sandpit then, where she left her bucket before, and begins to dig furiously there, chatting in her own babble of half-coherent language as she does so.

I can hear the sound of the North Circular thundering by from here. It's not that far from our flat either, but closer to this playground, Livi's favoured one. I don't mind it, despite all the news reports about the dangers of bringing up children in London. I worry about her lungs sometimes, breathing in all that crap every day.

But most of all I worry that she has retained something of that day in the farthest parts of her baby memory.

I had to come home, after. Back to London, where I belong.

I couldn't stay in Casterbourne, of course, and now I'm

not even sure I want to be near the English coast for some time yet. No, I am happier here, in the stinky, anonymous heart of the city where I am just Mr Little again to the Year Twos I teach in the slightly struggling school. I'm not the 'tragic husband of multiple murderer Anya Ryland' as one tabloid put it. Zoe had pulled the iPad out of my hand and almost slapped me for reading that one, in those terrible, black days afterwards when I could barely function as a human being, let alone a dad.

We see her often, her and her new girlfriend Hayley. She's Scottish, loves kids. Livi adores her.

Livi is too young to ask questions about her mother but I know the day is coming, and not that far away. What can I tell her?

Patrick's fingerprints were on the gun as well as Anya's, but the police think these were older.

They say that Anya shot herself, then Julia shot Patrick, then herself. Gentle, cultured Julia, with a shotgun in her hands. I can't seem to picture this. Not that I try.

Although no one can ever know now exactly what happened, it probably played out like this:

I picture her walking to the front door and using her key to go into the house she grew up in. Maybe Julia was napping, the chemo having taken a lot out of her that day.

Maybe Patrick said something like, 'What's up, sweetie?' but she ignored him and went to where he kept the shotgun. She knew how to load it because Patrick had shown her once.

I think she wanted to be with them, when she did it. It had to be there. And they wouldn't be able to live without her.

It was all or nothing, when you were a Ryland. Julia knew, I think, more than I ever understood, what Anya was capable of. I think she was trying to warn me that day in her study, when she suggested I let her know if Anya's behaviour ever 'worried' me. At the time, I thought it was concern about Anya's well-being.

But maybe it was fear of what Anya might do.

Patrick, it turned out afterwards, was under investigation for defrauding investors in his company. Julia was much sicker than any of us had known.

I think about the picture they had on top of their piano sometimes, taken on a French holiday when Anya was a child. They are sitting at a sunlit table outside a café, the table crowded with baskets of food. Patrick has a tall glass of beer in front of him, Julia a glass of red. Anya is holding up a glass of Coke and making a silly face at the camera.

The perfect middle-class family on holiday.

They would always be together now.

A wave of grief hits me, as it often does, and I take deep breaths. One day at a time. That's what my counsellor says. I may never get over this, but a time will come when I can live with it.

I get angry at Anya sometimes. I was so very grateful that she chose me, you see. I thought she was better than me inside. But I don't know whether she would have been able to change.

I still miss her, despite everything she did. But when I try and imagine a different outcome – knowing she had killed two people – I don't think we could have survived that.

Anya wasn't 'better than me', after all. This is a strange, unsettling thought. I guess if I have learned anything, it's that remorse *means* something. You can never undo a terrible act. But you should at least carry its weight.

'Daddy! Daddy!'

I am jolted from my gloomy reverie by small daughter, who is lying on her back and making angels in the sand with her chubby arms and legs. She is cackling like a lunatic as she does it and my heart is packed with love.

From a passing car I hear a blast of music – 'Have a Nice Day' by Stereophonics. I used to find this song thoroughly annoying because of its ubiquity. But now, I feel something that I can only describe as not exactly pleasure . . . but like the shadow of a familiar feeling I may have again.

I haven't been able to listen to music since it happened. Every song had an association with Anya and our life together. It's only now I realize how painfully I've missed it.

Perhaps I'll get Spotify or Apple Music going again and try to find something new to listen to. A brand-new genre of music. I mean, I've never really given jazz much of a go.

There's a teacher at school, Evie, who says she likes jazz. She's very nice, and I think there is a possibility she likes me. Maybe it's time I paid this more attention.

I have been living in the dark for so long. You could say, I was here even before my wife and my parents-in-law died; my marriage weighed down by secrets. Maybe it started that night when I was twelve and I played a part in Mrs Mack's murder. This even resulted in a certain blindness on my part; an inability to see beyond my own guilty conscience.

But perhaps there comes a time when you have to give yourself a break and step back into the light.

I walk over to Livi and lift her from the sand, then hold her squirming body high in the air, turning her in circles in the air. Sand tinkles gently onto me and she laughs and laughs, hands outstretched, her halo of red hair caught by the late afternoon sunshine.

Acknowledgements

Considering what dark imaginations they all have, the crime writing community is such a supportive and kind place. I think that with this book more than any other, they helped get me to the finish line.

Aside from the daily laughs, gossip and support, I had expert advice from the writerly ex-cops I know. Thank you so much, Clare Mackintosh and Rebecca Bradbury, who assisted me with the authenticity of certain scenes. I owe a massive debt to Katerina Diamond, who came up with the book's title. I couldn't quite find the right one this time, but as soon as she said, 'What about *The Killer Inside*?' everyone went, 'Ah . . .'

I am also grateful to private eye Mike LaCorte of Conflict International, who gave me advice on tracing someone who's quite determined to disappear. (I'll be bearing this in mind, should I ever have the need . . .)

I hadn't been in a primary school for a few years when I started writing this book and chatting with Peachey David helped me craft certain scenes. Thank you, too, to Anthony David for letting me visit St Paul's Mill Hill School to shadow a teacher in Year Six. Michael Biggs was a lovely person to spend the day with and is clearly, rightly, adored by every one of his pupils (Mr David, I think he probably deserves a pay rise . . .)

I'd like to thank Emma Haughton for being such a huge support and reading this book when I wasn't even exactly sure what it was going to be.

Inbali Iserles, Geri Ryan and Rosie Thornton were all immensely helpful with Cambridge knowledge I needed for this book and any faults there are definitely my own.

Thanks to the publishing professionals I rely on so much in this funny old job of mine. Mark Stanton, my agent (Stan, you are indeed The Man), my amazing editors Sarah Hodgson and Finn Cotton, publicist Emilie Chambeyron and eagle-eyed copy editor extraordinaire Rhian McKay. You are all bloody brilliant, basically.

Pete, Joe and Harry, you're the absolute best. I'm so proud of each one of you and immensely grateful I get to hang out with you all.

Finally, to every reader who has got in touch to say they have enjoyed one of my books, you have no idea what this means. Please don't ever stop!

Caroline Green, London, May 2019